Dear Clemmie

Rare is the book that will
— hopefully! — **DAISY** be a pleasure
to both of you... **IN** That said, I do
hope you **EXILE** both enjoy
this. Daisy is a total
imp of the juice + joy this story
has given Paris of Paris's fancy
d grotty famous + back alley street
is supreme. I met JT Allen when
I first started my company d
on twitter I ⎯⎯ invited this
"Daisy Tannenbaum" to a treasure
hunt at the louvre. Turned
out by D.M. JT Allen is a 50
year old screen writer in LA (who
wrote the lion king) d NOT a

Published in the United States by SUMUS PRESS.

SUMUS PRESS and the moth design are registered trademarks. No kidding. Seriously. But you can use them as a tattoo design next time you're at the tattoo parlor. Just tell them Daisy sent you.

ISBN: 978-0-9986805-1-4

For Cora, Lily, and Laura.

The French got into the bad habit of speaking French a long time ago, so since this story takes place in France there's some French in it. But don't worry, I didn't speak a word of it when I got there and you can mostly puzzle it out, plus I put a little glossary in the back if you're curious.

# 1. A Room of My Own

My own room.

First time ever.

I'd always been thrown in with my older sister, Clymene. It's the most amazing thing having your own room, your own desk, your own desk lamp you can turn on in the middle of the night without anybody biting your head off; and nobody texting all night with their toad boyfriend, messages swooshing away at all hours; or flinging your underwear at you just cause you forgot to pick it up.

Not to say I didn't miss Clymene. That's the weird part.

Right after we got to the apartment and I'd heaved my suitcase onto the bed, Aunt Mill stuck her head in the door and said, "Do you want to call and tell them you've arrived?"

"No thanks," I said.

"Are you sure? I have unlimited international minutes on my cell phone."

"No thanks," I said again.

Aunt Mill cocked her head. "Okay, well, I'll just give a quick call so your mom won't worry."

Knock yourself out, lady, I wanted to say. And she could tell that's what I wanted to say. She seemed pretty sharp, Aunt Mill, like a lean, mean math teacher. But no way I was ever talking to any of my family, ever. They could just get whatever updates they wanted from Aunt Mill, with her unlimited international minutes. Pretty soon they'd lose interest and wouldn't even pretend to care. Years from now, I'd meet my new little brother and they'd say, this is your sister, Daisy, and he'd go, "I have another sister? Really?"

So, okay, let me go back a little.

When we returned from Moken Island, which you can read about in my first book, I'd missed about three weeks of school and had to jump right in. You'd think maybe after you'd been shipwrecked, fought off pirates, recovered a stolen treasure and survived a typhoon or two, your classmates would give you some social cred. Not likely. Sixth grade cliques at the Fairfield School had formed faster than buboes on a plague victim.

I got tossed in with a new girl named Lucia Sarir, who was tall and thin and walked like a giraffe and never said anything to anybody. Her parents were from two different countries, like Estonia and Kazakhstan, so she wore weird clothes, purchased in Bulgrungastad or something. But once you got past her shy-wall, Lucia was clever and funny and played killer chess. Trouble was, she got picked on constantly. Especially by Martin Blindenbok.

Martin would follow behind her and mimic her walk while everybody laughed. Even I pretended to laugh too, so Martin wouldn't pick on me, which made me feel like a worm.

So no big surprise really when, one Monday, after a weekend of feeling entirely wormy for betraying Lucia, I socked Martin Blindenbok in the nose. He'd snuck up behind her and knocked the books from her arms. Martin is a whole head taller than me and weighs twice as much as me, but I didn't think about that. I just let him have it. His nose exploded blood and he fell back and hit his head on a locker and crashed down in a blob.

Next thing I knew I was in Principal Smootin's office, getting expelled.

Good move, Daisy.

Dad came over to school.  Mom, who was monster preggers, had to stay home cause she had something called preeclampsia pre-term labor, which meant she couldn't get out of bed.  After Dad talked to them, the school agreed to send me to some child psychologist lady.

The evening after my visit with the psychologist lady, who asked me a million dumb questions, Mom and Dad had a humongo argument.  He's a professor of archeology and she works for a textbook publisher, so you'd think they could talk in a civilized way, but forget it, tons of shouting, cups breaking, the works.  From upstairs, I couldn't tell what they were saying except for a few times when they got crazy loud, like when Mom yelled, "Over my dead body."

Next day, at breakfast, they said they'd made a decision. They were sending me to be home schooled by my mom's sister, Aunt Millicent.  Since I suck at math, and Aunt Mill is a math teacher, Mom and Dad thought it would be a good idea.  Only trouble was, Aunt Mill lived in Paris.

I argued with them for like an hour.  It was so unfair.

But later that night, Clymene came over to my bed when the lights were out and whispered that she heard Mom and Dad talking.  She said they felt terrible.

"Good," I said, "they should."

"No, Daisy, you don't get it.  Dad was talking about how the school psychologist thought you were suffering from post-dramatic trauma disorder from the experience on the island and that you should be put on medication before returning to school."

"Gross.  No way I'm doing that."

"That's what Mom and Dad said.  Mom was so mad Dad told her to calm down, which of course had the exact opposite effect.  That's why she was screaming, "Over my dead body.""

Oh.

Phone calls were made.  E-mails flew back and forth.  It was settled.

What did I know about Aunt Mill?  She lived in Paris.  She was Mom's older sister.  She wasn't married and didn't have kids.  She'd only visited a few times, when I was little.  She always gave us weird gifts like Becassine and Bleuette dolls, which are old French dolls that nobody ever heard of, but which Mom insisted were collectors items and hid away somewhere.

So I really didn't know anything about Aunt Mill.
Dad gave me his old laptop.  Clymene lent me her digital camera.  Mom gave me her original 1985 addition of *Agatha Christie's Complete Miss Marple Mysteries* to read on the plane, which I loved.  But then she ruined it by getting all teary and reaching up from the bed to hug me before I left.

Because I was twelve and traveling alone, the Air France people put a plastic pouch around my neck with my ticket and passport inside.  I got to be escorted onto the plane by my own stew.

Go geek girl.

All the little French families sitting around me on the jet seemed so happy, kids talking in French to French moms, while French stews in their pale-blue uniforms, hair perfect, scarves perfect, everything about them French and perfect, handed out French magazines and French earphones.

I tried to read *Miss Marple*, but the stories just made me worry about Lucia.  Who would protect her?  Plus, I was ticked with my mom for packing me off and then getting all sobby about it.  Halfway through the flight I look down through the clouds and saw icebergs, little cold things bobbing in the vast blue. That's the way I felt inside.

Aunt Mill—dressed in the same kind of trim suit as the stews, only in pine green—stood at the customs exit to greet me. She spoke to the Air France people in fluent French as they signed my paper work. She's not much older than my mom and looked a lot like her, though younger somehow, thinner, blonder hair, more—I don't know—stylish. She has an ever-so-slight limp, which you only notice really when she's going up or down stairs. She practically smothered me with her hug.

We took a taxi from the airport. As we neared the center of the city, the streets got smaller and the buildings more old and crooked until pretty soon we turned down a street that was barely wide enough for a single car. Aunt Mill told me the French name for her neighborhood but I promptly forgot it. She said it meant swamp in English and that they drained a swamp four hundred years ago to build all these big fancy palaces for all the rich fancy people who then got their heads cut off with a guillotine. That part I remembered.

The taxi stopped in front of these huge green doors that Aunt Mill called carriage doors. In the old days, people would drive in with their horses and carriages. But now, inside one of the big doors was a smaller door that we walked through.

I dragged Big Bertha, my monster suitcase, across the bumpy courtyard as Aunt Mill led the way. She called out, "Sief," and like magic, this scrawny, dark-haired, Raggedy-Andy of an eleven-year-old came loping out from the opposite side of the courtyard. "We need help with the suitcase," Aunt Mill said.

We entered an archway and climbed these crooked steps, so worn they sagged in the middle. Aunt Mill hobbled up, hanging on to the rail. Sief tried to grab Big Bertha out of my hand.

"I can do it alone, twerp-o," I said.

Aunt Mill looked down from the landing above and said something in French. Sief promptly let go of the handle and went down and started pushing from below. We clunk-clunked up a flight and then he started easing off without appearing to, then pushing again, easing off, pushing, till I almost fell on him. He grinned.

I shoved Big Bertha down on him. He missed a step and knocked his chin. I yelled, "Hey, watch out, klutzoid."
Sief just grinned again. Eventually we got to a landing ten thousand steps up. Aunt Mill had the door to her apartment open and while I rolled Bertha in, she gave Sief some money. I wanted to barf.

When I asked Aunt Mill about him, she said Sief was half Algerian, half Mohican, and half Puritan. When I asked her what that meant she said Sief's mother died last year and that he and his father lived across the courtyard and that he was a very sweet boy and spoke fairly good English and that if I didn't insist on trying to kill him with my suitcase we might become friends.

She must have eyes in the back of her head.

Aunt Mill's apartment was ancient. The living room had a marble fireplace and walls with carved wood that looked like decorations on a cake. There were books everywhere: books in cases that ran to the ceiling and books piled in corners around potted plants and books on the faded green couch and books piled on the fireplace and in the fireplace too, old books, new books, French books, art books. You could build a castle with all the books.

The living room gave into a dining room with another fireplace and a round dusty table ringed with dusty gold chairs. A chandelier with real candles instead of light bulbs hung down from a plaster rosette in the ceiling. Across the hall was a tiny kitchen with hardly anything in it and down the hall were three bedrooms, one for her, one for me and the last for her study. The study had more books, along with scrolls and charts and piles of paperwork, plus, in a corner, a ginormous steel safe.

"What's that for?" I asked.

"It's just an antique," said Aunt Mill. "Too heavy to move, so there it sits."

## 2. Le Saint Gervais

Aunt Mill woke me at seven in the morning, Paris time. I'd been asleep about six seconds. She said she was taking me to her school to do some testing. I had five minutes to shower and throw clothes on. The shower heater either scalded you or doused you with ice water, with no in between, unless you had the touch of a safecracker. Then we sat down to warm milk with coffee, and yesterday's stale baguette with jam. Aunt Mill smoked half a cig by the open kitchen window, telling me the whole time what a disgusting habit it was.

I borrowed an umbrella for the dash to the Metro. She kept a dozen in a brass holder by her door—a good thing because it is always raining in Paris. Always.

The sky was dead-mouse gray. Wet cobbles glistened under vapor lights. People walked hunched over, dragging on their cigarettes, bumping you off the sidewalk as they passed. Handing me a Metro ticket, Aunt Mill passed through the fare-barrier and mashed into the morning crowd. I had no idea where we were going but it was pretty cool to be on the real Paris Metro, even if everyone was churlish. Aunt Mill is not a morning person, but I didn't realize that at the time, so her silence on the ride over made me feel like I was something heavy she had to lug around.

A brass plaque marked the entrance to the Embassy School. Early kids, dressed in school blazers, said *"Bonjour Madame Millicent"* as we came in. They eyed me, exuding posh.

I got whisked into a cubical with a glass wall and four

computers, next to the principal's office, while Aunt Mill talked with an office bee named Mademoiselle Villand, a young woman with angelic hair and a cherub face who could roast you alive with her booming voice, which she used on kids running in the hall.

Aunt Mill went off to teach. Mademoiselle Villand set me up to take tests on a computer. The keyboard was different than an American keyboard, with the letters all mixed up, but luckily it was just scroll and click and fill in A, B, C, or D—same hyper-boring tests we take at Fairfield, except the computer would lock you out when your time was up. I had a headache three minutes in.

Mademoiselle Villand came in occasionally to check that I still had a pulse, and to set up the next torture session. Normally, I would have thrown myself out a window, but I was so jet-lagged I zombied through. At noon, Aunt Mill and I walked around the corner to a tiny café where she had a twenty-minute chat in French with the guy who ran the place, while I sat listening, understanding not a word.

After lunch it was more torture. I even took a French test, which was a total joke. Then I waited for Aunt Mill, watching the rain stop and start, watching the lead-colored daylight disappear, watching knots of students traipsing out, gabbing in French and English and even Japanese.

I must have fallen dead asleep. Aunt Mill woke me and apologized for taking so long and asked if I wanted to grab a bite of dinner. Sitting up on the bench outside the principal's office, wiping drool off my cheek, I had to think for a few seconds where I was.

We metroed back to Aunt Mill's apartment and ate at a place around the corner, called Café Saint Gervais. She talked with *both* owners of this place. The man shook my hand. The woman kissed my cheeks and spoke English to me, telling me that her name was Rose, and that my name, Daisy, meant *Marguerite* in French, so we were both flower-named girls, the best kind of girls in the world, and that if I ever needed anything, or was hungry, or wanted to get out of the rain, or wanted a *chocolat chaud,* or anything, just anything, I should stop in and ask for Rose.

Le Saint Gervais was kind of a dump really, unless you think of grungy furniture from the 70s as a trend. But Madame Rose knew how to cook. We had *saumon rillettes* and *gratin dauphinois* and *rôti d'agneau aux herbes* and then *figues chaudes à la mousse d'amandes.* I remember all that because Madame Rose wrote the names of everything down when I asked her to. She was excited that I was excited about the food, but who wouldn't be—it was amazing. Aunt Mill ordered a bottle of wine and poured some in my glass. I told her I was just a kid and didn't drink wine, but she said that kids in France could drink a little wine under adult supervision and that it was a shame not to drink wine with such a good meal. It didn't taste that great, kind of sour, with a worn out smell. I had more fun swirling it in my glass the way Aunt Mill did.

She asked me to tell the whole story about Lucia and Martin Blidenbock, including about punching Martin, so I did. She laughed. "Good for you. Unofficially of course," she said. She started talking about crazy things that she and my mom did when they were young but she made me swear never to tell anyone. I had no idea my mom was such a terror.

At the end of the meal, when we were stuffed to our eyeballs and Aunt Mill was drinking an espresso, she pulled out the scores from the tests I'd taken. She looked them over, sighed gravely, and said, "A French scholar you are not, mademoiselle."

She said I tested well in reading comprehension,

vocabulary, history, geography, and life sciences. "Math, as predicted, is a problem and your French, shall we say, is robustly remedial, contrary to your mother's claim."

"She probably fibbed about that. I've never taken a day of French."

"Yes, well, I suspect at that point in the conversation she was afraid I'd refuse to take you on because of the language barrier."

"So am I going to the Embassy School?"

"Heavens, no. That place is for diplomat brats. You'd wilt there. Your parents and I agreed that I'd home school you. But you're already testing past tenth grade in most subjects now. You'll need to take the sixth grade accreditation exam in the spring but you could pass that tomorrow. So here's what I propose:

"For math, I'll give you a set of problems each morning. After you complete them, whether it takes five minutes or five hours, the rest of the day is yours. However, you can do nothing else until they're completed. You'll also be required to read independently, picking a book from my library or, in any case, a book I approve of, which can be almost anything, as long as it's not completely idiotic. We'll call that your honors independent study. In addition, you'll be required to keep a journal on Paris— on what you've seen, heard, smelled, read about, what puzzles you about the city, what annoys you, what the people look like, eat, wear, what the design of the city tells you, and so forth. You will be required to write at least five pages a week in this journal, but I suspect that won't be too great a burden for you. In the meantime, I'll look into an appropriate language school."

I nudged a bit of almond cream around on my plate. "So, when you say 'the rest of the day is mine' you mean like I have to sit in the apartment all day or am I going to be at the school with you?"

"Neither.  Of course, you can sit in the apartment if you choose, since it is technically part of Paris.  Your journal will get very tedious if you do."

"So I just wander around?"

"If you choose.  However, having a plan or goal each day will probably make it more interesting."

"What if I get lost?"

"I'll give you a *Paris Par Arrondissement* map book, and also a cell phone, in case you really get stuck.  Of course, getting lost is one of the best ways of discovering things.  Plus, as you've probably observed, there are people living here, and though they speak French, they're quite helpful, especially to polite little girls."

"Won't the police arrest me for cutting school?"

"Why would they?  You're a foreign tourist."

This was clearly too good to be true.  I knew there had to be a catch.

"What's the catch?" Aunt Mill said.

"Huh?"

"You're thinking, 'what's the catch?'"

I nodded.  Was she a mind reader too?

"Well, you will have to finish your math homework each day, which won't always be easy, but aside from that, we're in a city with 204 museums, 407 gardens, 7,000 cafes, 60,000 shops. There's a historic plaque on every other corner.  Let's take where we are now.  You're dining in a restaurant, a seemingly unremarkable one, named after a Roman martyr from the Second Century, when Jesus was still considered the hero of a fringe cult. Victor Hugo bought his daily bread around the corner.  Louis, Duke of Orleans, was murdered a few steps down the way, sparking seventy years of war.  Up the street, the Knights Templar had their headquarters, until they were all arrested, accused of witchcraft, and burned at the stake. This city is literally an open book, with infinite pages, written in code, waiting to be deciphered. Now some people, perhaps most even, wouldn't know how to take advantage of that. But based on what I know of you, I think you will."

I said nothing. I was stunned. Aunt Mill paid the bill and said a chatty goodbye to Rose and her husband. We all double-cheek-kissed, an awkward thing for me, which made them laugh.

Aunt Mill and I walked home under umbrellas, everything varnished by the rain, then chuffed up the bowed steps to her apartment. I got ready for bed. She went into her study, "to do some late work." I had a long look in the bathroom mirror after I brushed my teeth. Sometimes you just look in the mirror and don't recognize the person, or don't like them particularly, or wonder why they do certain things, like punch people in the nose and refuse to telephone their mother.

When I came out of the bathroom, I saw Aunt Mill seated at her desk, examining an old piece of paper—like really old, like the kind pirates made their maps on—with a magnifying glass.

"Good night, Aunt Mill," I said.

She looked up. "Night, Daisy. Get a good rest now."

I nodded and padded off down the hall, brain not quite registering what I'd seen until after I'd turned away: there was that safe, steel door swung open, stacked high with old papers like the one Aunt Mill was eyeing with her glass. The safe might be an antique and "too heavy to move" but it was doing more than just sitting there.

# 3. You See, Grace Kelly?

The smell of warm milk woke me. I stayed under covers, listening to Aunt Mill knock around the kitchen. Out the window all was gray.

It had taken me half the night to fall asleep—listening to all the sounds that somehow disappear during the day—lone car engines echoing off stone buildings, the buzz of door locks as people came in late, the faint notes of someone somewhere playing jazz piano, muted by the sound of rain.

Aunt Mill knocked and stuck her head in the door. "I'm off. *Tartines* and *café au lait* on the kitchen table. Nuke the coffee if it's cold. There's cheese, apples, all sorts of *truc* for lunch in the fridge, or you can just go round and see Madame Rose if you'd like. Math problems for the day are on the table, too, with instructions and a little surprise. See you around four."

She disappeared. The apartment door clacked and her steps faded down the stairs. I sat up. The floor was icy. I pulled on socks and padded around the place, looking everything over again. The door to Aunt Mill's study was closed. I tried the knob—locked.

The milk and coffee were still warm. I dipped the grilled bread in and looked over the nine problems she'd left. They looked like: "7 x (10 – 1) = X." She wrote out instructions for adding the answers together to get three numbers that would, "open the safe."

For a moment I thought she meant the safe in her office

but then I noticed, right in front of me, a gray tin cube with a black plastic dial, and a slot for coins. The kid who first owned it probably ran a bank now. I gazed at the problems.

Math.

I won't even tell you how long it took me to find the answers. Eventually I did though, added them up, and got the safe open.

Inside I found a key to the apartment, five euros, four Metro tickets, a cell phone, a *Paris Par Arrondissement* map book, and a hand-drawn map with directions to various places: the Picasso Museum, the Place des Vosges, the Centre George Pompidou.

Umbrella in hand, I slammed the door and ran down the stairs, thrilled to be on the loose. I didn't care where I ended up—I just wanted to be out. As soon as I hit the courtyard, the cold smacked me. The sky had cleared. The temperature had dropped. I ran back up, chucked the umbrella, grabbed mittens, hat, coat. I was midway across the courtyard when Sief darted out, big smile on his face, "Where you going?"

"Out."

"Where out?"

"Just around."

"I will come with."

"Um. You don't have to."

"I don't mind."

Some people can't take a hint. I pushed through the carriage door and walked off, not waiting for Sief. Aunt Mill's rue was tiny, just a dash on the map, one way leading toward the Café Saint Gervais, the other, who knows.

When Sief caught up he said, "Do you know who you remind me of just now?"

"No."

"Grace Kelly."

"Who?"

"You never hear of Grace Kelly?"

I shook my head.

"But she is American."

I shrugged.

"But she is a princess."

"We don't have princesses in America."

"She was Princess of Monaco. You never hear of *To Catch a Thief?*"

I shook my head again as a truck rattled past.

"Best movie ever."

"So she was a movie star *and* a princess?" I pivoted suddenly and crossed at a right angle.

When Sief caught up again he said, "How can you not know of most famous, beautiful actress in the whole world?"

I stopped. I was lost already. The doof was distracting me. I wanted to pull out my *Paris Par*, but not in front of him. I looked up at the blue street sign.

"Lost already?"

"No."

"Where you trying to go? I will walk you wherever you wanting." He smiled. Ear-to-ear. Big ears. Cute freckles. He looked half African and half Arab or something. I could see why Aunt Millicent called him a Mohican, but Puritan?

I sighed and said, "Where did you learn English?"

"Detroit. Best city in America. I live three years there."

The sun sliced shadows on the buildings. We were standing on the dark side of the rue, the cold side. "Can you take me to the Pompidou Museum?"

"*Le Centre Pompi?*"

I nodded. Sief took off, saying nothing about anything we

passed—boutiques, cafes, tiny alleys, ornate doors. I tried to remember the street names but there were far too many and Sief was zigzagging fast: rue Charlot, rue des Quatre Fils, rue Geoffrey something-or-other.

Suddenly, he halted in front of a tiny store. I knocked into him. He up-nodded and said, "You will like this." Chipped gold letters on a shop window spelled out, *Gausson Bottier, fondé 1831.* Displayed inside were a dozen pairs of expensive riding boots, and pictures of jumping horses, along with a row of riding crops and equestrian trophies. The boxes stacked on shelves, and the machines inside, looked liked they'd been around since 1831.

"Big chedda for those boots," he said.

"I'll bet."

"You ride horses in America?"

"At summer camp."

"How many horses you own?"

"Own? None."

"Me either. But someday I gonna own a dozens. Then I coming here to get my boots. See that sign? Says, boot maker to the king. I gonna say, 'make me the same boots the king wears.'"

A bald man inside the shop looked up from his workbench. He couldn't possibly hear what Sief was saying but he gave us a smirk.

"You wait and see, Homer Simpson," said Sief. "I walk in someday with big chedda and buy two for me and two for Grace Kelly. Which you like best, Grace Kelly?"

"How far are we from the museum?"

His lip curled down. He walked off, flicking a hand for me to follow. A few more zigs and we broke out of the medieval streets to the *"Centre Pompi,"* which looked like a flying oil refinery crash-landed among the ancient buildings. Crowds of people watched a fire-eater guy, so we watched too. Further on,

toward the entrance, two girls in overcoats played violins, cheeks
pink, glasses fogged-up.

"You want to go in the museum?" I asked.

"No. You go. I wait outside."

"But it's cold. Your ears are red."

"I'm okay."

"You want to get a *chocolat chaud* at the café? Aunt Mill
gave me money."

"No. You go. I wait for you."

This was ridiculous. All he had on was a ratty sweater with
a muffler round his neck. Twerp that he was, I couldn't just
leave him to freeze to death.

He gazed up at *Le Pompi*. "It's *cool*, huh? Like inside out
world."

"Like what?"

"Like upside down world. You want to see something *très
cool?*"

Before I could answer, he flicked his hand and set off again,
zigging and zagging. We passed Tour Saint Jacques, then crossed
rue de Rivoli to rue des Halles, stopping midway down. Sief
pointed into a shop window.

Dead rats. Two rows of them, huge things, hanging in
traps, dusty and tattered like the moose head in granddad's rec
room. A sign in the window said: *vers 1925*.

"Super-cool, hunh?"

I squinched my nose.

"You see how they is the same as *Le Centre Pompi?*"

I shook my head.

"It is so simple, Grace Kelly. The rats own down below.
The Under Paris. And these, *bon-bien*, they were foolish to leave
their land and come to ours. So we make them on view, on
*exposé*—as a warning to their brothers below that this is our

world, not theirs.

"But long ago, we bury our dead in their land and they say, okay, we will care for your dead. Then we build the *égouts*—the sewage pipes—and the Metro too. We dig down more and more into their world so that it is impossible for them to escape. We take what is theirs. So the rats and humans are making conflict now. And that is what *Centre Pompi* is talking of *le conflit*—the conflict—between two worlds, above and below. You see?"

I shrugged. I did not see.

# 4. Rossignol C

"He's a bit obsessed with rats and sewers," said Aunt Mill. I had told her about my weird walk with Sief while we sat eating *poulet en pot-au-feu* at Le Saint Gervais. "But there's wisdom in what he says, too," she added.

"Like what?"

"Paris lost half its population during the Black Plague, transmitted by fleas, carried by rats. So rats have a connection to death, the underworld, the afterlife, all that. Rats mark the border between above and below, light and dark. Plus, there actually *is* a vast, other Paris below us. Victor Hugo called *L'égout*—the Paris sewer—'the conscience of the city, a trench of truth, where the immense social sliding ends.' Plus there're the catacombs. You'll have to put the catacombs on your list of things to visit."

"Like bones and skulls and stuff?"

"Bones and skulls—and rats—a whole, underground city of the dead. So Sief was making sense, in his curious way."

Madame Rose came over and asked how everything was and if we wanted dessert, or at least I think that's what she asked, and the two of them started gabbing in French while I watched. After Rose left, Aunt Mill sipped her wine a moment and said, "Have you e-mailed your mom yet?"

I shook my head.

"Why not?"

"I thought you talked to her."

"That's not the same as hearing from you."

I stared at my plate.

"Aunt Millicent, can I ask you something?"

"Certainly."

"Last night, when I was going to bed and you were in your study, you were working on an old-looking paper or something and your safe was open and there were other old-looking papers in there."

"Yes?"

"What were you doing?"

"Working on old papers."

"What kind of old papers?"

"Why should I tell a girl who can't be bothered to e-mail her own mother?"

"If I promise to e-mail her, will you tell me?"

She waved for the bill. We walked back to the apartment and climbed the bowed steps. Aunt Mill unlocked the apartment door then stopped outside her office. "You must promise not to tell anyone about this, Daisy, not even Sief."

"Promise."

She unlocked her office door then knelt and, blocking my view, twisted the dial on the big safe. It woofed as the door swung open. We put on latex gloves. She fished a piece of paper from between two sheets of tissue, and handed it to me. It was old, but not as old as some of the papyrys sheets my dad has shown me. You could see crease marks in the paper where it had been folded, to make it easy to carry in a small pocket, like a note that got passed around at school. Faded brown numbers were written over someone's handwriting. The numbers were grouped in twos or threes like: "22, 412, 878, 21, 67" and so on.

"Are the numbers written in invisible ink?" I asked.

Aunt Mill looked pleased. "They were, yes. It's iron sulfate ink, developed with sodium sulfide. The handwriting was meant to mask the invisible message below. It was written around the time of the French Revolution."

"What's it say?"

"I don't know yet. It's like a math puzzle."

"Who wrote it?"

"That's part of what I'm trying to determine. It was in a package of such things that came from the estate of a British minister in the early nineteenth century, a man in charge of keeping track of French émigrés and diplomats."

"So this is in real secret code?"

"Rossignol C code to be precise, or, well, as precise as we can be at this point."

"Aunt Mill, this is so cool. Are all these papers in your safe secret messages?"

"No. Most are not, but they're from the same time period, written by people we think may have been involved in some way. I'm hoping they'll provide clues or show us whose handwriting this is."

"So is this like your hobby? I mean, why are you doing it?"

"I've been hired to."

"By who?"

"By a man with a lot of curiosity."

I looked at the paper again, squinting. "So are these orders to steal a secret formula or something? You must know something about what it says."

Aunt Mill smiled, considered a second, then said, "Have you ever heard of Jeanne de Valois, Comtesse de la Motte?"

I shook my head.

"What about Marie Antoinette?"

"The queen who got her head cut off?"

"Right. But before that she was involved in—or maybe

ensnared is a better word—what the French call 'The Affair of the Diamond Necklace.'"

"Cool."

"And the Comtesse de la Motte, most believe, helped steal the necklace, a huge, magnificent thing, worth a king's ransom, or, put another way, worth enough to buy a million loaves of bread for the starving people of Paris."

"Did this Comtesse lady get away with it?"

"She did. She fled to London, wrote her memoirs, and lived happily ever after. Until someone pushed her out a window."

"No way."

Aunt Mill laughed. "Way."

# 5. Comtesse de la Motte

I could hardly sleep for thinking about stolen diamonds and the Comtesse de la Motte flying out her window and splatting on the pavement. My days and nights weren't right yet anyway, so it didn't take much to keep me tossing and turning. I thought I heard that piano playing again among the night noises. But maybe I just heard the notes in my head.

A rainy dawn came too soon. I padded into the kitchen in robe and socks and caught Aunt Mill looking frantic, cig hanging out the side of her mouth, scribbling my math problems for the day.

"I couldn't stop thinking about that Comtesse de la Motte last night."

She nodded, gulped down coffee, handed me the page of problems. "Running late. Here's a little geometry review. See you tonight." She dashed off, door locks clicking behind her.

Like before, there were nine problems divided into three groups, only I had to identify angles made by two lines. The answers were multiple choice, each choice assigned a number, so when I added them it gave me the three number combination to the safe.

A cell phone rang. I flinched, till I remembered it was mine.

"Hello?"

"Daisy. Mill. Forgot to tell you about the books. I set them out on the table there. Thought you might enjoy them.

I'm at the Metro entrance. Have a fun day."

At the end of the table were two books, one on the Comtesse de la Motte and one on the French Revolution. I spent the rest of the morning curled up on Aunt Mill's green couch reading some pretty wild stuff and the more I read the more I realized how cool Aunt Mill's old messages were.

Apparently, this Comtesse Jeanne Valois de la Motte, (which is only part of her name cause they had ridiculously long names back then) was a poor, forgotten descendant of some long-dead king and spent her childhood running around barefoot, begging for food. When the then-current king, Louis XVI and his wife, Marie Antoinette, heard about the barefoot comtesse, they felt bad for her and sent her and her sisters some money. Probably a bad idea, since once Jeanne got a little money she just wanted more. She was quite good-looking and had at least three, um, toad boyfriends when she grew up. One was her husband, who was some kind of policeman, the other was a sinister dude named Rétaux de Villette, and the last was Cardinal Rohan, who was like the richest man in France at the time and not very religious, even though he was a cardinal.

Before that, though, a different Louis was king, Louis XV, and he had a girlfriend named Madame du Barry. Madame du Barry was a super hotty, and Louis XV really liked her, but for various complicated reasons she could never be the queen. The king wanted to buy her something really nice, and he asked these two jewelers, Mr. Boehmer and Mr. Bassange, to make Madame du Barry a necklace fit for a queen. Of course, Mr. Boehmer and Mr. Bassange wanted to please the king, so even more people would come to their jewelry store. They bought up every monster diamond they could find, borrowing wheelbarrels of money to do so, creating a truly amazing necklace. But just before they were going to deliver the necklace, Louis XV died.

Madame du Barry was politely asked to get lost, and Louis XVI and Marie Antoinette became king and queen. Boehmer and Bassange now had this monster necklace and no buyer. They went to Louix XVI and asked if he might like to buy it for *his* queen. Marie Antoinette said, basically, that she didn't want a necklace that was made for her husband's uncle's hooker, end of discussion.

Into all this swims the beautiful and sneaky Jeanne de la Motte, who is circling around Versailles, trying to talk to Marie Antoinette so she can weasel more money out of her. But Marie Antoinette learns that Jeanne has three boyfriends, one of whom is Marie Antoinette's old enemy Cardinal Rohan, who like insulted Marie Antoinette's mother when they were in high school or something, so Marie Antoinette is done giving handouts to Jeanne.

Jeanne doesn't give up, though. She knows that Boehmer and Bassange are *desperate* to sell the necklace and that, really, only a king or queen could afford the thing. She also knows that, with Marie Antoinette now on the throne, smarmy Cardinal Rohan is *desperate* to patch things up, since the queen is in a position to do Rohan some serious dirt.

Desperation, Jeanne knows, is not to be wasted.

Though the queen refuses even to speak to Jeanne, Jeanne tells the Cardinal they've become secret best buddies and that Marie Antoinette loves the necklace, is so obsessed with it she can't sleep, but doesn't want the starving French people to think she's just a spoiled, Austrian twit. Before long, Cardinal Rohan gets it into his pea brain (or maybe de la Motte just suggests) that if he secretly bought the necklace for the queen, she would forgive him for insulting her mother. Jeanne even tells the Cardinal that the queen has a crush on him.

On top of that, Jeanne gets her boyfriend, Rétaux de

Villette, who among other things is a good forger, to write fake notes from Marie Antoinette to the Cardinal. The notes confirm all the lies Jeanne tells. In one, the queen writes Cardinal Rohan that if he buys the necklace for her she will pay him back, secretly, in installments, so he won't even be out any money. The Cardinal writes back that he's willing to do so but he wants to talk it over with the queen, in person. Of course Jeanne is supposedly delivering all these notes back and forth from the Cardinal to the queen. Marie Antoinette, however, has no idea any of this is going on.

At this point, Jeanne, or maybe Rétaux, digs up some dim-bulb, out-of-work actress, Nicole le Guay d'Oliva, who looks just like Marie Antoinette and has even played her on stage. Jeanne sets up a secret midnight meeting in a garden at Versailles where Rohan and the fake queen talk, make up, and even make kissy-face. Totally crushing now, the Cardinal goes to Boehmer and Bassange and says he'll buy the necklace and pay them in installments, but only if they keep the deal hush-hush. They agree. They have unpaid diamond merchants sending gorillas after them and figure if you can't trust a cardinal to pay on installments, who can you trust?

Boehmer and Bassange deliver the necklace to Rohan, who gives it to Jeanne to secretly deliver to the queen. And that's the last anyone sees of the necklace.

Rohan never hears back from Marie Antoinette, not even a thank you card, and he can't seem to contact Jeanne, so he sends a note directly to the queen asking her if she likes her little present. The queen has no idea what he's talking about and doesn't even bother to write back, since we're talking about the guy who insulted her mother. Rohan writes her again, then again, and she finally tells him to buzz off. He gets miffed and tells Boehmer and Bassange to get the rest of their money from the queen.

Suffice it to say, the whole thing blows up: public scandal, media frenzy, celebrity trial. Comtesse Jeanne gets thrown in prison but somehow escapes to London, dressed as a boy. Cardinal Rohan lawyers up and walks away, everybody believing he's just a rich idiot. The queen, who had nothing to do with any of it, gets the worst. No prison time of course cause she's a royal, but everyone comes away believing that she's just a spoiled, Austrian twit who just had to have this monster diamond necklace, no matter that half of Paris is starving. Let them eat cake.

# 6. Nina's Song

It was late morning when I put down the book about Jeanne de la Motte and faced my math homework. It dawned on me that instead of doing the problems, if I just added all the variations of numbers I could get two of the three combo numbers. Then I dragged the dial and listened for the click of the third tumbler. Easy.

Inside the safe were more Metro tickets and euros. Not wanting to alert Sief, I ghosted down the steps, snuck across the courtyard, and slipped out the carriage door.

The only sites I'd seen in Paris so far were a schmancy boot shop, some dead rats, and a museum that looked like an oil refinery. So this time, *Paris Par* in hand, I hit Notre-Dame, the Louvre, the Quai d'Orsay, and even the Eiffel Tower.

I made a mess of the Metro getting to the *Tour Eiffel*, but I didn't mind. I loved looking at all the people in the Metro and hearing the roar and squeal of the trains. I loved the blur of color as they zipped in and out of stations and even loved the weird Metro smell, slightly different at every stop.

By the time I got to the base of the Eiffel Tower it was raining again, and getting dark, plus the ticket line was huge-long, and the top of the Tower hid in the clouds anyway. I turned around.

When I climbed out of the Metro at Filles du Calvaire, near Aunt Mill's, night had fallen. My cell phone dinged. Someone had called while I was on the train. I stood on the top step of the entrance staring at the phone. You'd think a French cell phone would work the same as in the US, but no.

A woman came up behind me and screeched at me for blocking the way, so I shuffled along, fiddling with the phone. It had to be Aunt Mill. Who else even knew I had a phone?

Clouds brushed the rooftops now. Fog drifted along the street. I thought I knew the way back to Aunt Mill's but everything looked different in the dark. Without realizing, I took a wrong turn, or maybe a few. None of the rues in Aunt Mill's *arrondissement*, er, neighborhood, run straight and their names change every five feet, and half the shops that were open in the morning were closed now, metal doors, like garage doors, pulled down over their windows.

I reached in my pocket. No *Paris Par*. I searched every pocket three times while people walked around me, carrying groceries and baguettes, chatting on cell phones, talking in French of course. I've been in places where people don't speak English because of Dad's work, but every once in awhile it can creep you out. Not creep you out really—that's not it—but like, make you feel suddenly very alone and lonely.

I walked to the end of the rue and looked up at the blue sign: rue de la Verrerie. Sounded familiar, like one of the streets Sief took me down. I turned around to see if I could at least make it back to the Metro stop.

I walked for ten years. Everything looked familiar. Everything looked strange. I passed rue Quincampoix.

*Quincampoix?* Really?

For some reason I started thinking about Lucia and Mom and even Clymene, about how I was such a miserable friend and miserable daughter and sister, a psycho really, who needed to be on meds for punching people. Maybe the best thing to do was just keep walking in circles till I starved to death and became a ghost, blending with the fog that rushed along these tiny rues.

Voices echoed out of nowhere. I was sure they were evil French gangsters, getting ready to pounce. No doubt when they discovered I had nothing but used Metro tickets and a handful of euros, they'd slice me up and throw me down the sewer to feed Sief's precious rats.

Then I heard the piano. Same song I'd heard tossing and turning at night. I had to be near Aunt Mill's. If I followed that piano I'd be close. I rounded the corner onto rue des Lombard.

That didn't sound familiar, but the piano got louder. I walked on.

The song emanated from a club called Le Baiser Salé. Outside stood a girl of thirteen, talking on her cell phone. I guess you would say she was put together. Black stockings, high-heel boots, a fitted coat, big scarf wrapped round and round, almond eyes, huge lashes, perfect amber skin. Plus, she was gabbing on the same model Samsung cell phone that I had, in English.

"Excuse me," I said.

She held up a finger, spoke into her phone, "Got to go. Text you. No, hey, don't be doing like that. *Bizou.*" She clicked off, pocketed her phone, smiled.

"You speak English," I said.

"I do."

"Have you ever heard that song—the one playing inside there?"

"I have."

"I hear it sometimes late at night."

"Me too."

"Really?"

"My dad plays it all the time."

I must have looked like a dim puppy cause she cocked her head and laughed, then stopped and said, "Are you all right?"

"I lost my map book and I've been wandering around like six years and I, um, I heard your, your dad playing and I think I, I mean—do you know where the Café Saint Gervais is?"

"Around the corner from our apartment."

"Really?"

She nodded.

Now I laughed. She raised a sophisticated brow.

"Sorry. My name's Daisy. I'm acting like a total doof, but I don't always." I whipped out my cell phone. "Can you tell me how to retrieve the message on this thing? I've had it for less than a day and I don't know how it works yet."

She took the phone and tapped a few numbers. "I'm Nina. How long are you in Paris?"

"Till the end of the school year. Like May or June, I

guess."

She handed back the phone. I put it to my ear, listened to the message. Aunt Mill was at home and wondering where I was and if I was hungry. Beep. Nina put out her hand, took back the phone, touched the keypad a few more times. "This saves the message. Hit seven if you want to delete it, star when you're done."

"Are you American?"

"French."

"You speak amazing English."

"My dad's American. Mom's French. Come meet my dad." She walked into Le Baiser Salé, right past the door guy, right up to the stage. A drummer was setting up. A bass player tuned his bass.

"Hey, darling," said a tall, black man with a dark suit, wire-framed glasses and smooth-shaved head. He was sitting at the piano, drinking coffee.

"Dad, this is Daisy. She listens to your music all the time."

"Really?"

"She lives near us. Hears it whenever she's trying to sleep."

He looked over his glasses at me, then at his daughter, then laughed a deep, lovely laugh. Nina kept a straight face but you could tell from her eyes she was pleased.

"I hope it doesn't keep you awake."

"No," I said. "The opposite. It reminds me of all the good things about home."

He smiled, leaned down, stuck out his hand. We shook. "Pleased to meet you, Daisy. I'm Louis. Stick around for the show if you want."

"I'd like to but, um, my aunt is probably wondering if I'm dead."

"I'm going to walk Daisy home, if that's okay," said Nina.

"Sure. Homework finished?"

"Not yet. I'll do it when I get back."

He nodded. We walked out, her dad playing what I would

later learn was "Nina's Song."

Nina glided straight out of the club, straight down rue des Lombards, which turned into rue de la Verrerie, then made one turn, left, on *rue Vieille du Temple*, and that was it. I was at Aunt Mill's. Simple.

We gabbed the whole way there, she texting at the same time and somehow seeing cars in the fog at the cross streets.

Her mom worked as a financial something-or-other. Her dad traveled a lot so it was a treat when he was home and playing in Paris. She attended a *collège* (junior high), hated school, loved boys (especially Gilles, Jean-Claude, Philippe, Bruno), loved clothes (especially Chanel, Dior, Balenciaga), loved New York City, her mother's cooking, and President Obama. She loved that I was being home-schooled by my aunt, love-loved that I had survived on an island and had a face-off with pirates and a shark. She announced, "You are a true *fauve*, Daisy, a *femme sauvage*." I had no idea what she was talking about half the time, but somehow it didn't matter because it was just so fun to talk to her.

When we arrived at Aunt Mill's carriage door, she said, "Give me your phone." I handed it over. She tapped away at it, then handed it back. "I put my number in for you. Call or text when you're lost. Day or night. Or just call and we can hang. Okay?"

"Thank you so much. You saved my life."

"Nah." She gave me a double-cheek kiss and glided off into the fog, the coolest person I had ever met.

# 7. Aunt Mill is a Nazi

"Lost it?" said Aunt Mill, with an exasperated-teacher frown. I was sitting at the table, eating a slice of cold pizza she'd brought home from a place called Pink Flamingo.

"It must have fallen from my pocket in the Metro or something. I'm really sorry. And then I couldn't figure out how to retrieve your message and then I got all turned around in the fog and ended up in this place called Le Baiser Salé."

"You went to the Basier Salé?"

"Is that bad?"

"They let you in?"

"I was with Nina, the girl who showed me the way home."

"How old is Nina?"

"Like thirteen. She lives nearby. Her dad is the guy who you hear playing piano late at night."

"What guy playing piano?"

"You don't hear him?"

She gave me a look I could have gotten from Principal Smootin back home and saved everybody a lot on air fare. Then she shoved forward the work I did that morning. "So this is a curious approach to solving your math problems. It appears you just added the various answers until you got the combination to the safe."

"Yeah?"

"You didn't do the problems."

"I got the answers."

For a nano it looked like she might laugh, but she kept a straight face.

"You can send me home if you want."

"That's not a valid option, Daisy. You're so angry with

your mother right now you won't even contact her, even though I've asked you twice."

"I'm not angry with her."

"No?"

"I just forgot to do it."

"Conveniently."

I wanted to barf pizza. "I'll go do it right now if that's what you want."

"Why don't you then."

I left the room. Stormed out really. The wood floors creaked. I went right to my computer, fired it up, my toe tapping like a mechanical beaver while the laptop did its start-up thing. I clicked open the e-mail and wrote: "Dear Mom, having a wonderful time. Rain never stops. Always dark. Rats everywhere. Food weird. French pizza makes you want to barf."

I deleted that one and wrote: "Dear Mom, Aunt Mill is a Nazi. Why didn't you warn me? She has an armband and a little mustache and everything. She's teaching me how to goose-step. Otherwise everything is just super. Hope you are doing swell. My name is Daisy in case you've forgotten me already."

I deleted that one too, took a deep breath and wrote: "Dear Mom."

But nothing would come after that. My mind blanked, fingers freezing over the keys.

Then I noticed e-mails flooding the inbox. There were a few from my mom and three from Lucia. I didn't want to read them. They would just make me feel worse. But one was from someone named Pauline Dumeril.

It took a moment to place her. She was one of a group of graduate students that adored my dad, which usually made me hate them, but Pauline, who was French, didn't—I don't know— salivate like the others. Tart and snippy was more her thing.

I clicked on her email and read: "Daisy. Do you remember me from the Ban Pak Galley project in Thailand? Your dad wrote and said you were coming to Paris. That's so exciting. I work at the Louvre now, in the restoration department. Would you like to come for a visit? Maybe we could have lunch."

Clearly my dad had emailed this poor woman and said, "Do me a favor, my total-reject, out-of-control daughter has been exiled to Paris, so can you meet up and pretend to be nice to her for an hour or two." I mean, Pauline was like thirty or something, and French, and like a grown up with a job, so we'd obviously have tons in common.

I wrote back: "I remember you, Pauline. How much is my dad paying you to do this?"

I hit send. Zoom. Off it went.

Before I could even start to think of an excuse for not looking at the other emails, a new email arrived from Pauline. She must have been sitting at her computer.

"He's paying me millions. How about we split the money? Come by on Thursday at noon. Porte des Lions entrance at the Louvre, on the Quai François Mitterrand. Look for the bronze lions. Tell the guard you're there to meet me."

I wrote "okay" and hit send. In two seconds Pauline had dug me out of my pity party. I wasn't ready to read my mom's emails yet but I thought I should at least try and look at Lucia's.

Big mistake.

In her first one, Lucia wrote, "Daisy, how is it going over there? Things are the same here. Worse really. Martin is out of control. It seems he has a grudge against me now. Everyday he says something about what I'm wearing or about my body. His remarks are disgusting and getting worse. I don't dare take books out of my backpack till I'm actually seated in the classroom because they'll end up on the floor. Yesterday, after school, when I was walking between two buses, Martin pulled my whole backpack off while everyone just stared. What I don't get is: why me? How did this happen?"

In the next e-mail, Lucia wrote, "Daisy, I haven't heard from you. Are you okay? I miss you so much. Nobody at school talks to me anymore because Martin will start in on them if they do. And now Michael Cornish and David Pebbles have joined Martin in calling me names. They are very sneaky about it too, so the teachers never seem to notice. I don't feel comfortable saying ugly stuff back, so I just try to avoid their eyes and ignore them. I tried telling Mrs. Guffelenta about it and she said, "I'll look into it," and then did nothing. I don't dare cry because it just makes them worse, but I feel like crying all the time. I go to sleep crying and I wake up in the morning and cry. I can't think while I'm in class anymore and when I get home, doing my homework just makes me think of them, so I don't do it."

In the next one she wrote, "Daisy, are you even there? Or have you decided not to talk to me either. Maybe I shouldn't blame you. These are just my problems anyway. You are far away in beautiful Paris. I think about you a lot, having a good time, enjoying the French food and going up in the Eiffel Tower. But maybe you don't even want me to do that. Maybe you don't want me thinking about you because you think I'm such a loser like everybody else. I understand if you don't like me. Even I know I'm a loser."

I didn't know what to write back. I climbed into bed and pulled the covers over my head and cried. My emotions had been snapping up and down like a jump rope all day. What a wreck. After a while Aunt Mill knocked on the door and came and sat on the edge of the bed. I tried to pretend I was asleep, but that was lame.

"Daisy, are you all right?"

I nodded from under the covers.

"You want to talk about it?"

I shook my head.

"Daisy, listen, I'm sorry I was harsh with you. I get testy sometimes. Occupational hazard. I just know your mom really worries about you. More than you know. Your dad too. This probably all seems very strange to you, them sending you here and all, but someday you'll understand."

She thought I was crying because of what she'd said to me earlier. I was tempted to tell her about Lucia's emails, but I didn't. Aunt Mill didn't know Lucia and wouldn't get how responsible I felt.

She said, "It's not a perfect situation, but for right now, let's make the best of it, okay? I'm actually rather glad you're here, believe it or not." She rubbed my shoulders through the blanket. "Come the weekend we'll go do tourist stuff. Sacré Coeur, the Arc de Triomphe, or maybe we can sneak into one of the fashion week ready to wear shows. We'll go anywhere we want and do whatever comes into our heads.   We'll have crepes and roasted chestnuts and a fabulous lunch at La Coupole. Okay?"

I nodded again.

"Get some sleep now. Everything will work out."

She adjusted my covers and left, clicking the door behind her. I listened to her footsteps on the squeaky floorboards. I was already learning which squeaks meant what. I could tell she'd gone into her office. Her chair creaked as she sat at her desk. Somehow her talk had made me feel better again. I hopped up, grabbed the laptop, climbed back into bed and adjusted the covers as the computer woke up.

I wrote: "Dear Lucia, how dare you think you are a loser or that I might not want to talk to you and how dare you think that there is anything wrong with you. You are wonderful and beautiful and smart, much smarter than Martin Blindenbok or Michael or David can ever hope to be. They are worms, Lucia, and they prove their worminess every time they call you something disgusting. Someday we will look back and pity them, that is, if we don't destroy them first.

"I am not the best friend, I know. I have been having a giant pity party ever since I got here and not looking at my e-mails. I wish I was there to stand beside you. But you don't really need me.

"This is a game of chess, Lucia. And as we both know, you are a great chess player. I doubt Martin even knows how to play. So first thing, learn the board you are playing on.

"What are the squares? Think about where Martin lives and how he moves to get to school and where he hides. You already know there are places he doesn't dare bother you, like in the classroom and in front of certain teachers, so start remembering every last one of those places. Those are your safe zones. There is nothing cowardly about using these zones wisely. It's strategic. No one moves their king out into the middle of the board. So, between the school buses is obviously a place to avoid. We learned that the hard way. But you can learn to avoid Martin, even if he tries to set traps.

"Next, learn the pieces. Who are his pawns? Who are his bishops? How do they move? You know David and Michael are his pals, so maybe you wait and take them out when he is not around. Plus, who else does he pick on? Maybe you haven't even noticed them because you are so worried about yourself. But they are there and if you keep your eyes up, you will spot them. Those are your potential allies. Find any person who is being picked on by Martin and make friends with them. Collect them. Tell them how great they are. Say hello to them in front of everyone. If you get picked on for it, so what, you're getting picked on anyway.

"David and Michael might even become your pawns. They pick on you because they don't want to get bullied by Martin. You will find them in a corner some day, without their king (or queen) and you can capture them. Who is the smallest of them? Who is the stupidest? Is there one of them, if you got them alone, that you could say something to? Maybe you will need to rehearse your words, but I think maybe David especially you could take out. All he seems to do is repeat what everybody else says so you can come up with something like, 'Are you just Martin's butt-puppet or can you actually think for yourself?'

"Now who are your queens and rooks? Think about it. The teachers. Okay, so maybe they are really only pawns in this game. But there is no shame in using all your players. That's how you play chess. I admit, Mrs. Guffelenta is as helpful as a turnip, but what about Mr. Reese, or that new art teacher, Ms. Cunniff? Talk to them. Make them listen. Even Mrs. Guffelenta. Go back to her. Go back every day if it takes that. Be dramatic. Say, 'I am losing my hair. I cannot sleep. They pick on me every day.' Even if you don't like to think about it, tell the teachers exactly the words Martin uses. Do it over and over until the teachers have to pay attention. Go to Principal Smootin. Better yet, write him. Write him every time Martin does something.

"It's very late here and I feel like half of what I'm writing sounds crazy, but I'm serious. Most of all I am serious that you can stand up to Martin. You are better than him. Someday, this will be so apparent that he won't even dare come up and speak to you, but for now, stand up straight, have courage, yell your lungs out when he comes near you. And don't you dare think there is anything wrong with you. Don't you dare."

I hit send. I didn't even reread it. Maybe it was crazy stuff to write. But it made me feel better. I hoped it would have the same effect on Lucia. I closed the laptop and squiggled under the covers.

# 8. Art Hospital

On Thursday, I woke up late and barely managed to finish my math problems before noon. Grabbing an umbrella from Aunt Mill's collection, I raced out. Rain pelted down. My sneakers were soaked by the time I found my way to the river. I followed along the Seine to Quai François Mitterrand until I came to the Porte des Lions at the Louvre. I spotted the two bronze lions, then the guard.

After getting buzzed through an iron gate and some thick steel doors, Pauline led me into the *Centre de recherche et de restauration des musées de France.* She explained that it wasn't part of the Louvre, just in the Louvre, though the museum was their biggest client. Basically, it was a hospital for art. She suggested we eat at the employee café instead of slogging through the rain, then led me past offices and workrooms and storage areas with racks and racks of old paintings. One area bulged with crated statues in various states of decay, another with dozens of tapestries. A colleague stopped Pauline to discuss something and I got to peep into a room where a crew in lab coats seemed to be x-raying the parts of an altarpiece.

We ended up in a French version of my school cafeteria, bland and boring, but with Old Master paintings on the wall. The place was jammed because of the rain, but we managed to squeak into a table as two people left. I held the table while Pauline went to the lunch line. She had free lunch coupons or something, and brought back a tray with two *croque monsieurs*—a kind of open-face ham and cheese sandwich with white sauce that's out-of-this-world yummy, especially on cold, damp days.

We spent the first minutes talking about how un-tan we'd both become since the last time we'd met, and about Ban Pak

Village and Dad's Roman galley and what had happened to my family and me on Moken Island. I hadn't seen Pauline since that summer, and though I didn't really spend any time hanging out with her then, it was cool to hear her story of how the dig crew totally freaked when we disappeared. She couldn't believe all the stuff I told her about life on the island and about the pirates and all that. She kept saying, "*Mon Dieu, Daisy, mon Dieu!*"

Eventually, she told me about how she got the job at C2RMF, which is what they called the place, and what they did there. Actually, we talked about all kinds of stuff, too much stuff really, and when we looked up the café was empty. Everyone had gone back to work.

Pauline asked if I'd like to take a look around. She introduced me to a dozen people whose names I promptly forgot, but the work they were doing—pigment stability analysis, 3-D mapping, multi-spectral imaging—was totally cool.

We ended up in her office. She explained that she was in charge of database management for several of the restoration and documentation teams. People kept ducking in to ask her this or that, but she didn't seem in any hurry to kick me out, so we kept talking.

She asked how long I was staying in Paris, so I had to explain the whole kicked-out-of-school-and-sent-to-live-with-my-aunt thing, which, like Aunt Mill, Pauline found amusing. Was I really *that* funny? To change the subject, I asked her if she knew anything about the Comtesse de la Motte.

"Of course. We learn about her in school at the same age you learn about Martha Washington."

"So what do you think happened to the diamond necklace?"

Pauline smiled. "That's the million-euro question, isn't it? How do you know about *L'Affaire,* Daisy?"

"I've been reading a book. It said some of the diamonds were probably sold in London, but it sounded like most of the necklace was never found."

"That's one theory."

"There're others?"

"Some say the diamonds were recovered and secretly returned to the two jewelers because the king didn't want more scandal. Others say they were cut into smaller diamonds and sold off by various, um, *receleurs*—what's the word?—fences."

"Fences?"

"Someone who sells stolen goods. However, a girlfriend of mine in grad school wrote a thesis suggesting the eighteenth century French underworld was too infiltrated by police spies for the diamonds to go unnoticed if they'd been sold."

"Really? She wrote that for school? So cool."

"There are other theories too—that the diamonds were smuggled to America, that one of the participants, perhaps Comtesse de la Motte herself, hid them—buried them, tucked them under a floorboard."

"What about the husband and boyfriend?"

"Retaux and Villette?"

I nodded.

"They both died before Jeanne, so they might have taken a secret with them, but it seems unlikely since they were both tortured by the police. If anyone took a secret with them, it would have been de la Motte herself, when she plunged from the window."

"Do you think she was murdered?"

"Absolutely."

"It couldn't have been an accident?"

Pauline smiled. "There's an old saying that no one ever accidentally falls from a window."

"Really? Who says that?"

"Spies mostly."

Some man stepped into Pauline's office without knocking and they got into a long conversation in French. I couldn't tell what they were saying, but I could see anxiety growing on Pauline's face as they talked. When he left, Pauline puffed out her cheeks and exhaled.

"I better go," I said.

She nodded and stood up. "But this was so fun. You have to promise me you'll visit again." She walked me to the entrance.

We did the double-cheek thing before parting and this time I actually did it right.

Outside, I phoned Aunt Mill to check in. She was just leaving school. We met on rue de Rivoli to walk home together. It was still raining so we walked along under the Rivoli arcade, among the throng of tourists.

"Aunt Mill," I whispered, "I've been reading about it and I have to ask, are you looking for the diamonds or are you trying to figure out who killed Jeanne de la Motte?"

Looking amused, she spoke in a normal voice. "I'm just trying to break a code. If you worry about the other stuff it clouds your judgment."

"How do you actually break a code?"

"Depends on the code."

"What kind of code is this one?"

"It's a substitution code, combined with a complex nomenclature, with homophones to disrupt frequency analysis, using syllables rather than letters in the plaintext."

I must have looked gobsmacked because Aunt Mill laughed. "Let's see, where to begin? Antoine Rossignol was a genius code master who developed a nearly-unbreakable code for Louis XIV. Rossignol's son and grandson followed in the family trade, working for French kings down to the time of the Revolution. After that, the key to their codes were forgotten and nobody could break them for a hundred years."

"Seems funny to forget your own codes."

"Not when you consider there were three revolutions, a few enemy occupations, and—"

Aunt Mill whipped out her umbrella as a boy sprinted by, catching him in the throat, knocking him flat. It happened so fast and with such violence that I didn't believe my eyes. Just as the boy—eight, maybe, dark eyes, tangled hair, filthy clothes—smacked the sidewalk, a woman six steps away screamed, "My purse! He's taken my purse!"

Somehow Aunt Mill had spotted the kid making the snatch even before the woman knew. Poking her umbrella into his chest, Aunt Mill jerked the purse out of his hand, and held it out to the woman.

"Oh-my-god, thank you!"

The waif, or gypsy, or whatever he was, rolled over, popped up, and dashed away, lost instantly in the crowd. The woman—Dior sunglasses, Hermés scarf, Burberry coat—thanked Aunt Millicent a dozen times, offered to buy us dinner, pay us cash, have us to her house in the Hamptons, but Aunt Mill demurred and we scooted on, my mouth hanging open.

"Aunt Mill, how did you do that?"

"What? Oh. Situational awareness, my dear, that's all. Anyway. The point is there are lots of different ways to code messages. One way is to shift letters around, like in Pig Latin. Another is to replace the letters with numbers. But the trouble with that is that some letters, like E, T, A and N, appear in words frequently, while others, like Z and Q, hardly appear at all. So one way of breaking a code is to compare a lot of messages and see how often certain letters appear, or, in other words, what their frequency is."

I nodded, looking up in double awe.

"The Rossignols knew all about frequency, of course, so instead of assigning a number to each letter, they assigned a number to each *syllable*, which changes the frequency of numbers in the code."

"Sneaky."

"Plus they figured out which syllables were used the most, just like they figured out how many times E, T and A were used, and assigned several numbers to the most used syllables, to confuse enemy code breakers further.

"So the frequencies would be off."

"Exactly. Then they threw in other tricks, like placing certain numbers in their messages, called null numbers, that meant 'disregard the number right before this,' *and* assigning numbers for commonly used words—Paris, London, battleship—things like that—to further confuse anyone trying to read their message."

"Breaking codes sounds complicated."

"That's what makes it fun."

"You know what I think?" I said. "I think the diamonds are still out there, waiting for us to discover them."

"Really? Why?"

"I don't know. I just do."

She put a hand around my shoulder and squeezed me in.

"Aunt Mill, can I help you crack the code?"

"You need to be good at math to crack codes."

"I could get good. You could give me more homework."

## 9. Cat Burglar's Assistant

The next day was torture for Aunt Mill. She'd wrenched her knee flattening the purse-snatcher and overnight it swelled up like a Texas grapefruit. She put ice in a ziplock and wrapped it onto her knee with an Ace Bandage, but it kept sliding off. She had to call a taxi to get to school. She didn't even bother saying how bad smoking was when she had her cig by the window. I helped her down the stairs, her jaw locked the whole way.

Still, she managed to write out two dozen math problems before she left. I couldn't even solve the first one. I stared at it for six months. Great code breaker I'd make.

Escaping to the green couch, I read a book about Marie Antoinette for the rest of the morning. The sun got brighter. Math disappeared entirely. Just when I was thinking about getting up to spread butter and jam on a piece of baguette, Sief thumped into the window like a bird.

I couldn't believe it. He hung by a rope, four stories above the street, barely squeezing into the balcony that jutted out a few inches from the living room window. He signaled for me to open up. I just stared. He became frantic, tapping the glass, shouting, "Come on, let me in."

"Are you crazy? You could kill yourself," I said, forcing open the window latch. He tumbled into the room, looking up with a triumphant smile.

"Grace Kelly!"

"Don't call me that. What are you doing?"

"I come to see you since you never come to see me."

"Ever hear of knocking on the door?"

"This is more adventureful."

"What if I wasn't here? You'd just hang in the balcony like

a squished sardine till Aunt Mill came home?"

"I would make a cat burglar escape back to the roof. And anyways, I knew you was here. You want to go for a walk?"

"I'm busy."

"You are just reading of a book."

"Maybe I want to read of a book."

"Maybe I will read of a book too." He started looking through Aunt Mill's stacks, pretending to be interested. "Is there any books on cat burglars?"

"What is it with you and cat burglars?"

"That is what I am going to be—a famous roof man. I comes in like silence, steal the lady's jewels, and vanish into the night like a cat."

"Are you kidding? Turn yourself over to the police now and save the trouble."

"The police will never catch me."

I made an ugh-face. He turned and closed the windows.

"Do you know anything about math, Sief?"

"Like what?"

He followed me into the kitchen. I pointed at the problems. He studied them. "You got another paper?"

I went to my room and brought back a notebook, flipping it open to a clean page. He sat down, licked the end of a pencil, and started writing out the first problem, saying, "When I am done you must destroy of this paper so that Madame Millicent never knows I do this for you."

"Is that the correct answer?"

"Of course."

I watched as he worked, slow and steady, running through all twenty-four problems one after the other, never saying a word. I followed what he was doing the whole time and sure enough one problem after another became clear to me just by watching him. How could that be? How could he do them and I understand how he did them, and yet when I was alone I couldn't see past the first problem?

"*Fini,*" he said, handing me the notebook and pencil. "Now copy out the numbers with your own hand. Then I destroy my paper."

I couldn't do it. I stared at the answers, thinking about all the lies that would grow like weeds from this one lie. So what if I could never do math and break codes—better that Aunt Mill be disappointed with my math than with what a cheat I was. I tore out the page and handed it back to Sief. "Here, just get rid of it."

He didn't take it.

"Can you just forget about it? I'm sorry."

He nodded, took the notebook page and shoved it in his pants pocket.

"I think I've got to get out of here for awhile."

"You want to go for someplace super cool?"

"Does it involve rats?"

He shook his head.

"How far is it?"

"Not far."

"I just thought of something. The key to the apartment is in the safe. Without the math answers, I can't get the key to get back in."

"No problem," he said. He took the notebook, ripped out a sheet of paper. "Go get of your coat." When I came back he was standing at the door, folding the paper into a tiny square so it would keep the latch from catching when the door was pulled closed. I stepped out. He eased the door shut behind us. I started down the stairs. "Not down," he said, "up."

I paused. He darted up the steps, stopping at the top floor landing, where, around a bend in the shadowy hallway, an ancient ladder led to an open skylight. Up Sief shot, through the hatch, smiling back down at me. "Come on, Grace Kelly."

He took me under the shoulder as I came through the hatch. The roof was steep so we just sat there, my butt glued to the cold zinc. I could make out Notre-Dame and Le Centre Pompidou and even, way off, the Tour Eiffel, plus all the chimney pipes and antennas and satellite dishes and gray rooftops of Paris.

"Cool."

"Told you."

He crawled to a thick chimney with a dozen pipes coming out the top and untied a rope from around one of them, pulling up the rope from the edge where it dangled down to Aunt Mill's window. He coiled the rope and tucked it into a corner and said, "Come on. I show you round."

He sauntered off, bent low, staying to the crest of the roof. When he got to a chimney block that formed a barrier from one building to the other, he turned back and signaled to me. I crawled on all fours, moving like a crab. When I got to the chimney I grabbed hold of Sief, then let go, realizing how creepo that was.

He monkeyed up some metal handholds, balanced on the top of the chimney block for a second then disappeared down the other side.

"Sief?"

"Don't be afraid," he called back.

"I'm not."

"No?"

I grabbed the iron rungs and forced myself up, heart thumping, short of breath. I leaned onto the top of the chimney, squiddled my legs over, shimmied across on my butt.

Sief looked up from the other side. "I thought maybe you fall asleep."

I snailed down the rungs. He put out his hands and guided me then took off across this roof, strolling like he owned the place. It made me laugh. I walked upright. There were yards of roof on either side here and the angle wasn't very steep, so there was no way could you fall, but somehow the strangeness of being up here, or the badness of it, made me nervous. We scuttled around a smaller chimney block where the mansard roof dropped off steeply, sticking to the flat walkway on top. On and on we went, one building connected to another in an endless chain, until we climbed onto the bottom ledge of a slate-covered dome and sat side by side.

"This is my favorite place in the world," said Sief.

I could see why. We were all alone with a view that no one except pigeons could see, over a forest of slate and zinc and chimney pipes. Sief pointed out the Pantheon and Sacré Coeur and Tour Montparnasse and a dozen other things till there was nothing left to point out.

"Why did you come to Paris, Grace Kelly?"

"To learn math from my aunt."

"They got math teachers in America."

"Yeah, well, my mom's having a baby and she had complications, you know, like trouble with the baby, so they wanted me out of the house."

He puffed out his lips. "You missing your mom?"

"I guess. Not really. I mean, I don't know."

"All mixed up."

"I'm not mixed up."

"Maybe not you, but your feelings."

"I am my feelings."

"Maybe not so much sometimes."

I gave him a that-makes-no-sense look. He shrugged.

"So are you really going to be a cat burglar?"

"Maybe. Trouble is, when I *pique* somethings, you know, when I steals them, I don't feel so good after. I always worrying about the person, you know? But maybe if it was from a rich person, like diamonds that they don't need, that would be different."

"How do you know they don't need them?"

"Did you ever see someone begging for food?"

"Sure."

"Where?"

"Thailand. Turkey. Philidelphia."

"Did they ever wearing diamonds?"

I laughed, but then nodded. He shrugged.

"I'm freezing, Sief. Let's go."

He hopped off the ledge, held out his hand. I took it, stepped down, and followed him back the way we came. He walked fast now, zipping up and over each of the chimney blocks. He *was* like a cat burglar. I tried my best to keep up with him, pretending I was the great cat burglar's assistant, with pockets full of diamonds, the police in hot pursuit, with endless days of sunning on a tropical beach just ahead, if only we could make our escape.

I didn't notice the satellite cable, or whatever it was, till it snagged my shoe. Over I went, bumping down the roof, taking the end of the cable with me. To say I freaked doesn't come close.

I saw the edge of the roof zooming closer, felt the ridges of zinc panels smacking into my back, heard Sief shouting, diving, flattening himself as he slid down headfirst toward me. I did like a super gym class sit up, fingers to toes, grabbing onto the cable, still snagged on my shoe. It swung me down in an arc, while whatever little nails that held it popped out one after another—plip-plip-plip—till the cable snapped free and I lurched down again, holding a plastic coated wire tied to nothing.

As fast as Sief was coming to me, which was insanely fast, I slid faster, digging into the rib of a roofing panel till my fingernails burned from friction. And then I was at the end. Feet whisking over, then legs, breath stopped, Sief screaming. My fingertips clamped into the lip of metal for a fraction of a second while some voice inside me shouted at me to hang on.

I saw Sief's eyes. He saw mine. He was going to reach me and if he did, all he would accomplish was falling with me since there was nothing for either of us to hold on to. He looked so horrified, so determined, and I knew if I held on for even a nanosecond more he would grab on to me and go over with me, like a complete idiot.

So I let go.

## 10. The Tooth Fairy Crashes

I reached out for the fifth-floor balcony rail as it blurred by, got fingers on it, gravity yanking me off. This threw me forward so my head skidded along the building wall and my ribs crunched into a fourth-floor balcony rail, which jutted out maybe three inches more than the one above. As I bounced off the rail my hands gripped a flowerpot. I flew forward like a fish flopping into a boat, landing nose first on brown carpet in front of the windows, which were swung open while some lady vacuumed the place. She shrieked. Two toddlers—twins maybe, surrounded by building blocks—stared bug-eyed, then laughed.

The lady—grandma maybe, gray hair, faded dress—plastered herself against the wall so hard that a painting came down on her, which didn't help things. She started screaming at me and didn't stop. She's probably still screaming. I couldn't draw breath, couldn't think, couldn't have said anything to her anyway, was still processing the last few seconds while all kinds of weird end-of-life thoughts thundered through my brain.

Grandma shoved her vacuum at me. The kids picked up on her hysteria and wailed, matching the wail of approaching sirens and the shouts of people gathering on the street below. My body was so stoked on adrenaline I could have been cut in two and still walked away, which is what I did, scrambling up, hopping over the roaring vacuum cleaner, finding the door, negotiating the chain and deadbolt, walking right out.

I blew down the stairs three at a time, heard footsteps

pounding below, glanced over the rail and saw four *pompiers* in silver helmets and blue suits sprinting up, slammed myself into an alcove where a communal toilet used to be, and let them fly past. How they didn't notice me, I don't know. I got to the bottom of the stairs, shot down the entrance hall, and dodged out the door, sidestepping the gathering crowd, neck sucked into my coat like some cartoon character, eyes to pavement while everyone stared up.

I glanced back for a nano before darting around the corner. A fire truck blocked the rue, traffic backed to the corner, the crowd swelled, others hung out windows, shouting, disputing, pointing to the roof, to a flowerpot shatterd on the sidewalk. If I'd thought about it, if I'd been capable of thought, I would have realized that Sief was still up there and that my fall had happened so fast that people were still trying to figure out what occurred.

But I wasn't thinking, I was just limping away as fast as I could, vision wavering, heart banging out of my ribs, so freaked that it seemed like hours before I stopped in front of a window and stared in. Clarinets. I remember a row of clarinets. I started shaking, tears leaping to my cheeks, my whole body clenched.

I couldn't catch my breath. There wasn't enough air in the whole world. I'd been so sure I was a goner that I couldn't quite believe I was here. I pressed my head and hands into the icy window to keep from fainting and fought back the urge to vomit everything inside me.

Eventually, a man in an apron with a kind face came out and said something, asking if I was okay probably. I scraped myself off the window and hobbled away. Something navigated me, some autopilot I didn't realize I had. I knew those clarinets, knew that window, knew it was around the corner from Aunt Mill's. When I got close to the carriage door I wheeled suddenly—no way I could face Aunt Mill right now—crossed the street, and headed in the door of Le Saint Gervais.

I stumbled to a table, heard Madame Rose's sweet singsong, *"Bonjour, Daisy,"* and instantly regretted coming in. But I had to stop. Had to. Madame Rose came over, smile wilting.

"What's wrong, *ma puce?*"

"Nothing. I just slipped and fell down. It's nothing. Could I have a *chocolat chaud? S'il vous plaît?"*

She nodded, eyeing me, turning to her husband who, from behind the counter, puffed out his bottom lip and shrugged. She looked back at me and dabbed my nose with a napkin. Blood. I hadn't realized. She worked her tongue around in her cheek a moment, eyeing me, then walked off.

I could feel blood on the inside of my lip now, too. I must have bitten it. I felt the patch on my forehead that had been scraped off, then the burns on my fingers from grasping the zinc roof, then one hurt after another started phoning in—my palms from rasping across the carpet, my spine from twisting like a pretzel, my ribs from cracking into the balcony rail.

Madame Rose came back with the *chocolat chaud* in a wide white cup with a vast pyramid of foam and nutmeg on top. I smiled. She smiled back, put hands on hips, considering what to say no doubt. Luckily, two men walked in and sat at a table and she was obliged to go to them. I knew eventually Madame Rose would talk to Aunt Mill and Aunt Mill would grill me good, but I had some time before that happened, so I could work out what to say. The fact that I was even thinking about what I would say to Aunt Mill was a good sign, though the idea of lying to her or telling her the truth or even explaining anything, made me nauseous again.

I took a sip of chocolate. It was perfect. Warm. Lifting. But it made me feel like puking too, so I had to sip ever so slowly, balancing the life-giving sensation with the feeling that my head would spin off. I tried to imagine a time when life would be livable once more. I imagined pulling covers over my head. That's what I wanted more than anything—to go to Aunt Mill's and crawl into bed. I tried to work out how much time had gone by—it seemed like days. But when I was finally able to think it through, I realized I would be home way before Aunt Mill.

I heard a tap on the window. Sief stared in. He looked like he was staring at a ghost. His eyes got this funny look, like he might cry, then he dashed to the door and whisked in and stood at the table in front of me.

"You're alive! I thought you, you—I go crazy thinking it."

"Go away, Sief."

"*Je suis desolé*, sorry, so sorry."

"I don't want you near me right now."

"I feeling so terrible, Grace Kelly."

"Did you hear me? I just need to be alone."

He nodded just as Madame Rose grabbed him by the neck and yanked him around, yelling at him in a French that would singe hair off a monkey. Twisting away, he yelled back at her. Monsieur Rose came round the end of the bar with a length of pipe, growling like a bear. Sief retreated, shouting at them both, pretending he wasn't afraid of them, though clearly he was.

When he was gone, Madame Rose came and sat across from me. I put my hands below the table so she wouldn't see them shaking.

"What did he do, that filthy snake?"

"Nothing. Really. He bothers me sometimes. It's really nothing. I don't know what's wrong with me."

"Did he push you down? Did he hurt you?"

"No, nothing like that. I'm sorry I acted that way. I think maybe I'm catching a cold."

She glared at me. Not glared really, more like squinted with suspicion. I looked down at the swirl of chocolate and flecks of melted cream. Madame Rose flipped a hand, like she was dismissing the whole disgusting thing, then lurched off, back around the counter. I dug some euros from my pocket and placed them on the table. Madame Rose did not say *au revoir* when I left.

# 11. Bruno Pays the Bill

Two days later I dialed, heard Euro-ring-tone, static, then Nina's voice: "Daisy!"

"Nina, hi."

"Are you lost?"

"No, not lost, just—" I launched in before I lost nerve. "Nina, listen, I wrecked my coat and I need to buy another one and I can't spend much money and I have no idea where to go."

"Wrecked it how?"

"Long story."

"I'm just out of school. Can you get to the Bastille Metro stop?"

"Sure."

"I'll be waiting on the Opera steps." She clicked off.

I googled Bastille Metro and twenty-five minutes later I climbed out of the *rue de la Roquette* exit into a warming sun.

It had been an awful two days since the fall. I'd crawled into bed and basically stayed there, too wrecked to come up with a good lie, telling Aunt Mill I must have eaten something bad, revising my lie when she asked how I scraped my forehead, knowing it would only be a matter of time before she talked to Madame Rose and learned the details about my visit to Le Saint Gervais and the weird scene there with Sief.

I was so afraid Aunt Mill would learn somehow about my fall. Then she'd grill me till I cracked. She'd realize she couldn't leave me unsupervised and send me back home where they'd pack me off to some mental-girl hospital. But Aunt Mill didn't grill me. She inquired gently after me and arranged my covers and mussed my hair and took my temperature and was so nice it made me want to cry.

I woke up that first night thinking I was screaming my head off, muscles all cramped. Snapping upright, I realized I hadn't screamed and wasn't falling to my death. My ribs throbbed like crazy. Every time I fell back asleep the same dream came and I jerked awake again. Next morning, Aunt Mill continued being kind and concerned, even cooking me a soft-boiled egg, the only time I ever saw her cook anything.

Now, crossing a riptide of traffic, I spotted Nina reclining on the Opera steps with the poise of an Egyptian princess in dark glasses, red skinny jeans, black leather jacket, and a scarf twirled like honeycomb around her neck. She bounced up, gave me her wide wonderful smile then a double-cheek kiss. She introduced Gilles—sandy hair, khakis, shirttails hanging—who'd been attending her on the steps. Gilles said, "Very pleased to meet you," in English that was almost as bad as my French then he departed, after a double-cheeker from Nina.

"So what happened to the darling gray coat you had?" We were walking along rue de Lappe, or rather I walked and Nina glided in her graceful way.

"I fell off a roof and lost two buttons and tore the seam at the armpit and smeared the whole thing with something black and icky. Plus I got blood on it."

"Woah-woah, slow down. You fell off a roof?"

I nodded.

"Like the roof of a building?"

I nodded again.

"How high a building?"

"Five stories maybe, but I managed to fall into someone's

balcony."

"Daisy, are you insane?"

I shrugged.

"Well, go on, tell me."

I sighed. I felt better already. "Okay, so there's this kid named Sief who lives in my building. He's my age, has curly hair—maybe you know him?"

She shook her head. We turned down rue Keller, then started going into little boutiques with names like *L'idien* and *Moloko* and *Born Bad*. They had J-Pop clothes and French versions of Goth and a million t-shirts with skulls and Smurfs and Betty Boops. I told Nina about Sief coming down a rope and going up on the roof with him and then about my fall and the chaos after. She handed me jackets and coats and insisted I try them on, all the time peppering me with questions and saying, "ohmygodohmygod." We tried on coats at first but then started trying on everything—hats, boots, skirts. I *never* do this. But Nina was a pro. She could flip through a rack with lightening speed and pull out the only cool thing. It all got mixed up, the story, the clothes, the comments about the story and clothes, and pretty soon we were laughing like goofs and the boutique people were glaring at us. A few times Nina found me coats that looked perfect, but they were all way too expensive, even the ones marked half price.

"*Fauve*-Girl, how much have you got to spend?"

"Like twenty euros my dad gave me for emergncies."

"We can't buy anything for that. We can't even steal anything for that."

"Is there a flea market or something?"

"On the weekend. Not today. Come on, let's take a pause."

We walked down rue Keller. Along the way I stopped and

put my nose to the window of a store called *Bling-Bling* that had gobs of costume jewelry on display.

"Girlfriend," said Nina, nosing up next to me, "if you can't afford a coat, you can't afford any bling."

"Nina, do you know anything about Comtesse de la Motte?"

"Sure. We studied her at school. She ganked Maire Antoinette's necklace."

"Yeah. I was just wondering what the necklace actually looked like."

"Big and shiny."

"Seriously," I said.

"If you want to know about diamonds you should go see my Tante Benice. Well, she's not actually my aunt, she's like my mother's great aunt or something, but she's just like an aunt, and very cute, and old, and she works at Place Vendôme."

"What's Place Vendôme?"

"It's where you shop after you marry your billionaire."

We rounded the corner onto rue de Charonne and took an outside table at Pause Café. It was the last open table because the sun was out and people were snapping up the sunshine while it lasted. Everyone was young and arty or old and intellectual, with owl glasses and thick sweaters and pencil skirts and scarves wrapped like Nina's—a very different crowd than Le Saint Gervais.

A waiter came and we ordered and then Nina lit a cigarette and stretched out her legs in her long feline way. I noticed people looking at her—*men* looking at her. I was creeped out, but it didn't seem to bother her at all.

"I can't believe you smoke," I said.

"I don't really."

"What are you doing then?"

"It's Paris, *fauve*-girl. One sits in cafes and smokes cigarettes and looks and gets looked at." She opened her box of cigs, nudged it toward me.

"Those things are bad for you, Nina."

"Falling off roofs is bad for you. Anyway, you don't inhale, you just puff enough to keep the thing burning and you pose.

"Pose?"

She arched her wrist just so, elongated her neck, let one brow rise minutely higher than the next, let her chin go up a millimeter, let her lips part. She got a far off look, like she was thinking about somebody or something that wasn't there. She was gone from the Pause Café, gone from Paris, gone and yet utterly there. "It makes them wonder about you," she said. "Which is the whole point."

I picked up a cigarette. She came back from gone just long enough to light it for me then went off again while I blew out a stream of smoke, trying not to gag, trying this wrist position and that. I couldn't figure out were to put my elbows or my chin and my eyebrows would not cooperate at all. I wasn't sure I had eyebrows. I'd never paid them any mind before. Then the waiter returned with Nina's tea and my *chocolat chaud* and totally ruined my chance of finding a pose.

"So tell me about Sief," she said, sipping her tea, cig perched between elegant first and middle, lazy vein of smoke curling up.

"He's obnoxious."

"Aren't they all. Cute. Obnoxious. Obvious. Essential."

"Frankly, I don't get the whole boy appeal. My sister's in a constant state over them. She gets herself all frenzied and miserable and then has to make everyone around her miserable too."

"So is Sief crushing on you?"

"Eeeeuuuh."

"Adapt girlfriend."

"It's disgusting. He calls me Grace Kelly. You know who Grace Kelly is?"

She shook her head, parked the cigarette on her lips, took out an iPhone.

"Where did you get that?"

"Brand new. Don't you love it?" She tap-tapped, pirated some wifi, googled away, then turned the phone toward me, having found a net image of Grace Kelly. "Gorgeous," she said. "I see what he means."

"You do not see what he—"

Before I could say more, three boys appeared, borrowed chairs from nearby tables, and crammed in beside us. They were all our age and all infatuated with Nina. There was Gilles, from the Opera steps, and Bruno and Philippe, who went to Nina's school. Nina introduced us. They shook my hand and I said, *"enchantée"* and *"ravie."* For a minute or so they spoke English to me—"How long are you here? How do you like Paris? Where in America do you live? Have you been to California? Do you like California? Did you ever go surfing in California?"—but pretty soon they ran out of English lessons. Then they chattered away in French with each other, but mostly with Nina.

I wasn't totally lost. Somehow, even in the short time I'd been here, certain French words were falling into place. But I didn't need to understand to understand. I could see their faces, glances, gestures. Nina's eyes sparkled and she smiled and laughed and they loved making her laugh and didn't like when she pouted—fake-pouted really. She didn't show favorites and pulled each one of them into the conversation. She had more poise and charm in her little finger than I would ever have.

And somehow through all this conversation Nina was

having a conversation with me, throwing mirthful glances, raising a skeptical brow, rolling her eyes. "Cute, obnoxious, obvious, essential," she seemed to be saying. Then she said something to them that made their heads swivel toward me. All at once they said, *"Non, c'est vrais, un requin, vraiment?"*

"What?" I asked Nina.

"I told them you fought off a shark with a wooden spear."

"Is it true?" asked Bruno.

*"Mais, oui, c'est vrais,"* said Nina, *"Elle n'est pas comme vous mauviettes."*

They groaned. They waved dismissive hands. She looked at me, flicked her eyes upward—time to go—initiating a round of cheek-kisses and promises to meet soon. I started to reach into my pocket but Nina frowned and twicked her head microscopically and off we walked, leaving the three boys with our bill.

"We didn't pay our bill," I said when we got around the corner.

She shrugged. "I think Bruno's crushing on you."

*"Tu exagères, 'moiselle."* I said.

"Daisy, you spoke French!"

I stopped. She was right. Where did that come from? Nina laughed and hooked my arm and we walked down the rue.

"I've been thinking, *fauve*-girl. I have this perfect coat in my closet that I think will fit you perfectly. Want to come over and try it on?"

Of course I did.

## 12. Bad Trade Craft

The coat did fit perfectly. Nina said she'd outgrown it, but I don't think that was true. While I was trying it on, she switched out of her red jeans and leather jacket into a plaid skirt, white blouse, and black cardigan. Though I saw her doing it, I didn't think anything of it at the time. I did notice that her room was spotless.

Their whole apartment was spotless and modern, except for the grand piano in the living room. This must have been the one I heard on my first nights, silent now, since her dad, according to Nina, was playing a date in Prague.

Nina's mom, Anouk, came home wearing a trench coat, beige suit, and serious black glasses. She gave Nina a double-cheeker, but in a formal way, then handed off a briefcase and her coat. *"Dans mon bureau, s'il te plaît."*

Nina whisked off with her mother's things. This is when I understood the change of clothes, which went with a whole different manner and even posture. Gone was the Egyptian Princess with endless legs and a killer pose.

"You must be Daisy."

"Yes, ma'am." My posture straightened, too.

"Nina tells me you're being home-schooled."

"Yes, ma'am."

"Why?"

"Er, I got back to school late cause we, um, had a mishap over the summer—"

Nina returned and jumped in, "They got kidnapped by pirates and shipwrecked on an island and had to survive on canned food and sushi and she had to fight off a shark with a spear, and then they found gold and battled the pirates and everything."

Madame Anouk's brow shot up.

"Right, so when I got back to school I was doing horrible in math and since my Aunt Mill is a math whiz and, oh, also, since my mom is preggers, or pregnant that is, and has complications with the baby—"

I just stopped. The whole situation already sounded too weird for words and I hadn't even told about punching Martin or getting expelled or that I was considered too dangerous for the Fairfield School and, therefore, the last person in the world you would want your daughter hanging out with.

Thankfully, the phone rang: Nina's dad calling long distance before he went on stage. They got on two lines and talked to him, leaving me to stare down Ornette, the family cat, who made it perfectly clear he didn't approve of me either.

When the call ended, Nina's Mom asked her if her homework was finished.

"No."

"Started?"

"No."

"So you're counting on divine intervention?"

Nina didn't bother answering that one.

"Well, Daisy," said Nina's Mom, "it appears that it's time for you to go."

"For sure, totally."

"You must visit us again sometime."

"For sure, totally."

Nina's mom scared me. Classy and perfect like Nina. But

strict too, with eyes like the cat's that couldn't be fooled.

When I returned to the apartment, I could hear Aunt Mill in her study, talking on her cell phone in French, her voice just this side of shouting. At one point she broke into English, saying, "It can't be, Felix, it makes no sense. I'll bring the originals over so you can see for yourself."

I ghosted into my room, trying to avoid her, but a floorboard creaked. Phone call over, she knocked and came into my room.

"Daisy? You're back. Feeling better?"

"Much better, thanks."

"Where were you?"

"Hanging out with Nina. Who was that on the phone?"

"Hm? Oh. That was Felix. A friend. You'll meet him. We're going to have dinner."

"Is he the man who hired you to work on the code?"

"No, but he knows a lot about—about math and things. So now, Daisy, I talked to Madame Rose and she said you came into the café the other day and she thought you'd been in a fight."

"She did?"

"Yes. She said Sief came in and you became—*très déboussolée*—very upset with him."

"Oh."

"Well?"

She eyed me, but not like in a hyper-suspicious way. Still, part of me wanted to crack right there. "Well, I certainly wasn't in a fight. I don't think Madame Rose likes Sief very much. She and Monsieur Rose started yelling at him the moment he came in and then chased him out. To tell you the truth, *they* seemed *très déboussolé* with him."

"Yes, well, there's some history there. He's a bit of an urchin, Sief. An adorable urchin, but an urchin nonetheless. In any case, he won't bother you anymore."

I didn't say anything to that, since almost anything I could say might lead to another question. She eyed me a little longer then puffed cheeks and blew out a stream of air, a very French kind of expression, as I'd come to learn. "Listen," she said, "I've had a setback of sorts. My knee took a bad turn today. I need you to do me a favor tomorrow. There's a rare book dealer, Serge Lupatreaux, on rue Vivienne, near the Palais-Royal. He has a very old, very rare book, and I need you to pick it up for me."

"Okay."

"It's worth a small fortune, so no goofing around. Straight there, then straight back. The book will be wrapped up and padded but you must not drop it or get it wet or let it fall out of your pocket. I'll show it to you when you get home, so don't open the package. Understood?"

I nodded. "Is it a code book or something?"

"Or something. Keep it tucked under your arm and come straight home."

"Will I need to give Loop-a-toad money for it?"

"Lupatreaux. No, Felix made the arrangements."

"'Kay."

"Lupatreaux's an amusing man. Ask him to show you his Gutenberg Bible."

"Why's it so important to have this book?"

She pressed lips together, like she was fighting some habit within herself, some inclination to secrecy, but in the end she said, "The book is a series of essays on diplomatic issues by a minister named Jean-Marie Cournac, who was a spy handler for Louis XVI."

"Sixteen was Marie Antoinette's husband?"

"Right."

"What's a spy handler?"

"It's a person who manages secret agents in the field. In this case Cournac was the handler for an agent code-named Smythe, who had worked his way into *Jeanne de la Motte's* confidence when she was living in London."

"Smythe, really? They couldn't think of a better name?"

"Apparently not. Smythe's notes from Cournac were confiscated by British authorities when he was arrested in 1791. Very bad tradecraft not to destroy them, but our good fortune that he didn't. The notes Smythe sent back to Cournac in France were lost during the Revolution. Still, we can surmise from what we have that Jeanne de la Motte had run out of money in London and was looking for a trustworthy courier to pick up a package in Paris."

"A package of diamonds?"

Aunt Mill smiled. "There are a lot of gaps to fill in. Which is why I need the book. It's the way Cournac writes that's important, since we know he was familiar with the Rossignol codes and used them frequently. So much of usage and idiom has changed since then."

"You mean they talked differently back then, even in French?"

"Talked and wrote. I can analyze un-coded text the same way I can a secret message and learn the patterns of someone's thoughts and words. Sometimes those patterns will reappear in a coded text."

"Cool. Thank you so much, Aunt Mill."

"For what?"

"For trusting me with the mission."

# 13. Lupatreaux

Finding Lupatreaux's shop required a bit of work, even with Aunt Mill's written instructions. It was tucked away in the Galerie Vivienne, a shopping mall built two centuries ago with an iron and glass canopy over tiny streets. I wandered back and forth, passing boho boutiques and antique toy stores. I even uttered "Lupatreaux?" several times to a couple who worked in a used bookshop, but they just looked at each other and shrugged. Finally I located some crusty, spiraling stairs that led to a door with a bronze sign that read: "Serge Lupatreaux, Livres Anciens."

I knocked and stood in the stale gloom, getting the feeling you get sometimes in Paris, at certain hours and in certain places, that nothing has changed since the Three Musketeers stood waiting, at this same door, in this same gloom, on some important business for the king.

A towering man with a Neanderthal jaw, massive shoulders, and no neck answered the door. He wore a Nike tracksuit and trainers.

"Monsieur Lupatreaux?"

He nodded. Somehow I'd imagined, I don't know, a more hobbit-like person.

"I'm Daisy." I held out Aunt Mill's note. He blocked the door while he read, grunted, nodded for me to enter, and locked the door behind us.

If Lupatreaux disappointed in his un-hobbitness, his hobbit-hole did not. It must have been some grandee's library once, with busts of Greek smart-guys on pedestals, ladders to reach the upper shelves, and schmancy chandeliers. There were books on shelves that reached to the ceiling, books in locked cases, books stacked in freestanding towers like stalagmites. The place was sugarcoated with dust and had the most wonderful smell, like you would get smarter just by inhaling it. Despite the gloomy day, the skylight above created a broad streak of dancing particles like the hovering souls of departed books.

Lupatreaux led me to a desk that was a catastrophe of glue pots, obscure tools, spools of thread, and dismembered books. He handed me a package, spongy with bubble-wrap.

"Aunt Mill said I should ask to see the Gutenberg Bible."

"Enh?"

"She said you had a Gutenberg Bible. Gutenberg. Bible."

He cocked his head.

I did my best to sound French-like, *"Une bible de Gutenberg?"* But Lupatreaux waved a hand and made it clear that he was too busy to be bothered.

"No bible?" I kept on.

He shoved me toward the door, speaking in French. I picked up *"allez"* and *"au revoir"* and *"très occupé"* and a few other snatches. But the funny thing was it sounded more like Russian than French.

He locked the door behind me. I stood there with the package under my arm. It seemed so odd. Aren't you supposed to let people browse your store? Aren't you supposed to show off your Gutenberg Bible if you have one?

I plonked down the steps, dust poofing under my feet, then made my way out onto the rue Vivienne. Aunt Mill had suggested a different route back, saying that I shouldn't miss seeing the *Palais Royal*.

A geometric garden anchored the center of the Palais Royal,

with shrubs trimmed into cubes and cones, all surrounded by a covered arcade lined with curious shops selling antique buttons, or military metals or Japanese kimonos. Aunt Mill had gone on about how it was once a posh party palace, a sort of eighteenth-century Las Vegas that hosted Ben Franklin and Napoleon and some dude named Voltaire.

A photographer, with attending assistants, was doing a fashion shoot in the center of the garden, lights all over. The poor, skinny model was clad in a nighty, balanced astride a stone sphinx, and struggling to look like she wasn't freezing to death, though clearly she was. I stopped to stare.

That's when Sief grabbed me.

In the nano before I recognized him, I clutched the package so hard the bubble-wrap popped. He pulled me behind a column and shushed me.

"What the—"

"Give me your camera."

"What?"

"Quick. Someone follows you."

"What are you talking—"

"Keep walking. I take picture as he pass and meet you at home."

Part of me wanted to flatten his nose, but instead, I fished out the digital and placed it in his hand. He shoved me out from behind the column. "Go. I see you in a minute."

I turned to see who was following me.

"Don't look," he hissed, "just walk!"

I walked on, totally creeped. My legs felt like cream cheese. I pulled the package into my gut.

At the end of the arcade, I stopped. I'd forgotten where I was going. I crossed through the forest of black and white columns, cutting through to rue de Valois. I so wanted to look behind me. I stopped at the corner, swinging around, trying to look like a lost tourist. I saw a dozen people—kids and moms and nuns and workmen in blue coveralls, but no one who seemed to be following me.

It occurred to me that Sief had just stolen my camera. I'd handed it to him like a dope. The little slime had followed me. I got so mad I wasn't scared anymore. I walked on toward the Place des Victoires. Boy was he going to get it. Wait till I told Aunt Mill. He'd be hanging in that shop window on rue des Halles with all the other rats.

Out of nowhere, Sief appeared and yanked the book out of my hand.

He pulled so hard I smashed into a store window, crashing onto my butt. By the time I jumped up he was halfway down the block, turning into an alley.

I peeled after him. He led me down crooked passages and across courtyards and out into tiny rues. I won't even repeat what I shouted at him. It'll just get me in trouble. But it was ugly.

Sief pivoted around a corner. I slid down in a puddle trying to make the turn, ripping my jeans. I staggered up just in time to see a gray Mercedes stop right in front of him. A huge guy in a black suit and sunglasses jumped out and grabbed Sief by the throat. He ripped my book out of Sief's hand, tossed it to the ground, and tried to throw Sief in the car. I froze. This was so weird I couldn't process. Sief struggled like a spider going into a jar. The guy punched him—grown-up punched him. But somehow Sief wiggled free and ran. Another man inside the Mercedes shouted something, and the guy in sunglasses got back in, and the car tore off.

I stood there, mouth slack, brain stuck, until some woman came out of a store and bent to look at my package. I threw myself forward, snatched it up, and shouted, "Don't touch that."

The whole way back I kept looking behind me. Everyone seemed suspicious now—kids eating crepes, Chinese tourists, waiters in white aprons. As soon as the carriage door closed behind me, Sief emerged from his side of the courtyard. I almost screamed.

"I have your camera. I gets picture of guy."
He fumbled with the camera, trying to get it into playback mode. I snatched it out of his hands just as the first picture came up. It was a blur.

"Not that one." He looked over my shoulder as I clicked through blur after blur.

"That one." The picture showed a man in a dark passage. He was in silhouette. You could barely see his face at all.

"Great."

"I don't know how to use your camera too well."

"Sief, why did you take my package?"

"I was afraid. I thinking, I mean, I thought maybe those men kidnapping you. Or I thinked—thought—maybe they takes your package."

"So you decided to steal it yourself?"

"No. I was behind you and I saw the man in this picture talking to the man in the car and then the car drove ahead of you and you did not see it and I thought, run, Daisy, run, and then I thinked—thought—okay, make her chase me and so I take the package so you chase me and get away from them."

His nose was smeared with blood. His eye was puffed out.

"Sief, why did they want to put you in the car?"

"For stopping them maybe. Or for taking the package maybe. I don't know. But now you got the package back anyway."

"They left it."

"Why? It makes none sense."

"It makes no sense."

"What is in the package?"

"I can't say."

"Is it for Madame Millicent?"

"Sief, why were you following me in the first place?"

He looked at his sneakers.

"Why?"

"I don't know."

"It's creepy."

"But I like you, Grace Kelly. And Madame Millicent said I can't talk to you never again, or come near you or nothing, so I did not mean to talk to you or come near you but then I see this man following you."

"When did Aunt Mill say you couldn't talk to me?"

"After you tell her you falls from the rooftops. She had such anger with me and said I can't talk to you no more, never. You can't tell her I talked to you, Daisy. You please can't do that."

"Wait. I never told her I fell. I wouldn't dare."

"You didn't?"

"No."

"Maybe she talks to Madame Rose at Le Saint Gervais."

"Yeah, but Madame Rose didn't know I fell. She knew something was wrong, but she didn't know what. Sief, why did Madame Rose get so mad at you that day?"

He looked away and shrugged, "Cause I bothering you."

"It was more than that. She was really mad. Did you steal from them?"

His eyes snapped up. "Did she tell you this?"

"She didn't tell me anything."

Another shrug. "Maybe a little. Nothing much. From the

tables outside. Sometimes tourists leave *pourboire.*"

"Tips? You took tips?"

He gave me a glance like I didn't have a clue about anything then gazed at his feet. "I was hungry. When my father go away for awhile I, you know, I haven't got nobody around. My mom, she is just died and, well, so, I get hungry." He glanced over a second and shrugged. "But then Madame Millicent give me food and let me stay with her and, and my father come back after awhile."

"Where was he?"

"He goed away because of his sadness. But after some time he comes back." He looked so unhappy, I was sorry I asked.

His eyes would not return to mine.

"Thank you for helping me, Sief."

He nodded, but still his eyes didn't come back. I looked at my digital camera again, looked at the black shape of the man who had been following me. Sief saw me looking and gave a flick of his head. "He was Russian."

"How do you know?"

"I hear him talk. The other man, the one who hits me, he is Russian too. I saw a tattoo on his neck. *Un serpent*, a snake, *qui sort d'un crane et une croix entourée de barbelés.*" I shook my head. He searched for the words. "It's like a snake inside the, the dead man's head bone."

"A snake in a skull?"

"Yes, skull. And then a cross, you know, and then *des barbelés,* the wire for keeping animals in a farm."

"Barbwire?"

"Yes, barbwire. It is Russian criminal tattoo. They all has meaning. My cousin, Zyed, will know who is this man."

"How will he know?"

Sief shrugged. "He knows of these things."

# 14. The Sixteenth

Aunt Mill was in book bliss. As soon as I handed over the package she pulled on latex gloves, took up a razor knife, cut away the outer paper, the bubble wrap, and the inner tissue, revealing this little brown volume with brittle pages and a cracked leather cover. Didn't look like much to me. But she hunched over it, flipping on her work lamp so she could see it better, gently separating each page. Without looking up, she said, "How did you like Lupatreaux?"

"He seemed strange."

"How so?"

"Well for one thing, he was huge."

She nodded, but I don't think she really heard. Part of me wanted to tell her that Lupatreaux spoke with a Russian accent and didn't look like a hobbit and didn't show me his lousy bible and that someone followed me in the Palais Royal and someone else with a weird gangster tattoo tried to—to what? Kidnap me? Not really. Kidnap Sief? Well, maybe, but not really either. It seemed like they didn't want Sief making off with the book. But they didn't want the book either. It made, as Sief said, none sense.

So I didn't say anything more. If I told her *anything* it would lead to questions about what Sief was doing there and what he'd done to me before he came into Madame Rose's that day which would lead to the roof and me falling off. Couldn't go there.

Plus the whole thing seemed too weird. Was some guy

really following me? *Really?* I never actually saw the guy in the photo that Sief showed me. Sief could have taken a snap of any random guy. And for all I know the man in the sunglasses and black suit was a policeman with a tattoo who thought Sief was a gypsy thief. After all, Aunt Mill had clotheslined a kid on the rue de Rivoli without a second thought. Paris was full of pint-sized thieves and Sief, by his own admission, was one of them, stealing change off Madame Rose's tables.

It wouldn't leave me alone though. Aunt Mill spent the afternoon with her nose in the book while my head contorted with thoughts. I kept telling myself to get real. How would anyone know to follow me? And so what if Lupatreaux didn't look like a hobbit? Who ever said he would? Plus, who said he *shouldn't* have a Russian accent? Serge is kind of a Russian name, right? Maybe he emigrated from Moscow. And maybe he just wasn't in the mood to show off his Gutenberg Bible.

Brain churning, I turned on my laptop, brought up Google, and typed in Serge Lupatreaux. And there he was, a dozen photos: in his store, at an antique book festival, in a blog article about the Paris book-dealer's guild. He had a mop of white hair, thick glasses, a nose like a cork, sparkling eyes. A hobbit.

"Daisy, I lost track of time. We have to go." Aunt Mill stood right behind me.

"Go where?"

"We're having dinner with Felix. Do you have a nice dress?"

"A what?"

She rushed to the armoire, flipping hangers back and forth, extracting the ugly, gray dress Mom forced Dad to put in my suitcase. "In case she has to meet the president of France," Mom had said. Yeah, right.

"Here, put this on," said Aunt Mill.

"Do I have to?"

"We're going to the Sixteenth, darling."

"Which means?"

"Just put it on. We're running late and I need to get ready myself." She tossed the dress on my bed and thumped out.

The next twenty minutes were a horror of Aunt Mill dashing in and out to alter my appearance. She was worse than Mom. She brushed my hair, put a ribbon in it, criticized my shoes, was aghast at the hole in my tights—it was a nightmare. *Did I have any jewelry? Try this then. Let's try your hair this way. No you may not wear sneakers. I don't care if you hate those shoes. I don't care if you're crippled for life by those shoes. We're going to the Sixteenth, Daisy!*

We took a taxi because we were late and because Aunt Mill's knee was acting up. I felt ridiculous in the gray dress and tights and cramped black shoes and the scarf she'd tied into my hair and the silver necklace that made me feel like some pathetic, poser dweebette.

We scooted along the rue de Rivoli, passing the *Tuileries*, battling through the Place de la Concorde traffic.

"You look lovely, Daisy."

I gave back tight-lip.

"You're a pretty girl, you know, when you put a little effort into it and when your face isn't twisted into a smirk."

I wanted to roll my eyes. Instead I pressed my nose against the cold window.

"That's a pretty coat. I haven't seen it before."

"Nina lent it to me. She has a million."

Aunt Mill nodded. I could see her looking me over in the reflection of the window. She was dressed up too—pearls, blue suit, a humongous kaleidoscopic scarf.

"Who is this guy anyway?" I asked.

"Felix? He's a delightful man. My mentor in a way.

Intelligent, charming, knows just about everything there is to know and everyone there is to know too."

"So he's not your boyfriend?"

"Heavens, no. Just a dear colleague. You should ask him about his days in the French Underground. He was on the run from the Gestapo at age ten. Delivering documents, helping Jewish refugees escape. He's a *Chevalier de la Légion d'honneur,* no less."

We slid along the river, passing Bateaux Mouches, melding onto Avenue du Président Wilson, climbing up rue de Longchamp. We caught glimpses of the Tour Eiffel above long rows of elegant apartments. The streets were wider than in Aunt Mill's *arrondissement.* Each one had a lady in a stylish coat walking a pampered mini-dog.

"So, is this the Sixteenth?"

"It is," said Aunt Mill. We pulled up in front of a palatial building on a street of palatial buildings, with stone lions scowling down at us in disdain.

We were buzzed into a marble lobby with a bronze naiad in her own fountain, water gurgling from a cornucopia in her arms. An elevator, creaking lethargically, deposited us on the third floor. Aunt Millicent and Felix cheek-smooched about sixty times before he broke off and said, "And you must be Daisy."

"I must be."

A quick glance at Aunt Mill then he turned and smiled and extended a hand, "Felix Henri Chareau-Aghion de Pindenhaus at your service, Mademoiselle."

*"Je suis ravie, certainement, monsieur,"* I spouted like a nit. I put out my hand to shake. He bent and kissed it.

I flinched. He laughed, a bird twitter, and turned to Aunt Mill, "She knows French?"

"You've just heard the bulk of it," she said.

He guided us in. They started gabbing a mile a minute, in French, while I stood gaping at the place. The entrance gave into a ballroom with eggnog-colored walls, trimmed in gold. The rugs were a biege that made you afraid to walk on them. Everything was perfect: white lilies, gilt furnishings, a flawless mix of modern and ancient things. Right next to a plastic statue of Minnie Mouse was a real Picasso painting. Of a naked woman.

"Is that a Picasso?" I interrupted.

"Why, yes, it's of my mother. They were good friends, you know?"

Clearly I didn't.

"I have another of her, with more clothes on." He guided us into a room with built-in bookshelves and three life-size portraits in ornate frames. One showed an old guy in a black suit, the other a military dude with a brass helmet, the last a slender woman in a pale-green dress, diamond tiara on her head.

"There's the princess," said Felix. "It's by Philip de László. They were good friends too."

As we drifted toward the dining room, he told us how she'd married twice, first to the cavalry officer, who died in some colonial war, then to the banker, who died of a stroke and made her rich. She led a riotous life, cavorting with this painter and that poet, right up to April 1940, when the Germans invaded and she joined *la Résistance*. He saw little of her after. When he did, she would appear suddenly and command him to carry papers to some unknown address or deliver money to someone in a squalid café across town. Then she disappeared altogether. He was ten years old. An orphan. Wanted by the Gestapo.

"What happened to your mom?" I asked.

"Oh, I'm sure the Boche got her."

"But you survived."

"So I did. I was about your age when the Yanks arrived.

Skinny as an eel and living in the sewers."

We sat at a table arrayed with silverware and fine china. A tiny woman, gray hairs escaping at odd angles from her bun and dressed all in black, tottered in and delivered a *soufflé de crabe*. It looked golden and gorgeous but turned out to be tasteless.

Felix, dressed in a suit for the evening, was easily in his eighties. Magda, the housemaid in black, looked a decade older.

Aunt Mill and Felix started speaking French, drinking glass after glass of wine, and ignoring me. I could tell they were talking about the book and the diamonds. It was infuriating to sit there and *maybe* understand every twentieth word. Lupatreaux, I understood. They said that repeatedly. Diamond is the same word in English as French, so I got that. I picked up Jean-Marie Cournac's name a few times, and Smythe and de la Motte and Versailles and a few other things. They said the name *Samuelson* a few times too, whoever that was. They seemed to be arguing one moment and teasing each other the next. Infuriating.

Something crashed in the kitchen. We heard Magda cursing in Portuguese. Felix excused himself and went to the rescue. Aunt Mill refilled her glass.

"What were you guys talking about?"

"Oh, just shoptalk."

"Aunt Mill, which one was Felix's dad, the soldier or the banker?"

She gave me her amused look and said, "Actually, neither."

"So, does that mean his dad might have been Picasso?"

"You'll have to ask *him* that, my dear."

Felix returned with a platter of charred Châteaubriande. Magda followed with a dish of Coquilles aux Asperges. I held my breath as she tottered around the table with the wine, squinting as she refilled everyone's glass, including mine.

Felix and Aunt Mill went back to gabbing in French. The

meat was dry, the asparagus transformed into mush. Aunt Mill pretended everything was delightful. I took sip after sip of wine, just to see if she would give me the evil eye or something, but on they blabbed. At one point Aunt Mill broke into English. "I'll do a phonetic analysis of the whole book if I have to," she said. Then back they plunged into French.

Another crash came from the kitchen, this time with the wub-wub-wub of a bowl settling on the floor, and more flaming Portuguese. Felix threw up hands. Aunt Mill pushed back her chair, saying, "Relax, Felix. I'll take care of it." She slipped off into the kitchen. Felix glanced at me, then glanced away, embarrassed, I think. He stared into his wine glass.

"May I ask you something?"

He looked up, smiling. "Of course."

"Where is Monsieur Lupatreaux from?"

"Lupatreaux? Why, from Argenteuil I believe, where the asparagus comes from. Though I doubt they grow much asparagus there anymore."

"Where is Argenteuil?"

"Just outside Paris."

"Was Lupatreaux born there?"

"I believe so, yes. His family had a place there, not far from where Monet painted *Le Dejeuner sur l'herbe*."

Aunt Mill returned with a salad that had probably been scraped off the floor. Magda followed with a cheese platter and a monumental frown. Felix and Aunt Mill switched back to French again and I sat there thinking how strange it was that the neckless Russian in the tracksuit had said he was Lupatreaux when clearly he was not.

## 15. Peaches of the Devil

I woke the next day with fuzz-brain and sandpaper tongue. It had been a hideous evening, topped off by Magda nearly igniting us all when she lit up her *Pêches à la diable* after drenching it with a half liter of Kirsch. I'd been sipping the wine all evening, hoping they'd tell me to stop, but neither Felix nor Aunt Mill seemed to notice. Then I downed three helpings of the peaches with Kirsch. I'm not like some sneaky kid-drinker or anything. I only did it out of boredom, really.

By the time we left, I was feeling, I don't know, not like seeing pink elephants or anything, but a bit loopy. Aunt Mill had retreated to "the water closet" while Magda fetched our coats. Felix and I were standing alone by the naked mom painting and I was thinking how you would *never* get my mom to pose like that, but I didn't feel like talking about it, afraid I'd slur my words.

I guess Felix wanted to fill the silence so he said in a hushed voice, "Your aunt is a very courageous woman, you know. The only woman to be inducted into the Society of the Cincinnati."

"The what?"

"It's a military honor society started by officers who served under General Washington. Some were French, like Lafayette, but most were American. Only the oldest descendant sons of these officers can be members. Occasionally they induct someone for extraordinary valor, like your aunt."

I'm sure he expected me to ask what she'd done to get in, but at that point, after they'd ignored me all evening, I didn't care if she'd single-handedly saved a truck load of puppies from a sausage factory.

"Did you have too much to drink last night, Daisy?" Aunt Mill stood over my bed, amused smirk on her face, having opened the shade then the window, flooding the room with ghastly sunlight and icy air.

"I feel like a mushed dog turd on a wet Parisian sidewalk, if you want to know."

"Luckily, I don't really. I just wanted to see if you were alive before I left. Your math problems are on the table."

"Aunt Mill, who is Samuelson?"

She squinted. "Who?"

Too long. By just a nano. She was faking. "Samuelson. The guy you and Felix were talking about at dinner."

"We were talking in French."

"Duh. Noticed. All evening in fact."

"Does that bother you? That we spoke French in France?"

"Don't avoid the question. Who is he?"

She laughed. "Daisy, you must have imagined we said that. Sometimes, when French words run together in a random pattern an English word will seem to pop out. It's because of the tonic stress French puts on various words. And of course, drinking too much wine will have an aggravating effect."

"Good try. What's so important about Samuelson?"

She just smiled—a smile of pride?

"Is he the guy you're working for?"

"I promise, next time I take you to dinner we'll speak more English. Plus we never have gotten you into a French class. We really should."

"I've been studying on my own. On this thing called the Internet. Maybe you've heard of it. Does Samuelson know where the diamonds are?"

"We *know* where the diamonds are, Daisy."

"We do?"

"Yes. They're in the vault of a Swiss art dealer."

"I thought they were lost."

"I never said that."

*"Aunt Mill?"*

"I'm not trying to *find* the diamonds, Daisy. I'm trying to determine whether the diamonds Babinet has are the real thing."

"Who's Babinet?"

"The Swiss art dealer. He deals in old masters and antiquities. He sells to museums and big-wallet collectors all over the world. I think he's a tad shady personally, but he's managed to keep a good reputation."

"So you're telling me this Babinet guy has the real Queen's Diamonds?"

"Do you know what provenance is?"

"Sure, my dad deals with that. It's proving something is authentic."

"Exactly. And that's what I'm doing. If these coded messages can connect Babinet's diamonds to the Queen's Diamonds, then their value obviously goes up."

I took a moment to absorb that.

"Listen, I'm running late. We'll talk this evening. I left a tube of asprin near your math problems."

After she left, I stumbled out of bed into the kitchen. The math problems were long snakes of numbers and symbols. It was her way of punishing me. Downing a glass of water, grabbing a stale end of baguette to gnaw, I tinkered with the problems, half guessing the answers, but they were every bit as snakelike as they looked, humongous pythons squeezing the brains out of me like so much minty toothpaste.

I headed back to bed, dozing off, only to have the neckless

Russian guy in Nike warm-ups douse me with Kirsch and light me on fire. I woke up with a yelp.

Okay, so maybe he *was* a Russian gangster. Or maybe Lupatreaux had a very large intern. Either way, I had to know. Getting dressed, brushing my hair, ignoring my math problems, I tromped down the steps and headed back toward the Galerie Vivienne.

At the foot of Lupatreaux's stairs my heart started pounding and my breath got short. Part of me felt silly, the other part terrified. I climbed the steps, stopped in front of Lupatreaux's door, placed one foot behind the other in case I had to run, and knocked.

The locks ker-clunked and the door squawked open, answered by a little man with white hair, thick glasses, a cork of a nose.

*"Monsieur Lupatreaux?"*

*"Oui."*

I gushed like a balloon, "Hi, I'm Daisy, the girl who came by to pick up the book yesterday. My Aunt Mill is a friend of Felix Henri Chareau de Pindenhose, or something really long like that, but when I came here there was this other man, a big guy, and I was wondering if—"

His eyes went wide with fear when it dawned on him who I was. The door slammed in my face.

# 16. Court of Miracles

When Sief came home from school, I ambushed him in the courtyard: "I need to see your cousin Zyed about the tattoo."

He froze, didn't say anything, distressed look on his face.

"I know you promised Aunt Mill you wouldn't come near me anymore but we have to figure this out, Sief."

He thought about it, pressing lips tight, then nodded. "I be right back."

He disappeared up the stairs to drop off his book bag. When he returned he handed me a long scarf.

"What's this?"

"Hijab."

We rode the number three line, transferring to the number four. At the Gare du Nord station a crowd poured off dragging suitcases and another poured on. I was mushed in by a ginormous African woman in a bright print robe and three almond-eyed Arab sisters with scarves that made oval frames around their matching faces.

We wriggled off at Château Rouge to the thump of a *darbuka* drummer playing for change and chuffed up the steps into market stalls of prayer beads, tagine pots, portable gas stoves, Arabic chatter, and an endless stream of tan, chocolate, bronze, amber, and mahogany people.

"Where are we?" I asked.

"Goutte D'Or," Sief mumbled, pulling up the hood of his hoodie, slipping on dark glasses. "Put the scarf over your hair."

The way he said it hacked me off, but he marched away in his usual speed-meister manner. Between trying to follow him through the crowd and trying to wrap the hijab around my head, I almost lost him.

The further we marched from the Metro, the less people there were. We passed a fenced-off gap between buildings with a dozen charred cars in a big lump. Other cars dotted the *rue*, windshields broken, doors missing, wheels resting on cinderblocks instead of tires. Young men hung out in doorways, leering as we passed. Occasionally one would say something to us in a hushed voice.

"What did he say?"

"Nothing. Keep walking."

"Is he selling drugs?"

Sief didn't respond. He had on a mean face like he was trying to look tough to the guys in the doorways. The hair rose on the back of my neck.

Whole buildings were covered to head height with spray paint, one tag covering the next in stomach-churning chaos. We crossed a nameless rue with matching factory doors on either side, stopping to let some tanker trucks roar past, assaulted by the putrid odor spewing from them.

"What was that?"

"Blood trucks," said Sief, "from *l'abattoir*."

I'd had enough. "Sief, where are you taking me?"

"To my cousin's."

"What on earth does your cousin do?"

"Put your scarf back on."

"No."

"I telling you to protect you." He eased the scarf back over my hair. "Please, we are almost there." He walked off again and I followed, ducking through the loose joint of a tin fence into a cobbled passage that cut behind the drab buildings as if it had been walled up and forgotten. The buildings inside were crumbling. Weeds sprouted around mounds of trash and sodden mattresses. Glass vials the size of your pinky, scattered about by the hundreds, crackled underfoot.

The passage ended at a once-grand, crescent-shaped building, glopped with graffiti and crowned with faded letters that spelled out "Grand Bain La A--ttu—." On the steps of the place a teenager, named Hasan I learned later, stopped us. He was ginormous, with massive, gleaming muscles and a mushed-in nose. He glared at us like we were cockroaches—until he recognized Sief.

Hasan grunted and shook his head but ushered us up some rotten stairs and knocked on a door six times—twice quick, four times slow. Someone inside unlocked the door. Three men sat around a bowed table divvying up hundreds of credit cards and bundles of euros. They were dressed in warm-ups like the neckless man and look liked they'd been born scowling.

One of the men, cousin Zyed as it turned out, a twenty-something version of Sief, started yelling at us the moment we appeared in some slangy version of French. I could tell, in that way you can, that Zyed swore a lot. Sief started shouting back at him.

Zyed shot up from the table and cracked Sief across the face so hard I thought his neck would snap. Sief took the hit without complaint then fished a drawing he'd made of the snake and skull tattoo from his hoodie pocket. Zyed snatched it and tossed it to Hasan, all the while shouting.

Later I leaned that Zyed had told Sief he had no business coming, that if something happened to us on the way back it was not his blanking problem, that he'd made a blanking promise to Sief's blanking father and he would honor that promise, but not if Sief abused Zyed's authority. Zyed shouted that he was not interested in some blanking vory nonsense and if they decided to pull Sief's teeth out that was vory business, not his. Then Zyed laid into Hasan for letting us in which, considering Hasan was twice Zyed's size, was something to see.

I sensed things weren't going well, even if I couldn't understand the words, so when Hasan opened the door I pivoted instantly.

"You, girl," snapped Zyed. I pivoted back, trembling. "You know who I am?"

"No, sir."

"Don't play stupid."

"You're Sief's cousin."

"Does Sief's cousin have a name?"

"Um, Cousin Zyed?"

"I'm The Great Zyed El Hasi. What do vory want with you?"

"It has something to do with the book I was getting for my aunt."

"What book?"

"A book about French history."

That French history could be of any value seemed dubious to Cousin Zyed. He stared at me with dental-drill eyes then flicked his hand for us to beat it. We beat it.

Despite Cousin Zyed's saying he wouldn't protect us, Hasan walked us all the way back to the Metro stop. Suffice to say, no one dared bother us. Sief looked completely humiliated though. Myself, I wanted to lay into him for even bringing me to see his weird criminal cousin in this weird criminal hideout.

At the stairs to the Metro, Hasan pulled out Sief's drawing and handed it back to him. He said a few quick words and upnodded for us to take off.

We walked down to the platform. A rat scurried between the rails.

Before I could get a word out Sief said, "Hasan tell to me the tattoo belong to a *mec* named Yevka in Yursky Gruzdeva's gang. They traffics in diamonds. He say they *traînent*, er, hangs out, in Montparnasse, at La Rotonde."

## 17. Secrets Diplomatiques

Our train was packed, so there was no way to say anything to Sief above the roar without someone overhearing. When we were walking through the tunnel from one line to another, Sief said, "You cannot tell Madame Millicent that we sawed my cousin or even that we was together. Please don't say that we goes to Goutte D'Or. It's not such a bad place, really, but sometimes it says to people who don't know much about it that it is a bad place."

I nodded.

"And don't tell my father nothing neither, especialing that we sawed my cousin."

"I don't even know what your father looks like."

He pushed out his lip in grudging acknowledgment. His left cheek was red from the slap his cousin gave him and his right cheek was swollen blue from Snake and Skull's punch. Poor Sief. I seemed to be getting him in a lot of trouble. I don't know why he had anything to do with me. If he were smart he'd do what Aunt Mill said and stay away from me.

"So tell me why vory diamond traffickers follows you."

"I don't know."

"What is this book about that you brings to Madame Millicent?"

"I don't know."

"You says to my cousin it is about French history."

"That's what Aunt Mill told me."

He gave me a look that he'd cribbed from Cousin Zyed.

"Really, I don't know, Sief. She won't let me near it. Plus, it's in French."

"So finds out the title and we will find another of the

book."

"It's a rare book. You can't just buy it at a store."

"Find out what is the title. Tomorrow we can go stake out La Rotonde."

"Stake out?

"Yes—make waiting there to see if the vory shows up."

"I know what it means. Forget it."

He tossed his head like I was the lamest person in the world and turned away. He couldn't be bothered to say anything more to me. When we got close to our rue, just before we separated, he leaned over and whispered, "find out what is the title."

I made pug face and handed back the hijab.

At the apartment, Aunt Mill was in her study. She glanced back when I came in. "There you are. I ordered a pizza. Hungry?"

"Starved."

I moved to her desk, even more covered with papers now. In the middle of it all was the book.

I leaned over her shoulder. "How's it going?"

"Much better. The book's helped explain a number of things."

"Like what?"

"I found abbreviated words and idiomatic expressions that make sense in the context of the code. If I tie a few more together we may get a breakthrough."

"Can I see it?"

She fished some latex gloves from a drawer. "It's very fragile."

I stretched the gloves on. She handed me the thing like it was made out of moth wings. It wasn't remarkable, really—brown, worn, flecks of gold ink on the cover.

I opened the front page and read the title out loud, *"Aperçu des secrets diplomatiques dans l'histoire de France. Comprenant un point de vue philosophique sur la nature des actions menées avec discrétions et savoir-faire. A l'usage des futurs ministres royaux. Tome deux. Par Jean-Marie Cournac, Duc des Ongles.*

Aunt Mill laughed.

"What?"

"Your accent."

"Isn't the title kind of long?"

"Not by the standards of the day."

I flipped a page.

"Careful. Really. Very fragile."

The doorbell chimed.

"Must be the pizza." She got up, dug through her purse for her wallet, and went into the hall.

I jetted into her chair, snatched a piece of paper out of her wastebasket and started scribbling the title down letter for letter, since there was no way I could remember it. I pushed the title page flat to see the letters better. The book crackled. When I finished, I shoved the scratch paper into my pocket and stood up. I could hear Aunt Mill saying *"bonne soirée"* to the pizza man in the hall then the front door crunching closed.

I flipped open the book, paging through, trying to look natural. An old brown page, way in the back, drifted away from the binding as I flipped past. It had broken loose.

"Daisy, come on, get it while it's hot," said Aunt Mill from the kitchen.

Without even thinking, I stuffed the whole page into my pocket.

The pizzas came from a place down the rue called Pink Flamingo. One pie had gorgonzola and figs and *jambon*, the other had smoked salmon and *oeuf de lump*, a kind of orange caviar, with *crème fraîche*, which sounds weird but was really tasty. I took huge bites because if my mouth was full, I couldn't answer any questions Aunt Mill threw my way, or at least I'd have a second to think of an answer while I chewed.

Aunt Mill didn't say a word though, nibbling at a single slice, barely sipping her glass of wine. After a while she looked over my homework, harrumphed a few times, growing amused.

"Oh my goodness," she said.

"Those were impossible, Aunt Mill, and you know it."

She laughed. "Okay, let's go back and work on some fractions with unlike denominators. Then we'll return to mixed numbers with unlike denominators." She made me fetch a sheet of paper and wrote out the next day's problems while I looked over her shoulder. It took her two seconds. She folded the page in half and placed it under the sugar bowl. "Don't look at these till tomorrow."

"Don't worry."

"Did you get enough to eat?"

"I'm stuffed."

She smiled, finished her wine, and stood. "I think I'll work some more, if you don't mind. We'll do something fun come the weekend. Take the train out to Malmaison maybe. The leaves should all be turning bright colors."

She disappeared into her office. I mummified the remaining pizza in plastic wrap and entombed it in the empty fridge, expecting her to come charging out of her office and demand to know what I'd done with the missing page. Even after I retreated to my room, I flinched every time a floorboard creaked. I thought for sure I was in for it when I heard her steps approaching my door, but she'd just come to say goodnight.

"Night, Aunt Mill. Thanks for the pizza."

Off she hobbled, unsuspecting.

I pulled out the stolen page and examined it. I couldn't read it, couldn't really see anything special about it. It looked like a dry, brittle page from an old book. Suddenly all I wanted to do was return the thing. What was I going to do with it anyway?

The paper was cracked from when I shoved it into my pocket, so there was no way I could slip it back into the book without Aunt Mill noticing the damage. Who was I kidding anyway? Aunt Mill would keep the book locked away in her safe when she wasn't using it. Even the door to her study was locked when she wasn't around.

I told myself she wouldn't notice it was gone and if she did she would assume that it had fallen out a hundred years ago. But what a little jerk I'd become—lying, stealing, sneaking around with Sief. I'd never been Miss Perfect—far from—but even I knew I'd reached a new low.

To distract myself from feeling like a crud-ball, I fired up the laptop and googled Yursky Gruzdeva. He didn't have his own Wikipedia page but it ends up some warped teens in London had put together a world gangster appreciation site with bios of current top gangsters. It included a picture of Gruzdeva, bald and bushy browed, prison numbers running across the bottom. He wasn't particularly scary looking, though it claimed he was "a vicious Russian mobster, known more for brutality than brains, originally from Odessa, a suspect in the Van Cleef & Arpels heist in Cannes, in which two guards died." He was never arrested for that crime, however, in 2005, he was caught with undocumented Russian diamonds and sent to Fleury-Mérogis—the Sing-Sing of France.

While I was rummaging around the web, trying to find something better than the world gangster appreciation site, it came to me what I should do with the page from the book. I wrote an email to Pauline Dumeril, asking if I could come for a visit.

# 18. Stake Out

As soon as Aunt Mill left for work, I shot out of bed. I'd spent half of the night obsessing over the farfetched idea that a bunch of diamond-smuggling, tattooed Russians were messing with Aunt Mill, and scaring the pants off of Lupatreaux. By dawn, or what passed for a rainy Paris dawn, I was pretty sure the idea wasn't completely insane. Trouble was, even if I got the courage to tell Aunt Mill, which might actually make me feel better, she'd think the story was doofy or, worse, start interrogating me on how I came to know about it. I was in what my mom would call a real pickle.

After whipping through my math problems—Aunt Mill had gone easy on me—and doing some Google mapping, I dressed, grabbed an umbrella, charged down the steps two at a time, and dashed across the courtyard, opening the umbrella against pea-sized rain.

"You gets the name of the book?" Sief asked, appearing out of the shadows across the courtyard, hoodie pulled up, scaring the stuffing out of me.

"Yes."

"What is it?"

"It's too long to remember, but I wrote it down."

"Okay. I meet you here after school. We find it then."

I nodded. He adjusted his book bag, pivoted to go.

"Sief?"

He pivoted back. I held out the umbrella.

"But now you gets wet."

"Aunt Mill has a million of them."

"I don't want to stealing from her."

"It's not stealing. I'm lending it. You can bring it back this afternoon."

He thought it over, took the umbrella, nodding his thanks.

After snatching another umbrella from Aunt Mill's collection, I sloshed my way to the Quai François Mitterrand and the Porte des Lions entrance of the *Centre de recherche et de restauration des musées de France.* The guard, standing at the door under his own umbrella, notified Pauline, who did a pretty good job pretending she was happy to see me again.

When we got to her office though, she said, "I'm so sorry, I'm kind of swamped today. I sent you an email, but I guess you didn't see it. I can get you a pass to the Louvre though. Would you like that?"

"I just want to ask one question."

"Maybe we can meet later. I'm meeting some—uh—question?"

"Can you guys figure out if a painting is a fake?"

"You mean a forgery?"

I nodded.

"We're very good at it, actually."

"How do you do it?"

"With x-rays or autoradiographs, by evaluating pigments, by knowing the style of the artist and the material he or she used, by knowing who bought his or her paintings and who they were sold to or inherited by. Sometimes we just use a magnifying glass."

"What about this?" I set the page on her desk.

"Where is this from?"

"An old book. Or maybe a fake old book."

"Where did you get it?"

"I can't say."

"What do you mean? Do you know the title of the book?"

"I do, but I can't say that either."

She eyed me, then picked up the page and studied it, "Did you steal this from someplace?"

"No."

"Daisy, are you sure?"

"Could you run some tests on it to find out if it's real?"

She started to laugh but stopped herself. "Daisy, do you have any idea— " She exhaled, sat in silence a moment, then said, "Okay. I'll—uh—I'll have Dr. Baertich take a look at it."

"Who's he?"

"He's one of our experts who's very good at this kind of thing."

"Thank you. I really appreciate it."

She couldn't usher me out fast enough, which was fine by me because I wanted to get to Montparnasse.

I took the Number One Metro to Châtelet and the Number Four to the Vavin stop, climbing the steps into the rain. I knew the metro exit would be close to La Rotonde Café, where Hasan said the vory guys hung out, but I didn't realize it would bring me up right smack in front of it. Gruzdeva and his crew might be sitting inside, staring out.

Realizing my mistake, I flicked up the umbrella and spun it round, hiding myself from view, crossing to another café, Le Dome, which faces La Rotonde on the other side of Boulevard du Montparnasse.

At Le Dome, I settled into a table against the terrace window that gave me a view of La Rotonde. I ordered a *chocolat chaud*. It cost three times as much as at Le Saint Gervais, but at least the waiter didn't care if I sat there forever. Everyone seemed to be reading a newspaper or a book or checking text messages or scribbling in very important journals.

It took me a while to build up the courage, but after sipping my *chocolat chaud*, I eased out a pair of giant binoculars from my knapsack. I'd spotted them sitting on a high shelf in Aunt Mill's living room. Why she had gigantic spyglasses, I couldn't quite fathom, but now, wiping steam off the terrace window, I could see every wrinkle on every face inside La Rotonde.

And believe it or not, no one in Le Dome, the waiters, the texters, the boho ladies bent over thick novels, seemed to notice or care that I was spying on the people at La Rotonde. Maybe it was common to spy on people at La Rotonde.

But there wasn't much to spy on. The waiters and texters

and boho ladies bent over thick novels in La Rotonde looked the same as the ones in Le Dome. Nobody in La Rotonde had a tattoo. All of them had normal necks. None of them wore tracksuits. I sipped my *chocolat chaud*. The rain stopped and started. A bus blocked the view across Boulevard du Montparnasse, then a car broke down and three policemen came to give the driver a ticket. But no *vory* arrived. I reasoned that *vory* were probably late risers. If they'd been up all night planning jewelry heists, they probably got to sleep in late.

Minutes turned to hours. The cast of characters sitting around me changed. The foam on the side of my *chocolat chaud* cup fossilized. I began to wonder how Hasan knew that Yursky Gruzdeva hung out in La Rotonde.

But I kept at it. Aunt Mill's binoculars were so crisp and clear, I kind of lost track of everyone around me till I heard a Russian voice at a table across from me, saying hello to someone. I turned.

It was Yursky Gruzdeva. Same bushy eyebrows and shiny head, but smiling, dressed in a gray suit, silk tie, expensive trench coat, gold watch.

Instinctively I shoved the binoculars under the table, though the American man who rose from a nearby table to shake Gruzdeva's hand—who'd been sitting there for who knows how long—could easily have seen me with them. This man was thin and tall and wearing a suit too, with peppery hair and gray-framed glasses. He talked with the kind of East Coast accent that professor friends of my dad have.

After their first hellos, I didn't hear a word of what they said over the thumping of my heart. The waiter came and took Gruzdeva's umbrella and coat. Gruzdeva ordered without a menu and, after a short discussion, ordered for his American friend too.

I snatched a menu off the table next to me and hid behind it. Trouble was, after taking their order and bringing them drinks, the waiter noticed me with the menu and came by. *"Voulez-vous quelque chose, mademoiselle?"*

I didn't know how to say, "I just want to disappear behind

this menu," so I pointed to the lowest-priced thing. The old man at the table next to me paid his bill and shuffled out. I grabbed his newspaper, Le Figaro, and whisked that up in place of the menu. Strain as I might, I could not hear any more of Gruzdeva's conversation. The two men seemed to have professionally quiet voices.

It ended up I'd ordered a plate of sardines, which were actually tasty, but it was difficult to eat and keep Le Figaro upright. Ten minutes after Gruzdeva sat down with the American, just when I built up courage to bug the heck out, all three of the other vory guys paraded in—the neckless one who pretended to be Lupatreaux, the hulking one who followed me, and the snake-in-skull guy.

They didn't sit at the table with Gruzdeva and the American, they sat at a table across the restaurant, but they went over to pay their respects and even shook the American's hand. Clearly he was a big cheese. Gruzdeva seemed irritated that they'd introduced themselves and that they chose to eat at Le Dome that day. Meanwhile, I was freaking out behind Le Figaro. All three of these guys knew who I was. Hasan must have mistaken La Rotonde for Le Dome, or maybe the Russians like to alternate.

The waiter came by and took my plate away and said, "*Autre chose pour mademoiselle?*" I shook my head. He frowned, brushed breadcrumbs off the table with a tongue-depressor thing and said, "*C'est le croûton, Le Fig. Vous ne devriez pas perdre votre temps à la lecture.*"

Having only a vague idea what he'd said, I shrugged, hoping he'd go away. I nearly gagged when I saw the bill. Shelling out all the euros I had barely covered it. Fishing them from damp jeans while holding up a newspaper proved impossible.

Neckless, who probably knew my face best, had his back toward me. That was good. Snake-in-Skull and the guy who followed me were both half facing me. Sooner or later they'd look over. When their food arrived and they began to tuck in, I took a deep breath and stood, ballet-stepping between tight tables, trying not to knock anything over.

"*Merci, 'moiselle, à bientôt,*" someone sang. I did not answer, did not look back, bloomed my umbrella the instant I got out the door to hide my face. I walked straight down Boulevard du Montparnasse so I'd be out of sight as fast as possible.

Ten paces later I heard someone shouting, "*Mademoiselle, Mademoiselle.*" I must have looked terrified when I turned because the waiter flinched. He held out Aunt Mill's binoculars. "You forget these," he said.

# 19. Place Vendôme

My cell phone rang. "Daisy! I'm here!"

"Hi, Nina. I'm here too. Where are you?"

"Over toward the Chanel store. Where are you?"

"By the big column in the middle."

"I see you. I'm waving."

I turned in a circle around the Place Vendôme until I spotted her. Even in the pouring rain Nina looked turned out, shiny black raincoat, clear umbrella, to-die-for Paddington rain hat. I waved back and crossed the cobbled plaza, getting splashed by a limo racing toward the Ritz.

I'd phoned Nina shortly after escaping Le Dome, asking her if I could take her up on the offer to meet with her aunt, or great aunt, the diamond expert. She said sure then called back three minutes later and said Tante Benice was expecting us within the hour. Wow, she worked fast.

"How come you have binoculars?" she asked after we double-cheeked.

"Long story."

"I like long stories."

"Well, um, I wanted to see the Mona Lisa close up but knew the crowds would be huge because of the rain, so I brought these along?"

"You are *so* cute, *fauve*-girl," she said, hooking my arm, guiding me under a corner archway between Van Cleef & Arpels and Mauboussin. Both stores had windows chocked with diamonds necklaces—and not kid stuff either.

A locked door blocked our entrance into the archway. Even as Nina pushed the intercom button, a guard in a starched coat with gold buttons appeared, bellowing something that meant we were not welcome inside. From what I got of the conversation, Nina told the guard we were expected by her aunt and Benice's voice crackled over the intercom and Nina answered and the entrance buzzer buzzed, but the guard blocked our path and pushed the intercom button again to talk to Tante Benice.

But Tante Benice must have thought we'd just fumbled the door because she buzzed us in again without dialog and the guard started shouting into the intercom, which caused Benice to threaten to call the guard on him. He said he was the guard. She insisted he put Nina back on the intercom. She instructed Nina to find the *real* guard, who was probably off getting drunk somewhere, and that if he was not to be found then Nina should go next door to Mauboussin and ask *their* guard to sound the alarm. The guard took exception, stating that Tante Benice had no right to malign his dignity in such a manner.

While they argued, a woman in a fur coat slipped out the door and we slipped in. Up the stairs we ran. The third and fourth floors had progressively less-fancy jewelry stores, but this top floor, with its narrow, dusty hallway, held tiny garrets.

We came to a plain green door. Nina handed me a box of pastries she'd brought and knocked.

"Nina?"

*"Oui."*

*"Tu es seule?"*

*"A part mon amie,* Daisy."

The door buzzed open and we stepped into a postage-stamp lobby, framed by display cases. Tante Benice, gray brows just visible over the front counter, squinted through lenses that made her eyeballs look huge. She instructed Nina to close the door behind us and only then came round and gave Nina a hug.

Thin as a pipe cleaner, old as a pyramid, Tante Benice wore a vintage pink Chanel suit with black lapels that Nina instantly went gaga over. Benice had four rings on each hand and a ruby pendant around her neck. She adored Nina, wouldn't let go of her, stroked her hair and gazed myopically at her until Nina insisted she say hello to me. I got a standard double-peck and a nasally British, "How do you do?"

The place was strewn with tiny tools and bits of metal. Within reach of her chair sat several chests with hundreds of drawers and two safes, one on top of the other. Behind her stood a bookcase so heaped with books and binders that it would surely crush her if it ever fell. She had a magnifying light stand on her desk and a giant Sherlock Holmes glass and a set of goggles that looked like they had four-inch lenses, plus a microscope.

We talked for the next two hours, Tante Benice mostly in French, me mostly in English, Nina trying to translate. After a general exchange about Nina's mom and Benice's health, the old woman turned to me and said, *"Et alors?"* Through Nina, I asked how you could tell if diamonds were old. Tante Benice said all diamonds were old, sixty-million years old, shot up from the center of the earth through volcano shafts, faster than the speed of sound. After millions of years they washed down mountain streams, waiting more millions of years for humans to evolve from monkeys and discover them.

I asked if there was any way to tell the difference between a modern diamond in the store window at Mauboussin, down below, and one worn by, say, Marie Antoinette. Benice said that the diamonds themselves, if they were famous enough, might have characteristic flaws that an expert could recognize, but mostly one could tell modern diamonds from antique diamonds by the style and sophistication of their cut.

She explained the Round Cut and the Oval Cut and Marquise Cut. She had Nina fetch down a book to show us illustrations of each and even pulled out samples from her drawers, explaining that knowing the development of diamond cutting allowed experts to understand when a diamond first presented itself. She even opened her safe and showed us a two-carat, Teardrop Cut diamond from the era of Louis XIII.

I asked if it was possible to disguise an old diamond by re-cutting it. Benice said it was and that she'd done such cutting herself when clients brought in great grandma's diamond and wanted it made modern. Then I asked if it would be possible to cut a modern diamond to look like an old one. Of course it was, she said, if you had the skill and tools to cut in the old style—but no one did that.

When I asked Benice why certain diamonds became famous, she reached out and squeezed my hand. She was having a blast. She explained that a diamond gained fame because of its size and beauty and the celebrity of its owner, then launched into a story about the French Blue. Said to be cursed, the Blue was stolen from a temple in India and destroyed all who wore it, including Marie Antoinette.

I asked her what she knew about the so-called Queen's Necklace.

The poor, poor queen, she said. Innocent, completely innocent, set upon by that wolf de la Motte, she said, as if it had happened last week. She told us there were six-hundred-forty-seven painstakingly matched diamonds, the best the world had to offer at the time. Boehmer and Bassange's masterpiece. She had Nina fetch down another book with a drawing of the necklace, so we could see it for ourselves. All the diamonds were numbered, with huge Teardrop shaped diamonds at the corners and bottom of the necklace.

Benice told her version of how the gracious, frugal, beautiful Marie Antoinette refused to have her husband, Louis XVI, buy the diamonds for her, even though she had just borne him a son, the poor, doomed Dauphin.

She told how Jeanne de la Motte, after escaping poverty through the charity of the Queen, paid her back by conspiring with that fiend in red robes, Cardinal Rohan. Benice told of the forged letters, the midnight meeting, the secret purchase, and the final fateful episode when de la Motte was given the necklace for delivery to the Queen.

It was clear that Tante Benice loved telling this story. Her eyes got even bigger through her glasses as she recounted how the necklace was divided, how the she-devil de la Motte bought expensive clothes and a fancy carriage.

She said that the king should have slapped de la Motte in an iron mask, never to be seen again, but instead, honorable man, he gave her a public trial, a trial at which she ruined the reputation of Marie Antoinette.

I asked if she knew what became of the diamonds.

A few, she said, were recovered from de la Motte when she was arrested, but the rest were lost.

Intuiting my next question, Nina asked if it was possible that some of the diamonds might still be hidden somewhere. Benice smiled and said that if even part of the necklace was recovered whole, they would be the most legendary and expensive diamonds the world has known.

I asked how you would know they were the real Queen's Diamonds? Benice said you would have to prove provenance, establish a chain of ownership and acquisition, or link them somehow to de la Motte and her conspirators.

It was black outside Benice's tiny skylight. You could see she was exhausted from all the talk. Nina looked pooped too, from translating, and my head thumped from trying to piece the bits of French and English together. "Getting late. We should go," Nina said.

I thanked Tante Benice about twenty times in French and English. She shook my hand and proclaimed with her French-tinted British accent, "It has been a great pleasure speaking with you young lady, and a pleasure to know that Nina has at least one friend who is not a buffoon."

"Tante Benice!" Nina said, only to be engulfed in a hug.

When we hit the street, the Vendôme column glowed in shafts of yellow light. Glistening cobbles outshined the diamonds being stored in their vaults for the night. The sky, so it seemed, was out of rain for the moment.

As we turned up rue de la Paix, Aunt Mill called on her cell phone and asked where I was. I said I'd been hiking around all afternoon.

"Would have been sensible to hide in a museum. Are you soaked to the bone?"

"No. I have one of your umbrellas. Paris is beautiful in the rain."

"It is, isn't it?

She asked me to meet her at Le Saint Gervais for dinner

and signed off. Nina and I made our way toward the Marais, stomping in puddles and laughing.

"I love your Tante Benice," I said.

"She's crazy. But at least she doesn't pretend I don't exist."

"What do you mean?"

"My mom's family. Very old school."

"So?"

"So my mom and dad aren't married."

"Oh." We walked for half a block before I spoke again. "Really? I mean, really? You're like thirteen and they pretend you don't exist because of that?"

She shrugged.

"That's so entirely gross. You're the most beautiful, amazing person in the world. Do they have any idea what they're missing out on? I want to punch them in the nose."

She smiled and put her arm around me. "Anyway, I don't even know them and my dad's family is super nice, even if they all live in America. My Mom hasn't spoken to her mom in like thirteen years. She pretends it doesn't bother her, but come on. Her dad died and they didn't even tell her. She found out from a cousin six months later.

"Geez."

"Yeah."

"I mean, geez."

"Whatever. No family is perfect. The only hard part is my mom wants *me* to be perfect, as some kind of weird compensation or something."

I nodded. We walked on in silence, until we neared home.

As we came around the corner to Aunt Mill's apartment, Nina said, "Hey, Daisy, do me a fave and don't tell anyone about that, like Gilles or Bruno or anyone."

I entwined my arm with hers. "Of course not."

Sief appeared on the sidewalk in front of us. He stalked up, shoving his face into mine. "Where you been? I waiting all afternoon to go stake out at La Rotonde."

Nina glanced at me, puzzled.

"I went there by myself."

Sief's mouth came open. "How come you does it without me?"

"You were at school. And it's lucky I was alone, because they sat down right next to me."

"You goes inside? That's not the way you do it. You suppose to watch from another place, like across the street."

"That's what I did, Sief. I was in Le Dome. They were supposed to be in La Rotonde. Have you been to either?"

"You think I hangs out in boxes like that?"

"Why not? All the famous cat burglars do."

His lips turned down.

Nina took the opportunity to smile her most charming smile and offer her hand, "Hi, I'm Nina, Daisy's friend who she sometimes forgets to introduce to people."

He completely ignored her. "So does they see you? Does they know who you was?"

"I don't think so. I hid behind a newspaper and got out as fast as I could."

Nina's cell phone rang. She answered, said "*oui, maman*" and "*non, maman*" then hung up, her face losing all its natural joy. "Have to go."

She walked off.

"Nina, hold on a sec. Nina? I'll call you."

She didn't slow down or even glance back, crossing the rue like a deflating balloon. I knew she was hurt that I didn't introduce her and that Sief blew her off. I felt terrible.

"Did you see Yursky Gruzdeva?"

Eyes glued to Nina, I neither answered Sief nor saw Aunt Mill appear at the other end of the rue.

"Daisy?" she called out.

I pivoted around. Without a word, Sief strode off the other way.

# 20. Foie-Foie Gras-Gras

Aunt Mill called Sief's name three times but he ignored her, disappearing around the corner as fast as he could without actually sprinting. I, however, was trapped. I had just enough time, while she was shouting his name, to calculate that she hadn't heard what we said.

"What were you doing with him?"

"Me? I ran into him near Les Halles. We walked home together. I haven't seen him in a while."

"Why did he have my umbrella?"

Oops.

"Um, I lent it to him. This morning. It was raining and all he had on was a hoodie so I lent him the umbrella and got another one."

"I thought you hadn't seen him in awhile."

Oops again.

"I haven't. Just this morning and tonight."

She gave me a look that would broil cheese. It went on and on. Finally, exhaling with such colossal disgust that I felt my life shorten five years, she walked off down the rue. I stood there, feet welded to the sidewalk. She turned back, "Are you coming to dinner?"

Oh, sure. Like I could eat now. And at Le Saint Gervais no less. And what was I going to say? Or what part of it? If I even started I'd be a goner.

As I trailed behind Aunt Mill, I thought about what Clymene would advise. I could hear her saying, "Dummy up, moron, just dummy up." Funny how, whenever I was in trouble with grownups, I thought about my sister.

Aunt Mill stood at the corner across from Le Saint Gervais

waiting for me, so we could go in together. Madame Rose greeted us with her happy sing-song, but one glance and she could tell something was wrong. Aunt Mill made chitchat in French but Madame Rose wasn't fooled. She could tell I was in trouble and looked worried for me, but she didn't say anything other than, "So very good to see you, Daisy." Aunt Mill glanced at the chalkboard menu and ordered for both of us, not even asking what I wanted. Madame Rose whispered that she'd made *foie gras*, which she rarely did and never mentioned on the menu so, of course, Aunt Mill ordered some.

When the carafe of wine came, Aunt Mill poured herself a glass but didn't pour any for me. Madame Rose delivered a platter of cold salads—grated carrots in mustard dressing, chopped beets in vinaigrette, slivered celery root in *rémoulade*. I was too tense to eat. But Aunt Mill ate and sipped like some generalissimo who enjoys noshing before ordering an execution.

"Not hungry?" she asked.

I shrugged.

"May I ask what you're doing with my binoculars?"

"I was going to use them to look at the Mona Lisa. I thought there might be a crowd."

She looked perplexed a moment. "See that table over there?" She point with her wine glass to where I sat after falling off the roof, when I'd had my weird moment with Sief. Clearly Madame Rose had told her about it.

"Yeah?"

"What happened over there?"

"Napoleon ate a sandwich?"

"Recently."

"Johnny Depp ate a sandwich?"

She smiled for a nanosecond in spite of herself. She ate a forkful of beets, chewed slowly, leveling her microwave eyes on me the whole time. "The trouble with small lies, Daisy, is that they make us suspicious of everything one says, plus they tend to grow bigger on their own. Wouldn't you agree?"

"I couldn't really say."

She smirked or frowned or whatever she does, then said,

"Tell me what happened between you and Sief that day?"

"Nothing happened."

"He's not allowed in here. Did you know that?"

I shrugged.

"He's stolen from Madame Rose, so he's not welcome, which makes it rather remarkable that he came in to talk to you, don't you think?"

I shrugged again.

"He must have wanted to talk to you very badly."

"If you don't believe me why don't you ask him what happened?"

"I did. He said nothing happened. Which is obviously untrue. Which is why I told him not to go near you, or to talk to you, under any circumstances. And there he was, talking to you, holding an umbrella that you lent him."

"Is it a huge a crime to lend someone an umbrella?"

She sighed. She sipped her wine. "The other evening, I came home to find you in bed with a bruise on your head and a swollen lip and buttons ripped off your coat and you said you'd eaten something that disagreed with you. What am I to make of that?"

"That I'm a super klutz."

"Can I suggest that if you are going to lie, at least make it an amusing one, about, say, Johnny Depp or Napoleon?"

Luckily, Madame Rose whisked in holding a plate crowned with a slab of *foie gras*, surrounded by a halo of *cornichons* and toast triangles. The generalissimo forgot about her interrogation while she carefully slathered a triangle with the gray-brown putty, took a bite, and moaned with delight. The two of them discussed the *foie gras* in detail. Madame Rose looked very please with herself, so pleased she offered the condemned prisoner some of the *foie gras,* slathering it over a toast triangle herself, saying, "This is from the recipe of my grandmother and is too much work to make now-days, but you must try some, Daisy."

"Hmmmmm," I said. In truth my stomach tumbled like a dryer and I couldn't taste a thing. Madame Rose went off to tend to other diners and I was left alone with the generalissimo. She sipped her wine and ate *foie gras* with an ecstatic smile, and for a moment I hoped she might forget what we were talking about or maybe let it drop altogether so as not to mar her gastronomic bliss.

But no.

She set down her knife, dabbed her lip with a napkin, resumed her disappointed expression and said, "So, what happened between you and Sief?"

"I shoved him. And he shoved me back. And then it got to be kind of a fight. And then he felt bad and came in here to apologize but I was still mad at him so I told him to get lost. He's been bugging me from the first day I got here and he calls me Grace Kelly, which is so stupid it drives me nuts, but he won't stop and acts like a little third-grader who just wants to annoy me. But I realized he was just doing to me what I did to him, shoving me I mean, and so I guess I kind of forgave him.

"It's not like I have a whole bunch of friends, you know, like two really, though Nina has all these cool friends and I'm afraid they'll just find me boring eventually cause I don't speak French, so I'm kind of afraid of her, but Sief is, I don't know, different, annoying, but different, which doesn't mean I even like him, though I guess he's my friend, so even though I get mad at him, it's like the way I get mad at my sister, which I do all the time, like really mad, and she gets mad at me too, I mean she tried to crush my head with a rock once and I almost stabbed her with a spear and still we're sisters, you know, like I mean, like that's not the same as with Sief, but he's okay, you know, and he keeps me from being lonely. You know what I mean?"

"He calls you Grace Kelly?"

I tilted my head. *That's what she got out of all this?*

"Yes. And I've seen pictures of her and she's totally all gorge and that's totally not me and I don't like even being compared to her because I don't go in for any of that phony-baloney-romantic-French-guy stuff, even if he's like half Mohican and a trickster or whatever you said he is."

"He's trying to compliment you, Daisy."

"But did I ask him to compliment me? Did I? Do I even

need that complication in my life? It just creeps me out. And my life is enough of a wreck as it is, don't you think? I'm like exiled from my family and in a strange country and okay, I get that this is Paris, most beautiful place on the planet and all, but I'm lonely anyway and I feel like I've messed up everything and I'm so afraid that Mom and Dad will break up while I'm away and I won't be able to do anything to keep them together, like I could anyway, or even worse, *even worse,* that they have a better chance of staying together when I'm gone, which really scares me, because if that's true then I'll be here forever, which I don't mean as an insult to you or anything because I really appreciate what you're doing and I get that I'm like a thorn in your butt and that you'd like to strangle me half the time, which is the way I feel too, like I'd like to strangle myself half the time, but I *would* stay away from them, my parents, I positively would, forever, without even complaining, if it would help—if it meant they stayed together—because I get that they're afraid to have me around the new baby and I don't blame them."

"Daisy," she snapped.

I stopped. I'd managed to get myself all emotional. I had tears in my eyes. My voice had gone up six notes.

"What?"

She leaned over the table, speaking softly, "They aren't afraid to have you around the baby. They're just overwhelmed. Kids get sent away all the time when their mothers are having babies. It's practically a tradition. And I've never considered strangling you, ever. I like having you around. Granted, I'm a cranky bachelorette set in her ways, but you are such a ray of light, I can't even tell you. I worry about you is all. And I worry that I'll let down *my* sister—your mother. And as for the rest, as for if they'll stay together, that's a mystery that you and I can't fathom or control and we just have to trust that they can work out what's best. Does that make sense?"

I nodded.

"But you know, deep down, I believe they will."

I nodded again. I wasn't sure what happened or exactly what I'd said even. I felt warm and confused and guilty too, because somehow even though there was a lot of truth in what I said, about myself, about my parents, it was still a big messed up lie, because I couldn't admit I'd done something so totally stupid as fall off a roof, and because Aunt Mill was being so nice about it all.

We sat quietly. Aunt Mill took a sip of wine and did that little thing where she swirls the glass so there's a tornado of wine inside. "I don't want Sief coming near you, Daisy. Is that understood?"

I nodded once more. She nodded back.

"Oh, and I forgot to tell you, I found a French class for you. Strictly conversation. You'll have to go in the morning and do your math afterwards, but I think you'll enjoy it. It's all kids your age, so maybe you'll make some new friends."

# 21. Hôtel Rohan

Way too early the next morning we were up and out, marching under a coffin lid sky. A layer of mist hung in the Seine, making Notre-Dame float on a cloud, unattached to the earth. As we climbed rue Valette, the Panthéon towered above, silent and severe. The language school Aunt Mill picked was just across from it.

In the school's office, a wheezy lady asked me questions in French until a man in a rumpled raincoat entered, patting down the atoll of hair atop his head and muttered, *"Seydoux."*

Ushered down the hall, into a stuffy room with a ring of kids my age sitting in battered chairs, I was handed over to Mademoiselle Seydoux. She looked like a teenager, except for the crows-feet at the edges of her eyes, and could have written a blog on ugly sweaters from personal experience, but you forgot about all that the moment she laughed. She laughed every other second, at everyone and everything. She made fun of us without mercy when we butchered her language, or when we tried to make a joke in it, or even when we said our names, but there was never anything mean in it. She didn't have an ounce of mean in her.

We used no books, were not allowed to take notes, could only take away what we carried in our head. The lessons were all very practical: how to get change at a *Tabac*, how to find out if the train from Lyon would arrive on time. The students were from all over: China, Cuba, Canada, Colombia, just to cover the C countries, so we didn't speak anything but French. Mademoiselle Seydoux's genius was making all these kids from all over understand new words and phrases without ever saying them in their own language. So, from then on, for two hours every morning, three days a week, I attended Mademoiselle Seydoux's class. Every time I left, I felt happy. That was Mademoiselle Seydoux's real genius.

Over time, I became pretty good pals with Hirokiku and Chantou and Carlos and Edita, and I started feeling pretty good about my French, too. But that's another whole thing, and kind of getting ahead.

The night before my first French class, after our dinner at Le Saint Gervais and my visit to Tante Benice, I flopped around in bed like a bluegill on a hook, thinking about what to do, convincing myself I should tell Aunt Mill everything—about the vory, Lupatreaux, falling off the roof, going to the Goutte D'Or—and let her sort it out. She was the grownup after all. But part of me kept saying that if I told her any of that stuff I'd be packed off to some girl military school. I needed positive proof.

The slightest ghost-echo of piano broke into this mental möbius strip, and I knew that Nina's dad must be back in town. I got up and went across the hall to the bathroom, and on the way back I saw a thread of light coming from under Aunt Mill's door. I knocked.

"Daisy?"

I pushed open the door. "Still up?"

She glanced at her watch. "Oh, my. Two A.M. Lost track of time."

"How's it going?"

"Quite well. A breakthrough, I think." She seemed possessed by excitement. The safe was open. A spreadsheet thingy, made of sheets of paper taped end-to-end and crammed full of numbers and letters, draped from her desk across the floor. She picked it up. "Could be wrong of course but everything seems to be falling into place. Listen to this. 'Eight-seven-one says that three-two-three through six-four-seven, minus the tears, are in one-one-two.'"

"Numbers mixed with words," I said.

"Yes. But we know, or at least we're pretty certain, that Eight-seven-one is nomenclature for Jeanne de la Motte. They did that all the time—still do—assign numbers to key people and places. Easier than spelling out long words. So if we're correct, this means 'de la Motte says something or someone is still in Paris.' One-one-two, I'm fairly certain, means Paris, because Jean-Marie Cournac uses it that way in other messages."

"You mean the guy who wrote the book?"

"Right. So then we just have to figure out who three-two-three and six-four-seven are. They must have been aiding de la Motte in some way. This suggests they had a problem of some kind, thus the tears. Maybe they had a disagreement, but then they moved beyond it."

"Or maybe," I blurted, "it means that 'diamonds number three-hundred-twenty-three through six-hundred-forty-seven are still in Paris.' There were six-hundred-forty-seven diamonds in the necklace. That would mean about half the necklace, minus the big Teardrop Cut diamonds, which were at the corners and bottom. Maybe they cut off the Teardrop diamonds and sold them separately at some point, but left half the necklace hidden in Paris."

Her mouth fell open. She stared at me, slid her chair to a bookshelf, pulled down a thick tome, and flipped through it till she found a page with the same diagram of the Queen's Necklace that Tante Benice had in her book, with all the diamonds numbered.

She peered into the book then looked up, astonished. "How—"

"I read up on the necklace. I find it really fascinating."

"Oh my word, Daisy! You're right! Half the necklace. In Paris. Minus the Teardrop diamonds. I have to call Felix." She snatched up her cell phone.

"Aunt Mill, it's two A.M."

Her phone hovered mid-air a moment then she set it down. "Right."

We both went off to bed.

But of course I couldn't sleep. I lay awake thinking about the book.

The book.

It was clear. I had to get another copy to make sure Aunt Mill's copy was real.

Had to.

The next day, after leaving Mademoiselle Seydoux's class, while walking toward the river down rue Mazarine, I happened by the window of Librairie Pitollot. The brown tome in the window had its own hand-printed card saying, *"Première édition, Denis Diderot Encyclopédie, publié à Paris, 1765."*

I went in. The shop had polished shelves running up forever and jewelry cases full of first editions and, unlike Lupatreaux's, not a cobweb in sight.

*"Bonjour, Mademoiselle,"* said a woman in a burgundy suit, pearls, and tortoiseshell glasses, hardly glancing up from her computer, which was the only thing atop her rococo desk, aside from a rack of embossed business cards. I could tell from her bonjour, that she was really saying, "how dare you enter my store, you worm."

*"Bonjour, madame."* I said. *"Je cherches un vieux livre."*

"And what is the title of the book you search for?" she said in a perfect English accent that let me know I was a failure at both French and English.

I pulled out the slip of paper with the name of the book written on it.

She sighed, adjusted her glasses, and glanced at the slip. I'm not sure what she expected, but it wasn't *Aperçu des secrets diplomatiques dans l'histoire de France.* She looked up, startled.

"It's by Jean-Marie Cournac. I'm looking for volume two," I said, not able to keep from slipping into a boarding-school-princess accent of my own.

"And why do you seek this book?"

"As a gift for my uncle. He has all the airplanes he needs."

She turned to the green velvet curtain behind her and called out, "Monique." A second later Monique appeared, blond and in her thirties, wearing a younger version of the suit and pearls and even the tortoiseshell glasses. Her sister—for clearly they were sisters—handed her the slip of paper. Monique fixed eyes on the paper, then me, then on the paper again. The two got into an annoyed conversation in French that went right over my head until not-Monique turned and said, "Who is your uncle?"

"My uncle? Polonius Harringtonpottershire. Why?"

"We do not have this book here, but we may be able to acquire it. How long will you be staying in Paris?"

"Long enough."

They huddled again, yakked away, then not-Monique broke huddle and said, "We would need a hundred euro deposit to find this book."

"Oh, pull-leazze," I said in spoiled-princess. "I'll give you my cell number and if you find it let me know. Otherwise someone else will." I nabbed a biz card from the gold rack, pulled out a pen, and scribbled down my cell number.

"Young lady, this book is worth perhaps twenty thousand euros. A hundred euro deposit is really nothing much."

"So don't ask for it then."

I snatched another of their cards and was on my way out when Monique, who had a thicker though kinder accent, said, "This book that you search for is very rare. Perhaps you can find it in the *Archives Nationales*."

I nodded.

"*Bonne chance,*" she said as the door closed.

After getting back to Aunt Mill's and blasting through my math problems, I jumped on Google maps and realized the Archives Nationales was right around the corner. I'd walked by it a million times. It looked to be part of a bunch of rich-people houses from the 1600s, called *hôtels*, mashed together into a huge museum.

A *hôtel*, so you know, wasn't like a place you stayed in during vacay, where you could order room service and splash in the pool. It was like a fancy-pants house, like a *château*, only in the city. Aunt Mill's building, in fact, with its courtyard and carriage doors, was one of these *hôtels* that somebody had divided into apartments long ago.

The one in this bunch that grabbed my attention, though, was l'hôtel de Rohan, as in Cardinal Rohan, the guy that Jeanne de la Motte tricked into buying the diamonds. The Hôtel de Rohan was practically across the street from us!

I dashed down rue Vielle du Temple to the massive blue carriage doors of l'hôtel de Rohan. The little door inside the big door was open, so I stepped in. A guard in blue, with the standard guard mustache, wiggled a finger and made it clear that this wasn't a public entrance and that I should go around the block to the Hôtel de Soubise. I tried to say, "*mais, j'adore l'hôtel de Rohan,*" but he just puffed out his cheeks like that was an inane thing to say and pointed down the block.

They wanted to charge me two euros to get into the Hôtel de Soubise. I glanced in past the ticket booth to a long, perfect paved drive with perfect geometric bushes spaced at perfect intervals, bordering impossibly perfect squares of lawn. The drive led to a creamy palace that convinced you in an instant that it really was worth being a princess, even if you had to lose your head in the end. Nowadays the Hôtel de Soubise was a museum where they kept really old documents, like the proclamation of King Charles the Bald Guy and the *Déclaration des droits de l'homme.*

After expressing, in my limited French, that I wasn't there to see the proclamation of Charles the Bald Guy, the ticket lady directed me around the block to the rue des Quatre-Fils and the entrance to the Centre Caran. Built on the back side of the Hôtel de Soubise and Hôtel de Rohan and very modern, the Caran housed desks and computers and microfilm machines where people seemed deeply involved in researching whatever they were researching. Several librarians, amused by my half-French-half-English, passed me around like a hot potato before Madame Haron invited me into her office. Madame Haron couldn't have been a madame for very long. She had a smooth, pink face behind thick, frameless glasses and even though she was dressed in modern clothes she made me feel like I was talking to a reincarnated princess. She seemed slightly amused and a tad bored, but much too refined to be dismissive.

"So let me see if I understand," she said, referring to a form they'd made me fill out. "Your name is Daisy Tannenbaum and you are American and currently residing in France and you are looking for a rare book written in the Eighteenth Century. You have no scholarly credentials and no letters of recommendation. You don't really read French, especially as written in the Ancient Regime, and you refuse to tell us why you want this particular book, yet you say it is vital that you find a copy of it."

"Correct."

"Well, Daisy—it is Daisy?"

I nodded.

"Well, Daisy, I can see you are an intelligent girl. We have some wonderful programs here to acquaint young people with our collections. There is a workshop where we teach you to make a book the way they did in the Eighteenth Century and another that teaches you how to create the page of an illuminated manuscript and—"

"Not to be rude, but I just need the book."

She looked at the form again and read out loud, "'*Aperçu des secrets diplomatiques dans l'histoire de France. Comprenant un point de vue philosophique sur la nature des actions menées avec discrétions et savoir-faire.*'"

I nodded.

"But why this book? We could perhaps bend some of the rules about educational credentials, but everyone who uses our resources must state the purpose of their research. All those people you see," she nodded out her office window to the dozens bent over old documents or scanning computer screens, "they have all stated a specific reason why they are here."

"Can you keep a secret, Madame Haron?"

Madame Haron smiled patiently. "The purpose of your research must be a matter of public record. That is why you fill out the form."

"Well, could you keep the form in your desk drawer for awhile? Just for the meantime?"

"You have me intrigued, Daisy. Please tell me your secret."

"You have to promise to keep it secret."

"Can you promise me in return that you are not plotting to

overthrow the state? We frown upon people overthrowing the state."

"I'm serious."

"As am I," she said with a flashing smile.

"Okay, I promise not to overthrow your government."

"Then I promise to keep your secret."

"This is about the Queen's Diamonds."

She laughed—a wafer of a laugh that made it impossible to get mad at her. She put her hand up. "I'm so sorry. You took me by surprise."

"I'm serious. Jean-Marie Cournac was in Louis XVI's intelligence service. He was in charge of tracking de la Motte in England and getting back the diamonds. The book contains hints about the covert operation he was boss of. That's why I need it."

Her mouth hung open. "You know a lot about *l'affaire.*"

"More than a lot."

She picked up her telephone, hit intercom, spoke in hushed French with someone. I thought for sure a guard was on the way to escort me out.

"Are you working with someone on this search for the diamonds?"

"I don't need a partner if that's what you mean."

She laughed again. "No-no, I have my hands full, but you must be working with someone, no?"

"No."

She tilted her head to indicate I was a bad liar.

"Against someone, but not with someone, if you know what I mean."

Before she could say anything her intercom buzzed. She picked up her phone, listened, said, "okay" and hung up. She moved to her computer, moused around a bit, studied her screen and frowned. "I'm afraid we don't have a copy of the book, or books—*Monsieur le duc* wrote three volumes apparently. It isn't listed in the collections of the Bibliotèque Nationale either. It appears there are several copies in private collections."

"Like whose?"

"I can't tell you that."

"Are they here in Paris?"

"I can't say."

"But you know?"

"They are private collections. We are not permitted to give out private information."

"Just this once?"

She laughed again, but there was just the hint of annoyance to let me know.

"I'm sorry, I just really-really need to know."

"You could try an antique book dealer. Often they have contact with the collectors and can put you in touch with them. There's Monique at Librairie Pitollot, she's very good, and Loeb-Larocque, and Lupatreaux, too. He's excellent too."

"Lupatreaux," I sighed.

"Yes. I'll write them down for you." She pulled out a fountain pen and stationery embossed in gold and wrote out the names in perfect princess script, saying, "You know, we have a replica of the necklace here. Have you seen it?"

I shook my head.

"Would you like to?"

I nodded. She gave the stationery a crisp fold and handed it to me with her business card then got up, nabbing an ID lanyard from a hook near her door. We exited the Caran and walked across an inner *jardin*. Everyone we passed said *"bonjour"* to Madame Haron like they were delighted to see her and, I suppose, who wouldn't be? I felt special just walking by her side.

With a nod from the guard, we walked in a back entrance to the Hôtel de Breteuil and through room after fairy-princess room, passing life-sized mannequins dressed in flowing silk gowns with tiny waist and poufy hips, each topped with a towering white wig, until we came to a glass box with the mock-up diamond necklace. Even the fake looked amazing. I must have stared like a dummy for an hour.

"Have you ever worn them?" I asked.

She smiled and was about to say something when her cell phone buzzed. She studied a text message and frowned. "I must go. But it has been a pleasure meeting you, Daisy. I wish you good luck in your quest. You have my card so please give me a call and tell me how it turns out."

"Thank you Madame Haron," I said.

"Stay as long as you like. But promise me you won't steal our diamonds. They are only made of glass, but we like them very much all the same."

## 22. The Big Empty

That night I dreamed I attended a ball with Madame Haron. We both wore silk gowns with tiny waists and poufy hips, and glorious tall wigs with a million curls and ribbons, and while I looked rather odd and out of place, Madame Haron looked stunning, the six-hundred-forty-seven diamonds glowing like tiny fires around her neck. She kept saying, "Please don't steal our diamonds, Daisy, as we like them very much." Though not exactly a nightmare, it disturbed me enough to knock me awake.

Three A.M.

I lay listening to Aunt Mill moving about her study, obsessing over her code.

I'm not sure how she managed to drag herself off to the Embassy School the next day. I certainly didn't want to get up. She had to come in and wake me three times, the last time with a cig dangling from her lip as she pulled me out by my feet.

After she left, I padded down the steps and posted myself in the courtyard, hoping to catch Sief going off to school. No luck. Either he'd beat me out, or was waiting me out. Little twerp.

Shivering and hungry, I climbed back up and got ready for French class. Aunt Mill had been in such a hurry she didn't even leave me any math problems.

After Mademoiselle Seydoux finished ridiculing our wretched French, I tramped off in search of the book at Loeb-Larocque, on rue de Tolbiac, the last of the three places

Mademoiselle Haron said might have it. At Loeb-Larocque they barely let me past the door. Who was I? Did I have an appointment? Did I have truckloads of money? This was a private auction house, they said. This was for serious collectors, they said. This was not a place for young foreigners with germ-laden breath that could destroy priceless antique manuscripts with a single careless exhale. When I asked if there was anywhere else I might go to find the book, they said "*non*" and pushed their door in my face.

Peeved, I pointed myself toward Aunt Mill's by way of the river, trudging down rue de Tolbiac till I hit Quai François Maurice. Following the river ended up not being such a great idea because the roads along the *quais* were jammed with traffic and thick with exhaust.

Perfect, really, cause my brain was stuck in traffic too. Someone out there had the book I needed and I couldn't get it. If I was an adult, or spoke French better, or had gobs of money, it might be different. If Pauline would actually take me seriously, it might be different. If Madame Haron would tell me who the private collectors were, it might be different. But it wasn't different. I was just some loser kid who couldn't do math.

Escorted by my private cloud, I crossed a bridge over the Seine and bumped along till I came to a basin with a bunch of boats tied up, just below Place de la Bastille. I poked along a garden path beside the water, walking right by Nina, who was sitting on a bench. I almost didn't see her. She looked so sad she didn't look like herself, slouched and staring at the water.

"Nina?"

Her eyes rose, not surprised to see me, but not unsurprised either, almost as if she *didn't* really see me.

"You okay?"

I barely got a nod.

"Mind if I sit down?"

She shrugged. I plunked down next to her. She looked back at the water.

"What's wrong?"

I waited.

And waited.

"Hey, listen," I said. "I'm really sorry about the other day with Sief. I didn't mean to like ignore you or anything. It was rude and I feel really bad. It's just that he's kind of a brat about things sometimes and sometimes I react badly."

She didn't respond. Nothing.

"Nina, what's going on?"

She pulled herself out of wherever she was and eyed me. She seemed to acknowledge that she needed to be her social self, but then looked away.

I waited some more.

"Daisy, do you ever get the big empty?"

"The what?"

"The big empty. You know, like when everything becomes nothing so you try to fill it up. You buy clothes and shoes, you fill your closets with them, you study hard, then harder, you work till you collapse, you always try to look your best, better than your best, changing outfits, changing your makeup, your pose, your opinion, wanting to please, wanting to be the most beautiful, the smartest, the most clever, the very center of the swirl that ends up being just as nothing as everything else."

Wow. This was like a whole other Nina.

"Well," I said, not knowing what to say. "I mean. I feel lonely a lot. And confused. But I don't worry about being the most clever or beautiful. I guess I worry most about letting people down."

She nodded, staring back at the water.

"Did you have a fight with Bruno or Gilles or something?"

She half-smiled. "No." She sighed. "No."

"Well?"

She turned, eyes intense suddenly. "You know what I want? I want to get married."

"You will."

"No, I mean now. Like right now."

"You're thirteen."

"So, Bianca of Savoy married when she was thirteen. So did Lucrezia Borgia."

"They were like Dark Ages people or something. Anyway, getting married won't fill up the big empty."

"It might. It's worth a try."

"Not really. It sounds like a disaster. Especially when you're as amazing as you are."

"I'm not amazing. And even if I was I don't want to be. I don't want to have to fulfill someone else's great expectations. It's just exhausting."

"Well, that's fine. Or, not fine really, but I totally get it. And, if you promise not to hate me for saying so, it sounds like what you really want is for your mom and dad to get married, not you."

She looked at me. It was not a happy look.

"Nina, have I ever told you how screwed up my parents are? They actually got divorced and then got married again and now my mom's pregnant. I mean she's like a hundred years old and preggers. It's just cuckoo-gross-crazy. Parents are crazy. I don't know if we drive them crazy or they just come that way, but that's the deal."

She laughed. I was getting her out of her funk, which was good, but suddenly I felt overcome by sadness myself. I stared out at the water.

"What's wrong?" asked Nina.

"It just dawned on me. I haven't talked to my mom since I got here. I've been ignoring her. Like your mom and her mom."

"Oh."

"Yeah."

My cell phone rang. I dug it out of my pocket.

"Hello?"

"Daisy, I'm desperate," said Aunt Mill. "Felix is coming over in an hour to look at the code work and I promised him some dinner. I'm stuck at school with two lovely children who tried to poke each other's eyes out."

"Yikes."

"I'm waiting for their psychotic parents to come pick them up."

"You want me to make dinner?"

"You're so sweet, but no. I've already put in a big order with Rose. She's been cooking all day. I just need you to swing by and pick it up and then set the table and buy a baguette and maybe just make things look nice."

"Sure."

"I'll get home as soon as I can."

"No worries."

"Thank you. You're saving my life." She clicked off.

"Problem?" Nina said.

"We're having this guy over for dinner, but my aunt is stuck at school."

"Boyfriend?"

"Work friend. He lives in a palace though. I think Aunt Mill wants to make a good impression."

"Need a hand?"

Boy, did I.

When we got to Le Saint Gervais, Madame Rose staggered

out of the kitchen, pink faced and frazzled. "But the food it is not ready yet, Daisy. *Faut attendre*—need to wait."

Nina introduced herself to Madame Rose and they got into a mile-a-minute blab with so much slang that I didn't have a clue. Nina turned to me and said, "Let's go." We were out the door and halfway down the block before I spat out, "Nina, where are we going?"

"Madame wants us to buy cheese and bread. We can do that and then come back to pick up the dinner." She had her iPhone out and was dialing, waiting, leaving a message: "Mom. Daisy's aunt is having a dinner and needs to borrow a bottle of wine. I won't take anything from the top rack. Call you later."

We were already at Nina's front door. "I'll dash up and get the wine. You hit the *boulangerie.*"

"Wine?"

"Madame Rose said she couldn't give us any cause we're too young and she's pretty sure your aunt forgot all about it, so I'll dash up and grab some and meet you at the *boulangerie.* Go."

I almost saluted.

From five to seven, the local *boulangerie* changed, as everyone in the neighborhood stopped by to pick up fresh bread for dinner. The line tailed right out the door and down the sidewalk. This was not the time to linger over which cream-filled pastry you wanted. Aunt Mill, who explained the five to seven rules the first time we visited, said you were expected to step up, bark your order, nab your change, say a curt *merci* and get out. A tourist who wandered in at this hour to gawk, or who couldn't pronounce the name of the bread they wanted, would catch it from bakers and customers alike.

As I got close to the front of the line—with the smell of warm bread making my stomach twist with hunger, with people nudging up behind me, with everyone repressing dog-like urges to grab, scratch, shove—my mouth went dry with fear.

Four ladies worked the counter—one shouted your order, one made change, two filled your order.

*"Deux baguettes, s'il vous plait,"* I squeaked.

*"Deux bag'merc'mo'selle'l'suiv."*

Step left, dispense euros, receive change, step left, receive baguettes, hold vertical, step left, avoid next customer, swivel, shuffle, squeeze out the door.

I marched out as Nina marched up, canvas bag over her shoulder, bottles clinking inside. We scooted up rue Debelleyme to rue de Bretagne and into a cheese shop that had six million cheeses. There was cheese made from cows with three eyes, from goats with wings, from lambs that walked on water.

The *fromager* knew Nina by name and asked after her mother. Business, though not as insane as at the *boulangerie,* was brisk, so Nina remained business-like. The *fromager* wrapped everything up in white paper. I had just enough to pay him. He dropped the receipt in our bag and wished us a *bonne soirée.*

Off we scooted, back to Le Saint Gervais.

By the time Madame Rose finished loading us up, we could barely walk. The climb up Aunt Mill's stairs was like Everest. A cast iron casserole, weighing over a ton, wrapped in newspaper and stuffed in a plastic bag, burned a hole in my chest.

"Come on, clock's ticking," said Nina, trudging up past me.

We got everything into the kitchen and unwrapped. The casserole contained a rabbit and wild mushroom stew. With it, Madame Rose had sent along a mound of her *foie gras,* a lobster salad, a green salad, and a *clafoutis aux cerises,* a kind of French cherry pie. All these things were on dishes raided from Madame Rose's own china cabinet, so Aunt Mill could say she made all this stuff herself if she chose.

"How does your aunt rate such treatment from the café

lady?"

"My aunt can't cook a thing. So we eat there all the time."

Nina flipped on Aunt Mill's oven, shoved in the casserole, yanked open drawers to find silverware. She asked me so many *where-is-this* questions that my head fell off.

"The *foie gras* can be our starter, along with the lobster salad," she said. "Then we'll serve the rabbit as the main course then bring out the cheese and a green salad before the *clafoutis*. We should unwrap the cheese so it has a chance to warm and, oh, bottle opener, so we can let the wine breathe."

"Nina, how do you know all this stuff?"

She gave me a pat on the head like she was my French grandma.

We set out plates, found actual matching wine glasses, sliced the bread, grilled some into toast for the *foie gras*, discovered some candles buried in a drawer.

When Aunt Mill called you could hear panic in her voice. "Daisy, I'm just getting out of here. Did you manage to get the food?"

"All good. Table set. Cheese unwrapped. Rabbit in the oven. We even opened the Chambolle-Musigny to let it breathe."

"*Oh, merde*—I completely forgot about wine."

"We borrowed some from Nina's Mom."

"You what?"

"Nina's helping me. Do you mind if she stays for dinner?"

"Wait. She brought a Chambolle-Musigny?" gasped Aunt Mill.

"Plus a sparkling Vouvray that she swears by."

It was silent on the line. I think my aunt had to compose herself. "Of course she can stay. If Felix gets there before I do, just talk with him, will you?"

"Got it."

Aunt Mill clicked off.

I gave Nina a thumbs-up. We cleared away books, tossed out desiccated flowers, did a dust-bunny patrol. Finally, we lit the candles and took a look around. That's when it occurred to me:

"Nina."

"What?"

"Only speak English tonight."

"*What?*"

"Don't speak any French to Aunt Mill or Felix."

"Why?"

"Because they may start speaking French and not realize you understand."

"So?"

"In fact, when they speak French, look like you *don't* understand."

"How do I do that?"

"Look like I did when we were with Bruno and Gilles at the café."

"Why?"

The lock on the apartment door clacked.

I whispered, "Last time they talked French at dinner so I wouldn't understand what they were saying, so just play along, okay?"

"Hello?" said Aunt Mill from the hallway. "Daisy? We're here."

## 23. An Up-To-The-Minute Girl

I gave Felix, who was still huffing and puffing after climbing the stairs, a double-cheeker like I'd been doing it all my life and said, "Felix and Aunt Mill, I'd like you to meet Nina."

"Hiya," said Nina, shaking their hands like a farmer from Kansas.

"We have everything ready. Why don't you two relax and have a seat at the table," I added. "We'll serve."

Nina and I rushed into the kitchen and returned with the lobster salad and sparkling Vouvray, which is like champagne. Nina opened the bottle like a pro—POP—and filled their glasses. "Cheers," she said, as they clinked.

Felix and Aunt Mill were in *foie gras* heaven for the next few minutes, but took time out to ask Nina a bunch of *get-to-know-you* questions: "Where are you from? How long have you been in France? How do you like it here?"

It was the scariest part of the evening because Nina just made stuff up as it came into her head: "I have cousins in Queens and Malibu where we spend a lot of time listening to jazz and canoeing, and that's where I first learned to open soda bottles with my teeth... France isn't too bad but the language is impossible and why bother really because you just have to talk to your boring French grandparents, plus they are so fixated on cheese-cheese-cheese, always cheese, and none of it as good as peanut butter... I'm definitely moving to Oklahoma as soon as I'm old enough because it seems like the most American place there is in America and besides, they have Indians there and one of the really big drawbacks with France is no Indians…"

Soon enough, Aunt Mill and Felix switched to speaking French. I caught Nina's eye and flicked mine toward the kitchen. We rose together, clearing the first course plates.

"Such gentle-ladies," I heard Felix say, for our benefit, as we whisked out.

In the kitchen, as I eased the rabbit stew out of the oven and Nina chopped more bread, I whispered to her, "Don't look so interested when they're speaking French."

"But it is interesting."

"You can't understand them, remember. Try to look bored like me."

We returned to the dining room doing our best butler impressions, which probably weren't that good, but at least we didn't drop anything. The longer the evening went on the more relaxed Aunt Mill and Felix became. Just so it wouldn't go too smoothly, I'd break up their conversation by saying to Nina stuff like, "So do you like Beyoncé or Rihanna better?"

"I love them both. How could you not?" she'd say, throwing Aunt Mill and Felix off their conversation completely.

This went on through the rabbit and into the salad and cheese and *clafoutis*. Even though I didn't understand Felix and Aunt Mill, I had a vague idea of their conversation. They talked about Cournac and de la Motte, and about how useful the book was, and how Aunt Mill had a breakthrough with the code. Felix said things about Cournac and the French Revolution, but it was impossible to grasp what. What was easy to grasp was that they were both excited.

After the *clafoutis*, Aunt Mill took Felix into her study. When they realized Nina and I were following them, they traded a glance. Aunt Mill gave a shrug. When Nina saw Aunt Mill's safe and the spreadsheets and the old messages written in code, her eyes got huge but I managed to give her a stern frown and she returned to looking bored.

Aunt Mill walked Felix through her discoveries, showing him one old document after another, dispensing with the latex gloves on this grand occasion, the two of them getting entirely engrossed. This went on for so long I realized I had to say something.

"Aunt Mill, do you mind if I tell Nina something about this?"

"It looks like old-timey writing. Are they love letters?" said Nina. Was she a natural or what?

Felix and Aunt Mill gawked at her. I think they'd forgotten we were there.

"They are old-timey, yes," said Aunt Mill. "From the Eighteenth Century."

"So before airplanes," said Nina. "I get kind of vague on stuff before the airplane ages. I'm more of an up-to-the-minute girl."

"Oh," said Aunt Mill with a veteran teacher's non-judgmental face that never really hid the fact that she thought you dumb as a stone. "These letters are about two-hundred-years old, dear," said Aunt Mill, handing one to Nina. "They were written in code. See the numbers?"

"Cool. What were they writing about?"

"Oh, which king was saying what about this or that princess."

"So this was in the time of wigs and floufy dresses?"

"Yes, during the floofy dress ages," said Aunt Mill.

Felix couldn't contain himself and blurted a question in French and the two of them jumped back in, leaving Nina and I to bite back smiles.

Eventually Felix and Aunt Mill meandered into the living room, talking on, while Nina and I cleared the dishes. Nina got a text from her Mom and so she had to go. Felix gave her a triple-cheek kiss and promised to have us over to his place in the Sixteenth and thanked us for the "truly memorable" dinner. Aunt Mill hugged her and shoved a bunch of euros into her hands for the wine. I told them I was going to walk Nina home.

"Ohmygod, Daisy!" she screeched as we went down the stairs.

I shushed her and then shushed her again in the courtyard. She vibrated from not being able to speak. As the carriage door closed she grabbed me by the shoulders. "*Fauve*-girl, they're looking for the Queen's Diamonds!"

"I know."

"It's so cool. Those were all spy messages, those papers. Part of a secret plot to get the Comtesse de la Motte to reveal where she'd hidden part of the necklace!"    "I know."

"It's deliriously romantic, Daisy. This is like huge-huge-huge."

"I know, Nina. Don't talk so loud."

She put a finger over her lips then giggled like a six year old.

I grabbed her by the elbow and tugged her down the street. "Calm down and just tell me what they actually said."

"Your aunt said she'd had all these breakthroughs understanding the code. She was telling him what each message said. One talked about giving de la Motte a loan and another about rescuing her from some dangerous guy and another about how to pretend to be her friend so she would start telling them her secrets. Another was about getting her to trust them to transport the diamonds from a deposit box in Paris, and then I guess before it could all come down, they arrested the agent guy in London."

"Right."

"But then Felix started talking about some lady who was de la Motte's hairdresser. She knew the location of the depository, but de la Motte had the key. Jean-Marie Cournac, the guy who wrote all the secret messages, needed both."

"To get the diamonds?"

"Right. Some guy working for Cournac was going to pick them up and pretend to take them to de la Motte. Kind of the reverse of what she did to Cardinal Rohan. But that all fell through when de la Motte died. And then Jean-Marie Cournac got guillotined during the Terror."

"Him, too?"

She nodded. "Felix started talking about a chain of deposit box inheritors that led back to the hairdresser."

"De la Motte's hairdresser?"

"Yeah. I guess she disappeared during the Terror too. Then banks failed and Napoleon took over and then more historic stuff happened and then the vault, or bank, or whatever, burned during the Paris Commune and everybody thought the deposit boxes were lost."

"Oh."

"But they weren't. Not forever anyway. They were unburied at some point when they were rebuilding Paris and the new bank that was responsible for them tried to establish who the inheritors were. I guess they found some of the people who belonged to the boxes but after a hundred years the boxes were sold at a blind auction, which is like when you buy the box but don't know what's in it."

"When was this?"

"I don't know."

"Recently?"

"I don't know, Daisy. They didn't say. And I couldn't

exactly ask, could I?"

"Sorry," I whispered.

She shrugged. "Well, anyway, they were both pretty excited about it cause Felix says the messages draw a direct link from de la Motte to the deposit box."

"Did they say anything about the book?"

"The one Felix got for your aunt? She said she couldn't have broken the code without it."

I nodded. We were standing outside her apartment now.

"But then your aunt was saying she didn't care about the other stuff, the deposit box and the people who owned it now and the guy who hired her, because her job was only to break the code."

I nodded again. "I better get back before they miss me."

"Not so fast, *fauve*-girl. This is why you wanted to see my Tante Benice, isn't it? This is why you were asking her all those questions about old diamonds."

"Yeah."

Nina's iPhone pinged. A text from her mom. She exhaled in disgust. "Can I have a life or what?"

"I gotta go anyway."

She grabbed my sleeve. "Don't just slip off. I want to know what's going on."

"I don't know exactly. It's very confusing."

She gave me an exaggerated frown. "Is this how you treat your friends? Let them do things for you and then shut them out when you please?"

I sighed. "You remember the book my aunt was talking about, the one that helped her break the code?"

"Yeah."

"I think it's fake."

"Woah. What does your aunt say?"

"I haven't told her."

"Why not?

"Mostly cause I don't think she'll believe me and then she'll ask a bunch of questions I don't want to answer."

"Can't you just suggest it to her without getting into details?"

"She's spent months breaking the code. It's like her obsession, you know, so 'without getting into details' isn't going to work."

Nina didn't respond, except for a ghost smile while she gazed off, thinking it over. Her iPhone pinged again. She threw eyes upward and exhaled.

"You can't tell anyone, Nina. I mean it. Not Bruno or your mom or anyone."

"Duh."

# 24. Funny Tourists

A few days later, I sloshed my way through the rain toward the Porte des Lions entrance of the *Centre de recherche et de restauration des musées de France.* Traffic snarled along the Seine. Who would ever want to drive a car in this city?

As soon as Pauline Dumeril and I exchanged a double-cheek greeting I blurted, "Any progress on the page?"

She laughed. "Come back to my office."

Closing her door, sitting behind her desk, she said, "You've met Céline."

"Who?"

"Céline Haron, at the Archives Nationales.

"Madame Haron? How do you know her?"

"We went to school together. I was a bridesmaid at her wedding. Last night we were at a party and we started talking about funny tourists we'd met and she told me a story about a girl named Daisy who came into her office and I blurted, 'not Daisy Tannenbaum?' and she said, 'yes, Daisy Tannenbaum' and I said, 'I know Daisy.' Then Céline told me this crazy story about you searching for the Queen's Necklace."

"She was supposed to keep it a secret."

"Oh, I—we're pretty good friends. We tell each other everything. I was a bridesmaid at her wedding after all."

"So? Who else did you blab this too?"

"Don't be angry. We'd had a few drinks and—"

"I'd like to punch Madame Haron in the nose."

"Daisy."

"I suppose you haven't done any tests on the page I gave you?"

Her eyes narrowed, smile vanishing. But then she laughed a cat-purr of a laugh. "You're an imp, Daisy Tannenbaum. In Ban Pak we used to call you Professor Tannenbaum's Imp, did you know that?"

I didn't respond.

"What was the name of the book Céline said you were looking for?"

I'd memorized it by now: *"Aperçu des secrets diplomatiques dans l'histoire de France. Comprenant un point de vue philosophique sur la nature des actions menées avec discrétions et savoir-faire. A l'usage des futurs ministres royaux."*

She scrunched her brows—at my wretched accent no doubt—and slid her chair to her computer. "And the page you gave me is from this book?"

I nodded.

She worked her mouse and tapped out the title on the keyboard. "There it is. By Jean-Marie Cournac, Duc des Ongles?"

I nodded again.

"According to our database there are two known copies in private collections. Last copy sold for twelve thousand euros." She glanced up, "Seriously, you think this book is going to help you find the Queen's Diamonds?"

"It's complicated. But I need to know whether that page is a fake."

"Why?"

I hesitated.

"I won't tell anyone, promise."

I almost shouted, *that's what Madame Haron said.*

Instead, I said, "Can I just have my page back?"

She thought about it awhile or thought about something anyway, then stood up, saying, "Wait here a moment."

She left the office. Left me alone in the office. Left me alone in the office facing the back of a computer that had the addresses of the private owners of the book on the computer screen. I heard her footsteps fade down the hall.

I stood up, grabbing a scratch pad and pen off her desk.

By the time Pauline returned, I was back in my chair, trying to look innocent, but not so innocent that it looked like I'd been up to something.

Pauline introduced me to Dr. Alfred Baertich, a white-haired, crazy-browed, stoop-shouldered ancient wearing a frayed sweater vest. His English was almost as bad as my French, though not quite as bad, so Pauline did a lot of translating and we switched back and forth from French to English, sometimes mid-sentence. She explained that Dr. Baertich was very good with old documents and had helped unravel the Priory of Sion hoax, whatever that was.

She produced the page from a drawer in her desk, where it had no doubt been parked since I'd last seen her, handed it to him, and told him that I thought it was a forgery. He studied me with the most skeptical eyes I'd ever seen and said, "What make you think it is *une contrefaçon*?"

"It's complicated. I just have a feeling."

He snorted, then exchanged a rush of words with Pauline which went by so fast that I could only get the general sense that he thought I was a numbskull on a treasure hunt and why was Pauline wasting his time? I couldn't tell what Pauline said back, but it sounded like a combination of threats and begging. He smirked, pulled a tweezers from his pocket so that he wouldn't have to touch the paper and borrowed Pauline's magnifying glass for a close look.

He held the page to his nose and sniffed, ran a fingernail gently over the face of it, then held it at an angle parallel to his eyes so he could look across the surface, giving a running commentary which Pauline translated: "The paper is definitely of late eighteenth-century origin, very likely from local rag stock, produced in Paris. No watermark, which is odd, but not unheard of. The typeface is of a style used by licensees of the Royal Press prior to the Revolution. The ink looks right, though it could be faked easily enough. The writing style is typical of government functionaries of that period. The text seems to be something about foreign affairs, though it is hard to tell from such a small sample."

He set the page down, dismissing it like junk mail, asking the title of the book. Pauline told him. He looked at me, "How have you come to possess this page?"

"It fell out of a book my aunt owns."

*Tombée ou prise?*"

"He asks if it fell out or was taken," Pauline said.

"Both," I said. "Not that it was any of his business. Ask him how sure he is that it's not a forgery."

Pauline glanced at Dr. Eyebrows, who, instead of getting mad, seemed amused. "I don't say it is not forgery," he said. "I say, rather, it is impossible to conclude that it is not."

"So it might be?"     He puffed out lips and shrugged.

"Can I ask you something? Who is the greatest forger you've ever known?"

*Documents ou peintures?*

"Documents."

"Phillipe de Chérisey et Pierre Plantard. They made a complex of medieval documents *et*—"

His English failed him at this point so he went on in French as Pauline translated: "Which they planted in the Bibliothèque Nationale to be discovered. These forged vellums were very well made. They supported the claim that Plantard was a descendant of an ancient French king. They were very clever for their time."

"When was that?"

"In the 1960s," said Dr. Baertich, taking over again, "They are both dead now."

"What about now? Who's the best forger in France today?"

Pauline and Dr. Baertich shared a look. They both puffed out their lips. "Samuelson?" offered Pauline.

Baertich nodded, *"Mais il est à Fleury-Mérogis aujourd'hui."*

"Fleury-Mérogis? That's a prison, right?"

"Yes," said Pauline, "like your Alcatraz."

"Do you have a picture of Samuelson? Because I think I've seen him."

They eyed each other. Pauline sat down at her desk, mousing and keyboarding. We moved around to look over her shoulder. Her screen showed a non-public Interpol database. We watched a tumbling hourglass icon until a picture of Samuelson popped up.

"That's who I saw," I said, "at Le Dome."

"It's impossible," said Dr. Baertich. "He does—is serving—twenty years of prison for bank document fraud. I, em—how to say—*témoigné contre*—testified against him at his trial."

"I'm positive I saw him. Positive."

They looked at each other again. Dr. Baertich picked up the page and took another look. "Do you mind if I keep this so that I may make some testing?"

"Please do," I said.

Soon after, Dr. Eyebrows excused himself and Pauline said she had some pressing work. As she escorted me out, I asked how long it would be till I heard back about my page.

"Oh, well," she said, "we're worse than academia, with a five-year backlog, so probably not too soon. But I'll phone you the moment I hear something."

"So, like, never?"

"Professor Tannenbaum's Imp," she sighed.

## 25. Cheez Whiz & Jane Austen

Aunt Mill stopped off at an *epicerie* and brought home a rotisserie chicken and roast potatoes. It would have been wonderful had she not decided to go over my math problems while we ate. I'd rushed through them when I got back from seeing Pauline. I could see Aunt Mill growing upset. She put her fork down.

"Did you consciously construct these answers to ruin my day?"

"I'm not very good at math."

"You need to stop saying that, Daisy. Children, as a general rule, are not very good at anything. That's why we've invented schools. Which, granted, are not perfect inventions, though they certainly don't rank as the worst thing humans have invented, compared to say mustard gas and corsets."

"What's mustard gas?"

"Never mind. The point is—we are a school. You and I. I am the teacher. You are the pupil. I give assignments. You must do them. Must, Daisy. Is that clear?"

"I tried."

"You didn't try. I see no evidence of trying. I see evidence of a mind that is somewhere else, phoning in from Mars, feigning inability because exhibiting ability might require it to do something it is obstinately set against doing."

I almost said, *that's a lovely theory*, which is what my dad says when you say something stupid. Instead, I dummied up. Aunt

Mill flipped over the sheet of paper, pulled a pencil from the mug of them that sat beside the salt and pepper, scrawled out a problem and shoved it my way.

I stared at it. I don't know why, but when someone just smacks me in the face with a math problem, I blank.

"What's forty-five divided by nine?" she asked.

"Five."

"So we can reduce this to one and this to five. Right?"

I nodded. On she went, talking me through each baby step of the problem so it was simple and clear, until I could see the answer: "Eighteen and two-fifths?" I offered.

"Is that correct?"

"I dunno."

"Daisy, you *do* know. It's correct. And you know it is because you just did all the steps in the right sequence."

I stifled a yawn.

She took up her wine glass. "You are an enigma, my dear."

"Like a secret code?"

"Yes, you are your own secret code. It will take me years to decipher you. In the meantime I think I'll start locking up your key and allowance in the little safe again."

"But then I'll have to do the math problems before I go to French class."

"Won't kill you."

"It will, I'll be late every day, Mademoiselle Seydoux will ridicule me to death. Can't you just leave the key out and put the allowance in the safe?"

"I'll think about it," she said. "In the meantime, perhaps you could email your mother, like you promised."

"Does she like email you everyday and say, 'I haven't heard from Daisy?'"

"Every day."

"That's so lame."

She didn't say anything. I could tell I'd made her mad.

"Okay then, I'll go do it. No big deal," I said, stomping off.

As soon as I got to my room I clicked the email in box. The program fluttered alive and delivered ten million messages. My stomach crimped. There were several from Dad, most of them instructing me to write to Mom. Clymene contributed four, but I only read the first one, which was all about how horrible her poor pathetic life was and how lucky I was to be in France. Like she knew.

Mom had written two-dozen notes, some long, some short. The first ones were, I don't know, sorrowful and worried, but at some point Aunt Mill had started sending her reports on me because the notes got more happy and mentioned stuff that I'd been doing in Paris.

Pretty soon Mom started writing me about the maples in the front yard turning gold-orange and the first frost in the morning, and the trick-or treaters that came to the door (Holloween had slipped by) and about looking through an album of baby pics where I was wearing my pirate costume (which I wore for like, two years straight) and about feeling Baby-X kicking inside her. The emails made me homesick, and sad, and angry—all at once. I'm usually okay being sad and I do all right with angry too, but homesick makes me crazy.

I wrote her back saying, "I recognize that I'm the worst daughter ever in regards to not responding to your emails, but I do appreciate your writing them and promise that someday I will somehow explain my inexplicable silence." I even looked up inexplicable to make sure I was using it right.

Then I deleted the message.

Maybe another day.

I saved reading the emails from Lucia for last. I paced

around the room before I could even face them. If things with Mom seemed confused, things with Lucia were simple. I'd let her down. I fully expected to throw myself out the window after reading her emails.

But actually, Lucia was fine. More than fine. She wrote, "I absolutely cherished your last missive." That was the first clue. I'd sent an email, not a missive.

She said she put my advice to good use. "But some of the things you suggested were impossible to implement." *Implement?*

Apparently she had managed to avoid Martin Blindenbok most of the time and even isolated Michael Cornish and shoved him into a puddle. "There will be no revolution at the Fairfield School," she wrote. "There will be little rubs and disappointments everywhere, and we are all apt to expect too much; but then, if one scheme of happiness fails, human nature turns to another; if the first calculation is wrong, we make a second better: we find comfort somewhere."

My mouth fell open. Lucia had discovered Jane Austen.

Discovered was an understatement. They were living together. At Mansfield Park. Emma had moved in with them. Packed with pride and prejudice and swollen with sense and sensibility, Lucia had taken up with Miss Austen big time. They woke and ate together. They stayed up late into the night conversing. Martin Blindenbok stood not a chance against such an alliance.

Lucia, you may remember (my dear reader) was from Bulgrungastan or some such place and had slightly funny notions of America. Therefore, her discovery of and devotion to Jane Austen was not as surprising as her discovery of and devotion to Cheez Whiz.

It is surprising she found it edible, certainly, but more surprising that she discovered the nozzle of an eight-ounce, pressurized Cheez Whiz container could be crimped to a flat shape and still dispense a prodigious stream of whiz or cheez or whatever you call that stuff, into the vent of a school locker. She discovered, in point of fact, that you could dispense the entire eight ounces in a single long stream, late of a Friday afternoon, when the hallway was deserted, and that no one would discover it, because of Veteran's Day Holiday, until Tuesday morning, by which time the whiz or cheez, or whatever, had entirely transformed itself into rancid geck.

By Tuesday morning, Martin's locker was as whiffy as a skunk. The stuff had turned into green ooze that covered everything in his locker. He was livid. He was a laughing stock. He lashed out at those who laughed, including his allies Michael and David, and ended up visiting Principal Smootin.

And the brilliant thing for Lucia was the entirely liberating realization that, because he had terrorized so many other students and had made so many enemies, Martin had not the least notion of who had befouled his locker. The suspects were endless. In fact, she had heard a rumor later that Martin accused *me* of the deed.

For once I had a good alibi. I reread one of the weirder emails from my Mom, which I didn't understand the first time. She wrote saying she'd gotten a call from Principal Smootin, inquiring regarding my whereabouts that same Friday. She had informed Principal Nitwit that I was in Paris, as in Paris, France.

Next morning, I padded into the kitchen to find Aunt Mill clutching her coffee cup, dark circles under her eyes. I told her about Lucia's emails and how Principal Smootin thought I'd come back to haunt him. She smiled and then asked if, while looking at emails, I'd happened across any from my mother.

"Dozens," I said.

"Did you read them?"

"I did."

"Did you answer them?"

"I tried."

I got back a raised brow.

"I wrote a note and came this close to hitting the send button but I couldn't."

"Daisy, you're ridiculous."

"Probably worse than that, probably a psycho-job. But anyway, it looks like you've written her, so that's good."

"Not the same as you writing, though, is it?"

I shrugged.

She sighed, gulped down the rest of her coffee and milk, set her cup in the sink. "I have to make a quick trip to London. Just overnight. I've made arrangements for you to stay with Felix."

"What's up in London?"

"Some business."

"About your codes?"

She nodded. "I'm taking the Eurostar at nine. I told Felix you'd come by after French class."

"Can't I come with you?"

"I'm afraid not."

"I wouldn't get in your way. I could just walk around London all day and see stuff and check in on Kate and William."

"I'm afraid not."

"It would be very educational. I could write a paper on whether it rains more in Paris or London."

She laughed. It wasn't going to happen. A few minutes later we were out the door. Fog-ghosts cruised empty streets. Water gurgled down drainpipes. Everything dripped.

We walked together as far as Chatelet, pausing at the Metro steps. Aunt Mill's only luggage was an umbrella and a beat-up leather briefcase.

"You have Felix's address and number?"

I held up the instruction sheet she'd written out.

"My cell works over there, so call if you need."

"Okay."

"Call me even if you don't need."

"Okay."

She took me by the shoulders. She looked—I don't know—worried? It felt like a mom-moment.

"I'll be okay, Aunt Mill."

"I know you will. You've become quite the little *Parisienne*." She gave me a crushing hug and hobbled down the Metro steps as I turned toward the river.

Mademoiselle Seydoux wore a particularly hideous sweater that day. I made a comment that it looked like a *canard mort* (a dead duck) and she laughed and we spent the whole rest of the class making fun of each other's clothes in French.

When class was over, the sun made a rare appearance. Since Felix wasn't expecting me till later, I decided to walk to the Sixteenth. I wandered through the Jardin de Luxembourg, picked up rue Vaugirard, loitering with nose to store windows, then ambled along rue Grenelle for a long time, crossing in front of Place des Invalides, ending up on the Champs de Mars. I walked under the Tour Eiffel, bought some chestnuts and sat eating them, then crossed the river and climbed up to the Trocadéro, where the sun hid behind clouds and a snarling wind began to blow.

The whole time, I thought about the book. It was its own thing now, like a mythical beast. I knew Aunt Mill must be off to London to confirm her work with some fellow code expert. I'd heard her talking to Felix on the phone about some big meeting they were going to have so she could present her work to the rich guy who wanted to buy the diamonds. The guy's real name was

Berkman—I was pretty sure of that from eavesdropping. But really, why should I care if some rich art collector bought some phony diamonds from a Russian gangster?

After I'd found my way to Felix's apartment and gotten past the naked mom painting, while we were eating Magda's overcooked dinner, I said, "Felix, can I ask you something?"

"Of course."

"Is it possible the book Aunt Mill is using to crack the codes, the one she got from Lupatreaux, is a fake?"

"You mean a forgery?"

"Yes. And the messages too. Could they be fake?    So that the fake book would lead to translating the fake coded messages?"

He looked over his glasses at me. "That would imply that the code itself was a forgery."

I nodded.

He thought it over a moment. "Impossible."

"You're sure?"

"Well, unlikely in the extreme. What made you think of that?"

"It's just an idea I had."

"Based on?"

"Based on what if? Based on how much the diamonds are worth and how much time Aunt Mill has put into this and, and I don't know."

Felix sipped his wine, set the glass down, placing fingers just so on the base. "Have you mentioned this to your aunt?"

"No."

"I wouldn't if I were you."

"Why not?"

"Because she's worked very hard on this code.    She's struggled mightily. Good code-breakers are a special breed, you know. Imagine a vast picture puzzle with ten-thousand pieces, except the pieces don't really exist save as relationships of certain letters to certain numbers and vice-versa, and then only as an image in one person's head. It takes quite a head to hold all those pieces, you know, and sometimes that head just feels like it's going to—"

"Explode," I offered.

"I was going to say, drop all the pieces. But explode will do."

## 26. Getawayway

Felix put me up in a room with a canopy bed for a princess. Raspberry silk drapes billowed down over fluted columns to a matching duvet and pillows. The princess would not have found her pea, though, for all the other lumps in the mattress, plus the ancient dust would have made her sneeze all night. My nose clogged as soon as I got under the duvet.

It's a wonder I slept at all, since Felix (or maybe his mother) had decorated a bookshelf with a row of life-sized, wooden heads that came off the dolls that modeled clothes in Marie Antoinette's day. They had painted pink cheeks, creepy smiles, and no hair. A moonbeam sieved by lace curtains glinted off their glass eyes.

I had a 007 dream of Aunt Mill in London, karate-chopping her way through an army of bald, pink-cheeked assassins. I squirmed and shouted, "I'll be right there, Aunt Mill!" But I couldn't move—until Magda entered the room and woke me, setting down a tray with a pitcher of warm milk, steaming chocolate, and two insanely perfect croissants.

She motioned for me to sit up, fluffed my pillows, and adjusted the duvet, leaving me to enjoy my breakfast in bed, the first one I'd ever had when I wasn't sick. Later, she came back with my clothes, ironed and folded.

I found Felix, lounging in a silk robe with black velvet lapels, face hidden by Le Figaro newspaper, his slippers propped on a poof.

"Breakfast in bed was wonderful," I said.

"Forecast is for rain," he responded from behind the front page. "I believe I have one of your aunt's umbrellas in the stand. You'll have to take it with you."

I parked myself on a chair next to his. "Felix, how did Aunt Mill get into the Order of the Cincinnati?"

The paper lowered. "She didn't tell you?"

I shook my head.

He contemplated a moment then folded his paper.

"I'm a member of the Order. My great-great-great grandfather or something was an aid to Lafayette and fought with Washington and, of course, I'm the oldest living son and all, so I recommended her. It's mostly Yanks in the organization and they didn't like the idea of admitting a woman, never had before, made a world of fuss, but I insisted. Finally, they had to admit she deserved it."

"Why?"

"For heroism. Above and beyond."

"She was in a battle?"

"Of sorts, yes. We worked on a team together. I was her mentor, so to speak. We were charged with keeping some unsavory characters from doing unsavory things."

"What things?"

"Well, em, secret things, unsavory sorts of things."

"Can you be more specific?"

"Shouldn't really. Ask her again I should think."

I tried to give him my most disappointed look. It only made him smile, but then he exhaled and said, "This is top secret, you understand?"

I nodded and put a finger to my lips.

"We were charged with keeping certain weapons from certain organized criminal types who intended to pass them on to some bad players."

"Terrorists?"

"Depends on how you define the word, but it will do, I suppose. At any rate, the task was complicated by the dubious intentions of one of our own."

"You mean like a double-agent?"

"Er, yes, I suppose you would call it something like that."

"So what happened?"

"Well, em, double-er-agents are very hard to detect, very detrimental to success, making the whole job problematic—can't trust anyone, don't know why things are going wrong, setback after setback—and it's more difficult when you have players of many nationalities trying to cooperate. There's a natural tendency to distrust and when something like this happens—resources lost, people gone missing, operations botched—well, it's very discouraging."

"What did Aunt Mill do that was so special?"

"She devised a scheme to reveal the double and determine how he was sending messages. She decoded the messages herself because she wasn't sure whom else to trust. Then she set herself up as bait to lure the double into a trap."

"So she was a spy?"

"Oh, well, not—not a spy, not really—I never said that. Anyway, we never use that word. After all, I've never met a real spy, have you?"

"Not that I know of."

"Well, there you are." He looked at his watch. "Don't you have school?" He turned his watch so I could see.

"I better go. Thank you so much, Felix."

He leaned forward and we exchanged a two-cheeker.

"Don't forget the umbrella."

Because I was so tired, or maybe because I had all this stuff swirling in my brain, I kept spacing in Mademoiselle Seydoux's class, until she called me out, saying, *"Pourquoi as-tu la tête dans les nuages, Daisy?"* After that, the whole class revolved around on why our heads were in the clouds.

By the time class wrapped up, the rain had retreated, leaving behind the standard Paris gloom. I hardly noticed, though, cutting across the river behind Notre-Dame, retreating to back streets to get away from traffic. Unlike my first days, when Nina rescued me from walking to death in circles, it felt like all *rues* led to Aunt Mill's. I hardly paid attention, getting lost in my thoughts.

I had a lot to think about. Aunt Mill would be home from London today and I had to decide what to tell her. This Samuelson character, the best forger in France according to people who surely knew, was out of prison and lunching with Russian gangsters who terrified Lupatreaux into passing me a fake book. Plus, I now had the address of someone who had a real copy, in the suburb of Neuilly, a short Metro ride outside the city.

I'd just turned onto rue Vieille du Temple, a block from Aunt Mill's, so wrapped up in thoughts that I barely registered a car door shutting behind me. There were no cars up the *rue*, not that strange in the Marais where people regularly walk in the streets. That's why the gray Mercedes was able to back up and stop beside me.

A tinted window buzzed down. Yursky Gruzdeva gazed out. "I hear you looking for a book." My eyes flicked up the *rue*. The neckless monster in a tracksuit from Lupatreaux's marched toward me. I glanced back. The snake-in-skull guy closed in behind.

"Get in," croaked Gruzdeva, popping open the back door.

Yeah, right.

In less time than it takes to write, I tossed the umbrella at Gruzdeva, leaped onto the hood, bound onto the roof, and flung myself off the trunk. Neckless and Snake-n-Skull dove as soon as I moved, but got tangled in each other, giving me a half second lead. I could hear their footsteps behind me on the cobbles.

I raced up rue Vieille du Temple, hurdling over a tangle of pugs on leashes, dodging a taxi door as it opened to drop off tourists. I could hear the shouts of people behind me, who didn't like getting shoved out of the way by vory thugs, then heard a motor roaring and brakes screeching. I glanced over my shoulder and glimpsed the taxi driver shouting as the Mercedes backed up over the opposite sidewalk, but what I really noticed was Neckless just half a pace behind me.

As he lunged, I flung myself into the street, leaping over the front tire of a *Velib* rent-a-bike that slammed on brakes when the rider saw the Mercedes speeding his way. Neckless and the rider tumbled over in a heap. A second *Velib*, ridden by a screaming blond, plonked into them both. The riders sounded like a pair of Swedish tourists, based on their cursing. I would have laughed if I'd had any breath, and if Snake-n-Skull weren't two steps behind.

I sprinted across rue Barbette. I was hoping for one of those movie moments where a car blocks Snake-n-Skull's path right after I cross, but that didn't happen. I could hear his steps getting closer and even if he'd been wearing fleece slippers, I couldn't miss his non-stop cussing. You didn't have to know Russian to know he wanted to squeeze my eyeballs out.

I saw the big blue doors of the Hotel Rohan and the cutout door open. I pivoted across the street, zipping under the elbow of the guard with the big mustache, who didn't have time to react. Snake-n-Skulls smashed full speed into him. They hit so hard I think it knocked them both out for a moment. They stood eye to eye, blinking.

*"Alors?"* growled the guard.

Snake-n-Skull staggered back. The Mercedes screeched to a stop behind him. The guard reached for his walkie-talkie. Snake climbed into the Mercedes and it roared off, swerving around the screaming Swedes, who flung a bottle of wine at it.

I sat up behind the guard, picking pea gravel from my cheeks. He turned and hovered above me like an angry giant.

*"Alors?"*

*"Je veux voir Madame Haron, s'il vous plait,"* I said, or tried to say—who knows what actually came out in my gasping, heart-pounding state. The guard squinted at me. I repeated myself. He spoke into his walkie-talkie.

Other guards came running. Big Mustache Guard pulled me up and brushed me off. One of the other guards, who was like the guard boss or something, spoke English and asked me what happened and who I was and all those police questions, and then Madame Haron arrived and they all started yabbing and asking more questions and I had to explain everything all over again.

Clearly, Gruzdeva found out I was searching for the book. But I couldn't say that and I couldn't sort out who had told him while Madame Haron and the guards were peppering me with all these questions. Was it Pauline? Dr. Eyebrows? Sief? Sief's cousin? Nina? Monique at the Librairie Pitollot? Or someone else altogether, since, as I'd found out, nobody in Paris can keep a secret?

"Daisy, are you listening to me?" Madame Haron asked, hands on my shoulders. "Who were those men in the car?"

"I don't know. I never saw them before. Can I go home now? I'm really tired and I'm not thinking too well."

"You can go home in a minute—just answer Officer Bouna's questions."

"But I have, honestly I have. They just drove up and offered me a ride and I said *non, merci,* and they insisted and then one of them threw open the back door and the other got out and I took off running."

"And you've never seen them before?"

"No."

Madame Haron let go of my shoulders and turned to Guard Boss, puffing out her cheeks in frustration. They stepped off to the side and had a conversation that I couldn't quite hear while the other guards, including my savior, Big Mustache, stood by and had their own conversation. I stepped up to Big Mustache and stuck out my hand. *"Merci de m'avoir aidée, Monsieur, merci beaucoup."*

*"C'est avec plaisir, ma petite,"* he growled, shaking my hand.

My cell phone rang. I held up a finger and fished it out of my pocket. "Hello?"

"Daisy? I just got in," said Aunt Mill. "Where are you?"

"Down the block. Near the Hôtel Rohan. How was your trip?"

"Excellent. I'll tell you all about it when you get here."

"Be there in a minute." I punched off.

Madame Haron had finished her conversation and stepped over. "I'm going to walk you home."

And so she did, after I thanked Big Mustache again and shook hands with all the other guards and thanked them too. We walked across the perfect courtyard of the Hôtel Rohan, where Jeanne de la Motte had, once upon a time, conspired to steal the Queen's Diamonds, stopping in at Madame Haron's office for a moment while she made a quick phone call before leaving from the Centre Caran on rue des Quatre-Fils.

There was no sign of the gray Mercedes or of Gruzdeva's men, but Madame Haron caught me glancing up and down the rue for them.

"Expecting someone?"

I panicked, thinking it was Madame Haron who told the Russians. She wasn't walking me home, she was guiding me to them, having phoned just now to tell them what exit we'd be taking. I must have looked horrified because she asked, "Are you all right?"

"Do you know them?"

"Know who?"

"The Russians."

"What Russians?"

Oops. Of course, she didn't know them. If she did, she certainly wouldn't have gone blabbing about me and the book and the diamonds to Pauline. Plus, why would Madame Haron have anything to do with vory lowlifes? Get a grip, girl.

"What Russians, Daisy?"

"They were Russians. I could tell by their accents."

"Why didn't you tell Officer Bouna that?"

"Because—because I was confused. Everything was like smashed together in my head, if that makes sense."

She put an arm around my shoulders and said, "I think you may be lying to me. How are we to be friends if you lie to me?"

"Why would I be friends with someone who promises to keep a secret and then blabs it after a cocktail or two? Don't you think that encourages lying?"

That stopped her. She sighed. "So has this to do with your quest for the diamonds?"

"No."

"*Non?*" She shook her head with aristocratic displeasure. We were around the corner, approaching the doors to Aunt Mill's place.

"This is where I live."

"Ah. So close."

"Thank you for walking with me."

"I apologize for revealing your secret, Daisy. I admit I did not take you seriously at the time. However, from what the guard said, these men were not trifling."

"I'm home now. My aunt is waiting for me so I'll be safe."

She remained silent, lips pressed together, no doubt considering what to do. I didn't want her walking me up to the apartment and explaining everything to Aunt Mill so I pushed the cut out door open.

"I'll be all right," I said, slipping inside.

# 27. Breaking News

Aunt Mill was exuberant. Shoes off, feet on the couch, glass of red wine in hand, exuberant. She'd phoned Le Saint Gervais even before her train pulled into Gare du Nord, learned that Madame Rose was cooking *cassoulet,* and brought home an earthenware pot of tender white beans, duck confit, chubby sausages, roasted garlic, ham hocks and so many other things that only Madame Rose knew.

Running for your life makes you hungry, as does over-nighting in London apparently, so we went to the table and stuffed ourselves. Aunt Mill described the London subway and taxis and her near miss because she forgot that cars went the opposite way, and the divine Indian food and succulent bangers and the rain and fog—somehow altogether different than the rain and fog in Paris—and all the accents, ten-thousand different accents by her account, with hundreds of English words that she did not know the meaning of. Did I know that a *flannel* was a washcloth? Did I know that a *cheater* was a windbreaker, a *bap* was a hamburger bun, to *bodge* was to do a bad job, and that *rather parky* meant it was cold outside?

She'd brought me a tiny bottle of Floris Tea Rose perfume and a scarf in the same pattern that the Queen wears and a box of Fortnum & Mason tea. We made a pot of it and opened a box of lemon cream biscuits that she'd tucked in her briefcase. It was like mini-Christmas and for a long time I completely forgot all the trouble I'd been in just an hour before.

She wouldn't talk about *who* she met with, but she said she felt confident about her work after speaking with this particular friend and ready to write up her final report to submit to "Mr. Jones."

Here cell phone rang. Felix calling.

They reviewed her trip, Aunt Mill drifting into the living room while I cleared dishes. I couldn't hear all of their conversation, but got that Mr. Jones would be flying in on a private jet at the end of the week.

When Aunt Mill hung up she came in and said, "I should get to work. Can you tidy up?"

I nodded. "Aunt Mill, can I ask you a question?"

"Of course."

"Do you trust Felix?"

"Trust? Absolutely. Why?"

"It's just, I don't know, this is like a big thing with people who have tons of money, right?"

She nodded.

"So a lot of things can go wrong, right?"

"Things can always go wrong. But Felix isn't one of them. He may be eccentric and he's far too loyal to his housekeeper, but I would trust him with my life. In fact, I have on occassion."

She headed into her office. I washed up and for the rest of the evening, while she pounded away at her computer keyboard, I drove myself crazy thinking about who could have told Gruzdeva about me. I examined everyone. Felix didn't seem likely, based on what Aunt Mill said. Nina and Sief were off the list too. Sief had helped me discover Gruzdeva and Nina didn't really travel in Russian gangster circles. Same went for Pauline and Céline Haron—not really gangster-moll material. Sief's cousin? Did he even remember me? Doubtful. Plus he hated vory. That left Dr. Eyebrows at the Louvre, who I knew nothing about, and the two women at Librairie Pitollot, who I'd left my name and number with, like a complete nit.

Hours after I said good night to Aunt Mill, I was certain it was the two Moniques. Then I revisited Felix, from two in the morning till four, then I moved back to Dr. Eyebrows from four until I fell asleep.

The muffled ring of Aunt Mill's cell phone woke me. Rain tapped against my window. She picked up on the fourth ring and I could hear her saying in a hoarse voice, "What? When? Read it to me?" The hall light flicked on. My door burst open. Aunt Mill stood there, hair a shambles, holding her robe closed.

"Daisy, run down to the corner and get a newspaper."

"What?"

"There's a news box in front of the *tabac*. Get Le Figaro if you can." She thrust some change into my hand. I blinked at it. "Quickly! Get dressed!"

No socks, no umbrella, nose running, I nearly collapsed going down the stairs, thinking maybe a terrorist attack had occurred. The shops on rue Vieille du Temple were shuttered and the street was empty, save for a delivery van idling in front of the tabac. I slotted in the change, pulled out a paper, squinted at the unfamiliar format till the third headline caught my eye: *"Diamants de la reine retrouvés."* Even I knew it meant: "The Queen's Diamonds Found."

By the time I climbed back upstairs, dripping wet and gasping for breath, Aunt Mill had remembered she could read Le Figaro online. I found her, cell phone to ear, bent over her computer, "It doesn't say who the information comes from. It says a source familiar with international art dealings. Could be anyone."

She stood up, noticed me, put her hand out for the paper, making an effort not to shout into the phone, "Felix, this doesn't change anything. It's a ploy."

Listening to his response, she pointed at me and mouthed the words, "Go dry off."

"Yes, I'll come right over. Just take a deep breath. Felix, don't jump to conclusions. I told you, I can give a complete verbal presentation right now if need be. Yes-yes, I'm out the door, goodbye." She clicked off, pivoted, saw me lingering. "I said go dry off."

"What's going on?"

"Not a word till you're out of wet clothes."

After I'd toweled my hair and ditched my wet things, I found Aunt Mill in the kitchen, already dressed, blowing cig smoke out the open window.

"So what is it?"

"Oh, a huge lot of nothing. Someone leaked a story. Unknown source. Might be happenstance, but more likely the seller is trying to create pressure for the sale. Oldest trick in the book really."

"What do you mean?"

"The fastest way to sell something is to create competition between buyers. Buyers become less discerning if they fear someone may snatch their prize. So far there has been only one buyer, the fellow paying my salary. News like this will bring out a few more."

"Doesn't first buyer get first dibs?"

"Depends who else becomes interested. And it comes back to the question of authenticity." She stubbed out her cig, gulped the last of her coffee then took out her wallet and placed a wad of euros on the table. "Croissant money. I have to go see Felix. Mr. Jones is flying in today to confer with us."

"Don't you have to teach?"

"I've already called in sick."

"Aunt Mill," I said in faux-shock.

"Oh, please," she said, "from you of all people. I'll see you tonight. Don't punch anyone in the nose. Call me if you need anything."

She grabbed her briefcase and an umbrella and headed for the door, leaving the sodden copy of Le Figaro on the table. I couldn't help feeling that the story's appearance had something to do with my escape from Gruzdeva and yet it seemed preposterous that I could be involved in something that rated a story in a real French newspaper.

To be honest, I was kind of a mess. I couldn't think straight for all the mental tail-chasing I'd done that night. I felt pathetically homesick. How simple Martin Blindenbok and Principal Smootin seemed now. In a flash of panic, I imagined Snake-n-Skull crashing through the door to get me. I had to force myself to calm down.

*But they know where you live, Daisy,* my brain spun on, *they must know because they knew what street to look for you on, which means they know you live with Aunt Mill, which means they probably put it together that you saw them at Le Dome and Lupeatreaux's and they know you're after the book and they know that it is only a matter of time before you tell Aunt Mill.*

I dialed Nina, who picked up almost at once, her voice calming as always. "*Fauve*-girl. What goes?"

"I need you to come with me to Neuilly."

"What's in Neuilly, besides rich dorks?"

"A lady who has a book I need. I'm afraid my French won't be good enough so I'm hoping I can bribe you into helping me."

"Bribe away. I'll swing by your place after school."

"Can't you come now?"

"Not without my mom braining me. Can't it wait till

after?"

"Um, sure, never mind."

"No, come on. You have to go to your French class, right? I'll ring you at lunch and we'll pick a place to meet."

"Listen, Nina, where are you now?"

"Kitchen. Eating yogurt."

"So you're leaving for school soon?"

"About two minutes ago if I want to be on time."

"Do me a fave and when you leave your apartment, come around the corner to my building and just see if there are creepy Russian guys hanging out. They're driving a gray Mercedes. You can't miss them. They look like, I don't know, movie thugs."

She laughed. Then there was silence on the line.

"Are you serious?"

"Just walk past and see if you see them and call me on your cell."

"Daisy, this is creepy."

"Don't talk to them or anything and don't stare at them like you're looking for them. Can you do that?"

"Super-creepy. Has this got to do with the diamonds?"

"I'll tell you later, when we meet. Just call me once you've walked past my rue."

"*Fauve*-girl, you take the *gâteau*."

I didn't feel like I took the *gâteau*. I didn't feel like I took much of anything. After Nina signed off, I checked the courtyard-facing windows to make sure no vory were pacing the cobbles.

When my cell rang, I jumped. "Nina?"

"Nobody here that looks like a movie thug. In fact, nobody at all."

"No one hiding in the doorways or anything?"

"Daisy, geez, now you are really creeping me out."

"Well?"

"No. Nothing. I'm just coming to the end of the rue and there's no one lurking around the corner either. Do you want me to look in the sewers?"

"Hadn't thought of that. But no, they dress too nicely to get their clothes dirty."

"So they're well-dressed thugs? That's a relief."

"Go to school, Nina."

"I believe I shall. But seriously, are you okay?"

"Yes. I'm just letting my imagination get the better of me. But you've made me feel lots better. Thank you. You're my guardian angel, Nina."

"Heaven must be desperate. Call you later."

# 28. The Bulls

Nina was right. No vory.

Still, wanting to get off rue Vieille du Temple as soon as possible, I wove down rue du Marché des Blanc Manteaux and rue Des Hôspitaliéres Saint Gervais, tiny lanes that aren't even named on most maps, passing the school with the two bronze bulls. Aunt Mill took me this way once, on a ramble that led across the river and eventually to Place de la Contrescarpe. She'd paused in front of the bulls, though, and pointed out the plaque beside them that told the story of 260 Jewish children who had been taken from this school and sent to die in Nazis camps.

Aunt Mill became angry just looking at the bulls. I didn't know her from beans at that point. She was just this strange lady standing there staring down these bronze bulls. Without sympathy, incapable of remorse, they originally marked the site of a butcher's market. And she was mad at them. I didn't get it at the time and it freaked me out.

But now, this second time, hardly slowing as I marched passed them, and swimming in my own troubles, it seemed to me the bulls were an apt symbol for the evil that had been done here and that Aunt Mill, who, after all, wasn't even born when that evil occurred, nonetheless felt she was accountable. She hated *all* evil, past, present and to come.

Rounding the corner to rue des Rosier, I marched past the kosher pizza place and the Jewish butcher shops and the dueling falafel stands, while it dawned on me how much I'd come to love

Aunt Mill. I became so misty-eyed that I traipsed down to the Saint-Paul Metro before realizing where I was.

I took the Number One across town. A crowd of work-a-days battled their way off at Châtelet as another crowd battled their way on. We whisked under the Place de la Concorde and Champs-Élysées. Another crowd entered and exited at Étoile. On we went, out of the city, till we hissed into the Pont de Neuilly stop.

Hitting the surface, I trotted down rue du Château toward Avenue Sainte-Foy. The streets were wide, decorative fences high, sidewalks as big as our whole *rue* in Le Marais, with trees planted at even intervals along the grass parkways. The neighborhood seemed empty save for the occasional well-bundled nanny pushing a stroller.

It took me awhile to locate the château of Madame Geromina Henrietta d'Aubergine, tucked back between elegant apartment buildings. It appeared the apartments were built around the mansion, like an uptown version of the way Cousin Zyed's hideout was hidden by tenements, so that you could only glimpse the château behind the posh apartments. The front gate was locked, so I had to wait for a nanny to come out with a stroller. Once in, I scuttled down the drive, past hedges and flowerbeds, and up the steps to Château d'Aubergine.

No one answered the brass knocker or the doorbell. I retreated down the steps to confirm that there were lights on inside, then knocked and rang again. Eventually, several locks clacked, the door swung open with a haunted-house squeal, and someone who looked like Magda's older sister peered out—same hair, same precarious sense of balance, same *nun-but-not-a-nun* skirt and pilly sweater. Difference was, this version of Magda craned forward to hear me, leaning on a walker.

*"Madame d'Aubergine?"*

*"Hein?"*

*"Je cherche Madame d'Aubergine, s'il vous plait,"* I said a little louder.

*"Hein?"*

I looked behind me to see if anyone was watching, then turned back and shouted, *"Vous-êtes Madame d'Aubergine?"*

*"Elle n'est pas ici."*

*"Quand est-ce qu'elle va revenir?*

*"En Avril."*

"April? She's gone till April?"

*"Hein?"*

*"Elle revient en Avril?"*

*"Oui, c'est ça.*

*"Où est-elle?*

*"Oh, difficile a dire. Miami, peut-être, ou Les Seychelles. Elle a des maisons partout."*

I puffed out my lip and said, *"Bien, merci, au revoir."* I went down the steps. Gone till April. Owned houses everywhere. The book I wanted—no needed—stuck inside, guarded by a woman who could not hear and could barely walk.

On my way back from Château d'Aubergine, as I exited the Metro, Aunt Mill called to tell me I should get dinner with Madame Rose. When I asked why, she said that Felix, Mr. Jones and Mr. Jones's lawyers, were going back and forth with Christophe Babinet, the art dealer holding the diamonds, about the story in Le Figaro. She hadn't even started presenting her material about the code and predicted she'd be home very late.

Back at the apartment, I tried to concentrate on math problems, my window cracked so I could hear the carriage door buzz and the footsteps of people entering. Whenever someone did, I peeked out. At last, I saw Sief traipse home from school with his book bag.

"Sief," I shouted down.

He looked up, saw me, continued on, disappearing into the archway that led to his apartment. I shot down the stairs three at a time, shot across the courtyard and up the steps to his place. I turned the brass doorbell. The hallway lights, set on a timer, went dark after thirty seconds, casting me into darkness. As I turned to look for the switch the door came open, answered by a bald man in a sweatervest and slippers, newspaper in hand. Sief's father had the same basic face as Cousin Zyed, but instead of looking scary and nasty, he looked, I don't know, sad and puzzled.

"*Bonjour. Je suis Daisy. Je voudrais parler avec Sief, s'il vous plait.*"

The man nodded and padded back inside, door swinging closed behind him. I found the switch and turned the hall lights back on, waiting long enough for them to go off again. I half-heard voices inside. Arguing?

Finally, the door squeaked open just enough to frame Sief's face. He didn't say anything.

"What's your problem, Sief?"

"I got no problem."

"Why did you ignore me then?"

"You know why."

"You afraid of me? You afraid Aunt Mill will catch you with me?"

He made a "kuh" sound in the back of his throat to indicate I was ridiculous.

"You are. You're afraid I'll get you into trouble."

His cheeks pinked. "I likes your Aunt. I wishes she was my aunt. She does good for me. So if she says I to leave you alone, I leave you. But I not afraid of her or you or nothing."

"I'm sorry."

"You never likes me from the first time we meets. You

don't even likes that I call you Grace Kelly, which I don't calls anybody, ever. You always making me feel like, 'Okay, I got nobody else to hang with so I got to hang with this nerd.'"

"I don't think you're a nerd. I mean, maybe we didn't get off to such a good start and maybe I don't quite appreciate the whole Grace Kelly obsession but—"

"Just leave me alone."

He slammed the door.

Except I put my hand on it.

I know—you're supposed to put your foot in the door not your hand, but I didn't exactly think it through. Tears sprang into my eyes. My fingers burst into flames. But the door bounced back open. I clutched my hand and did an agony dance.

Sief looked horrified. "You crazy?"

"I need your help, Sief. I know I've been a jerk and a horrible friend and I don't blame you for wanting to avoid me like the plague. But this is important. I wouldn't bother you if it weren't. I need to break into a house in Neuilly and steal a book. The book, Sief. The one Aunt Mill is *supposed* to have. Those vory guys tried to drag me into their car the other day. If I didn't think Aunt Mill was in some kind of trouble I wouldn't even dare ask you, but you're the only cat burglar I know."

His expression changed, glow coming into his eyes.

"It wouldn't even really be stealing. More like borrowing. We'll mail the book back when we're done."

"In Neuilly, you says?"

"Yes. The lady who owns the house is gone and the housekeeper can barely see or hear. She moves around with a walker."

"When do we doing the job?"

"Tonight?"

He smiled. "Let me gets you some ice."

# 29. The Plan

I returned to Aunt Mill's apartment holding a Ziploc of ice cubes to my hand. A few minutes later, Sief knocked, marched in all business-like, commandeered my computer, and peppered me with questions about Château d'Aubergine. Looking over his shoulder, I watched him study Google Maps, an online Paris Metro guide, and the *préfecture de police* website, writing down cryptic notes to himself as he went. Then he started adding up numbers.

"What are you doing?"

"Counting times. How long is for all the steps."

"What steps?"

He ignored my question and zoomed as close as he could on Google Maps to the top of Château d'Aubergine. He made more notes, shifting the image from the dome of the château to the roof of the adjoining wings, and to the roofs of the apartments that surrounded it. He even studied the bushes and hedges in the garden near the house.

"What do you think?"

"Not so hard. I can goes in through the dome."

"Not just you. I have to go with, however we do it."

"But for sure they got alarm. We got to goes in over the roofs. *Alpiniste* job. You fall already once. Plus your hand is smashed."

"Don't worry about me. I'll be fine. Just figure out how to

do it."

He grunted, switched to street view and took a slow image-walk around the block, making more notes, then pulled a dilapidated book from his backpack.

"What's that?"

"*Les Grande Manoirs de Paris*. Edition 1952. No *alpaniste* can plan without. My cousin gives it to me for my birthday."

"Cousin Zyed?"

Sief nodded, paging through black and white photos of French châteaux until he landed on a section about Le Château d'Aubergine. He studied each picture like a scientist, flipping back and forth between photos, bending over one in particular, eyes two inches away, till he leaned up with a smile of triumph. "Got it."

"Got what?"

He pointed to a tiny thing in the picture, "*Thirard, marque vingt-et-un. Fabriqué*—er—made in the 1921. Inside-door lock. I got the key set."

My heart started thumping. This was so weird. Sief was good at this. I mean, I don't know what I expected. I'd asked for his help after all. But I'd never put much thought into breaking into a house before. Oh, I'd imagined it, sure, like you'd imagine flying the space shuttle or something, but Sief was preparing like a professional, like this really was or really would be his career.

My phone rang. I picked up. It was Nina, calling back to see if I still needed help with the lady in Neuilly.

"Who is it?" said Sief.

"Nina. You know, the one you were so rude to."

"How well does you trusts her?"

"More than I trust you."

"Let me talks to her."

He grabbed the phone right out of my hand and had a conversation with her. He looked at his page of notes and at his watch and told her when to meet us, and quite a few other things, in a kind of slangy teenager French that I'd heard before but could never make sense of. Finally, he turned to me and handed the phone back. "She wanting to talk to you."

"Nina?"

"Daisy. Is this guy for real?"

"What do you mean?"

"I mean he wouldn't tell me what you're doing. I'm just supposed to go to Neuilly at a certain time and hang out at a certain corner. Then I'm supposed text you if I see any police and say 'I have to go now because my boyfriend is waiting' instead of saying the police are there, and if I see Russian gangsters, I'm supposed to text 'I see my neighbor's black dog.' He calls it being *le mec extérieur*."

"What's that mean?"

"The outside man."

"Nina, if this sounds too weird you don't have to do it."

"Of course I have to. You saved my life the other day."

"I did?"

"Kind of, yeah. I was about to rush into an unwise marriage."

"You were not."

"Well, anyway, if you need my help, I'm there. But since cat burglar man wouldn't give me any details, just say yes if this is about getting the real version of the book your Aunt was talking about the other night."

"Yes."

"Okay. Except I'll probably tell my mom I left my homework over at your place so she'll let me go out."

"No problem."

"And one other thing. Cat burglar man said I'm supposed to go straight home after my part of 'the job' is over, but I want to meet up afterward, to make sure you're okay."

"Thanks, Nina. I'll call you right after."

Nina and I signed off just as Sief was gathering up his notes. He laughed.

"What?"

*"Merveilleux."*

"What?"

"This is goings to make us famous, Grace Kelly."

"No, it's not. No one's ever going to know about it."

He gave me his cat burglar wink, went into the kitchen, found Aunt Mill's ashtray, and set his notes on fire.

He tapped his head. "All up here now. How come you don't tell me this is house of seventh most richest person in France?"

"Cause you didn't ask."

"You said this old lady, she not too fast and don't see or hear too good, right?"

I nodded.

He smiled like it was no big deal, like nothing could go wrong, when in truth anything could. He looked at his watch. "I go home now to get tools. Find a disguise. Coat, hat, pants. But remember you throwing it away, so nothing you loves too much. A hat to makes you look like a boy is good cause the Metro cameras are not seeing so well.

After Sief left, I threw myself into the chair at my computer and wrote an email:

*Dear Mom,*

*This probably sounds really weird but I just want to write and say that I am so sorry for not writing sooner. Without going into too much detail I have to do something that might not be the best thing but seems to be the right thing. Now that I think of it, that's what happened with Lucia. I did the right thing but not the best thing. Or maybe that's not the way to look at it at all.*

I stopped, fingers hovering over the keys a moment, then hit delete. I started again.

*Dear Mom,*

*I am sorry for not writing sooner. I don't really know why I didn't other than to say that I was confused and hurt. But what's important is that I love you and miss you and that I've also come to love Aunt Mill. No matter what happens, please always believe that.*

I stared at the screen then pressed send.

# 30. The Heist

After making a big deal about our watches being set to exactly the same time, and checking that my cell phone was on vibrate, Sief announced that it was time to go. Just outside the carriage door, he gave me a phony tough guy nod and sauntered off down the rue. He seemed so calm. I could hardly breathe.

I walked up to Republique, Sief's bag of tools thumping into my back, then took a zigzag course: the Four Line to the Two to the Three. Sief had given me a baseball cap with the letters Z/F on the front. With my hair pushed under the cap, a sagging sweatshirt and a pair of sweatpants pulled over my jeans, I looked like a junior bag lady. I was sure everyone was staring at me. I was sure everyone knew I was on my way to do something illegal. Sweat poured out of me.

In the Barbes Rochechouart correspondence tunnel a blind man played a saw with a violin bow, bending the saw to make different notes, singing along in some language I didn't recognize. The effect was so mournful it nearly knocked me down. I dug into my inside pants pocket and gave him some coins. On the train platform two winos shouted at each other. Everyone looked liked they'd been working for days without sleep, shoulders hunched, chins stubbled, lipstick migrated off lips. A train swished in and we shuffled on, the winos staying behind to continue their debate.

At Villiers, I joined a car full of American kids on a school trip. They seemed so clean and bright-eyed, talking about seeing the Louvre and eating *crêpes*, snapping selfies. They must have been three or four years older than me, yet seemed annoyingly young. Their nonstop English overwhelmed me. I tried to tune them out but it had been so long since I'd had to do so—to cut out chatter in my own language so I could hear my own thoughts—that my head just shut down.

A few of them noticed me looking. I looked away. A blond-haired teacher or guide or whatever stood and studied the car's Metro map, then said, "I think we've gone wrong. I think we need to get off." She leaned toward an agreeable-looking man in a tweed jacket and asked, *"Excusez-moi, vous savez où est le hôtel Inter-Continental?"* The man shrugged. "I think we need to get off and change directions," repeated the blond.

Not only did they need to change directions, they needed to make two transfers. Their hotel sat across from Place de l'Opéra. Aunt Mill took me to the Café de la Paix once, part of the hotel, paying a fortune for a *chocolat chaud*, telling me a story about some guy named Hemingway dining there with his wife and not having enough money to pay their bill. I could have told them that, could have been the helpful stranger, and so young too, but since I was dressed like a bum and shaking like a leaf, on my way to break into a château with a sack of greasy tools, I remained silent.

The Metro stop Anatole France let out in front of a tiny café, filled with cheery locals. After floundering for direction, I found my way to rue Voltaire. What a relief to walk. I weaved down rue Danton, rue Kléber, Boulevard Victor Hugo, past modernish apartment buildings and nondescript medical offices. Sweat trickled down my legs inside the two pairs of pants. How could Sief be so sure we'd both arrive at the right moment? What if I had to circle the block ten times and someone noticed me and called the police? What if the police were already there, tipped off by somebody on the Metro or at the café? My heart started banging again. What a bad idea this was. This was so not going to work. Why hadn't I just told Aunt Mill the truth?

Ornate iron fences guarded the condos surrounding Château d'Aubergine, but just as I arrived, a young couple burst out the front gate. Smelling of cologne, the guy held the gate for his gal and then held it for me. He smiled. I smiled back, flashing on him describing me in perfect detail to the police.

My watch showed Sief due in two minutes. I made my way along curving sidewalks between the apartments toward the gate behind the château. Sief appeared, just as I arrived.

Once in, he patted my knapsack to make sure I still had the tools then moved off like he lived there. We made our way to a stone wall that separated the apartments from the château. Sief signaled for me to put hands together to form a step. I hoisted him up. He spun himself around and reached a hand down.

"*Sac*," he whispered.

I passed the knapsack up. He dropped it behind the wall then reached down and pulled me up beside him. He slid off the wall. I wriggled my feet over, felt his hands on my ankles and dropped down, smooth as ballet. So far, so good.

Sief took a methodical look around, then we moved off, cutting across the garden, along hedges, eyeing the buildings around us to make sure no one peeked out. In less than a minute, we stood against garage doors by the back of the château.

Sief leaned to my ear and whispered, "You okay?"

I nodded, even though I was the exact opposite of okay.

"How is your hand?"

Throbbing like crazy, but I didn't say that.

"Just go, Sief. I'm okay."

"You're not okay. Nobody is okay after a fall. So don't say you is."

"Don't be a jerk."

"Listen to me, Daisy. Look at me. We is a team now. We depends on each other. Don't look down. Don't look sideways. Think only about what you doing: hand-foot, hand-foot. Don't think nothing else. Nothing. Make the simple. Okay?"

I hate to admit it, but his pep talk did wonders. I answered by making a stirrup again with my hands, boosting him toward the top of the garage. He shot up in a second and reached down for me. Up I went like a Cirque du Soleil acrobat. He eased over to a drainpipe, checked the apartment windows around us, shimmied to the second story. A piece of twine dropped down. I tied the knapsack to it. Up it shot. Seconds later, a rope from the knapsack eased down, loop tied in. I eased the loop over my head and under my arms and monkeyed up the drainpipe as Sief pulled. We crawled up the back roof and over a sill, creeping on our bellies toward the dome. Hand-foot, hand-foot. At the bottom of the dome, we caught our breath.

I chanced a look. You could see the Arc de Triomphe, the Tour Eiffel, lights on the Champs Elysées, so breathtaking in that instant I wanted to cry.

"Best not to look," said Sief.

I nodded. "Hand-foot, hand-foot."

He smiled, "*Allez-oop.*"

The dome was covered in sections of green copper, each section attached to the next by an overlapping ridge of metal. By wedging fingers and toes into these ridges, we wormed our way up. By now we were above the apartments. Sief inched around the cupola, inspecting the tiny windows. Half way around he waved to me and I eased over, pushing the knapsack in front of me.

He dug into the sac, pulled out a gob of used chewed gum, and started chewing.

I made ick-face.

"You'll see," he whispered. He pulled out a screwdriver and scraped ancient putty from a windowpane, catching each piece as it cracked off.

The wind picked up. I glanced down at the streetlights below. Flurries twirled by. Seif leaned over and whispered, "*marteau*." I dug his hammer out. I wanted off this roof so badly I could've screamed, but Sief just patiently tapped the screwdriver into the putty clinging to the glass, oblivious to anything but his work. A chip fell, scuttling down the dome. He stopped to make sure no one had heard.

A few more tap-taps then Sief took the gum from his mouth and pressed it against the windowpane, formed it a bit, nudged the pane back and forth. Out it came. Genius.

Reaching in, he found the window latch and tugged open the window. In he went, wiggling forward till his feet disappeared in the black. I heard the clunk of a skull hitting metal.

"Sief," I whispered, "you all right?"

His face popped out of the dark. "I find the stairs okay."

I handed him the knapsack and leaned in the window, my knees just fitting on the tiny sill. If I slipped back now I wouldn't stop till I hit ground. Half way through my sweat pants caught on something. My heart started banging again.

"Sief, I'm stuck."

"No worry."

He grabbed my arms and pulled, the sweats peeling off me as I came through. I ended in a heap, pants clinging to my ankles. I could just make out his smile in the dark. We almost started laughing, but he put a finger to his lips. I did the same.

It was too dark below to see, save for vague forms of wood beams crisscrossing overhead. The staircase from the cupola, eighteen inches wide, swayed and creaked as we climbed down.

I heard the faint buzz of a cell phone on vibrate right above me.

Sief and I stared at each other. I felt my way up the stairs to the window where my sweatpants were and slipped the cell phone out of the pocket. I checked the screen to make sure it wasn't Aunt Mill.

"Is everything okay?" asked Nina.

"You're supposed to text, not call," I whispered. "Is everything okay out there?"

"No. I'm freezing my buns off."

"Is your boyfriend there?"

"My what? Oh. No, nobody's here. The streets are empty and it's starting to snow. Someone is watching *Koh Lanta* with the volume turned way up, but otherwise it's a ghost town."

"What's *Koh Lanta*?"

"Reality TV. They leave people on a desert island and see if they can survive. You'd be really good at it. Where are you? How's it going? How much longer?"

"All good. Hang in for a few more minutes. And text next time." I hung up before she could ask more questions.

Below me, Sief turned on a flashlight with a red lens, shining the beam on the steps so I could come down without breaking my neck, then swung the beam around until he spotted the door leading out.

He handed me the flashlight. "She is supposed to text."

"I told her."

While I held the flashlight, he pulling out a bag of old keys and tried one after another in the lock. The ninth key slid into the keyhole, but once inside it wouldn't turn. He kept it separate from the others.

"I thought you said you had the key?"

"Key set. Not key. They using maybe forty master blanks."

"What happens if none of them work?"

"Ssssh."   Another key fit into the hole but wouldn't turn. He put his ear next to the lock, listening to the sound it made as he twicked the key back and forth.  He slid it out, dug out a tiny file, filed away, examined, filed away some more, examined, filed, then slid the key again into the lock.  It clicked open.

We were in.

# 31. Le Grisbi

The door hadn't been open in so long that it crackled as Sief pulled. We could hear weird tropical music playing, like jungle suspense music.

Sief whispered. "Your lady likes watching *Koh Lanta*."

We tiptoed along a narrow hall with closely spaced doors—servant's rooms back in the day—then down a crooked staircase to another door. Sief eased the door open for a look. The jungle music got louder.

We emerged into a grand hallway. Streetlight ghosted in. Paintings of disapproving ancestors frowned at us. Down a sweeping staircase we crept, pausing at the bottom. The TV noise came from the right, behind a closed door. Sief headed left, inching open a pocket door, waving me into a formal library with shelves to the ceiling, full of old books, with rolling ladders to access them.

*Les Grande Manoirs de Paris*, Edition 1952, had a picture of Madame d'Aubergine's library in it, but I hadn't quite grasped the reality of it. There had to be three thousand books in here. I felt defeated before I started.

But Sief snapped me out of it, making a circular motion with his finger while he stationed himself with an ear to the crack in the pocket doors. I clicked on the flashlight and swept the light back and forth, looking for the right size cover.

They didn't believe in dust jackets in the Eighteenth Century or even putting the title on the spine of a book, so when I spotted one that looked the right size, I had to pull it from the shelf. Most books from those days didn't put the title on the front cover either. That meant I had to flip to the title page of each book.

After going for several books that *had* to be the one, I got methodical, taking on one shelf at a time, sweeping my flashlight from bottom to top, noting all the books that looked possible, going at them steadily. After awhile Sief came and looked over my shoulder.

"You want me to telephone for pizza?"

"Why don't you?"

I went back to work, but out of the corner of my eye I could see Sief approach a huge desk built like a Greek temple. He picked up a crystal paperweight, turning it in his hands.

"Don't get any ideas."

"Mind your bees-knees."

"Nothing leaves this house except the book."

He made a noise through his nose.

I pushed a ladder to reach some books on a high shelf— wheels squeaked.

"Quiet," hissed Sief.

"Sush. Help me lift it."

We lifted the ladder and placed it in front of the corner shelf. On the very top row sat twenty or so volumes the right size. While I checked them out he whispered, "What if the book is not here? What if it is locked up in a safe?"

"Shush." He was right, of course, but I didn't want to hear it.

"Or maybe—"

Something growled. I glanced down. A German Shepherd

the size of Rhode Island, teeth bared, stood inches behind Sief. I almost fell off the ladder. Sief didn't panic at all. He whispered to the dog, purred really, while he eased the knapsack off his back and dug out what looked like a dehydrated-mouse. He broke off a chunk of it and held it out. The dog stopped growling. Just like that. He inched forward, sniffing, took the thing in his mouth and started gnawing. Sief eased around and stroked the dog, giving me a thumbs-up. I slipped a book out, cracked open the front cover then froze as the TV volume dropped.

*"Grisbi?"* the old woman called out from across the hall.

The dog jumped to his feet, but Sief continued to purr in his ear, offering what was left of the black dog bar.

*"Grisbi?"*

We could hear the thump of her walker and the creak of floorboards. Sief pointed at me then pointed toward the door the dog came in, at the back of the library. I shoved the book back into place and grabbed the ladder rails to slide down, then stopped. I drew the book back out.

"Daisy, leave it," hissed Sief.

*"Grisbi? Viens ici mon chouchou."*

I flipped the cover open again, flipped to the title page: *Aperçu des secrets diplomatiques dans l'histoire de France. Comprenant un point de vue philosophique sur la nature des actions menées avec discrétions et savoir-faire. A l'usage des futurs ministres royaux. Tome deux.*

*"Grisbi,"* the voice commanded.

Grisbi wolfed down the last of the dead-mouse stuff and darted over to the pocket doors, whimpered like the most innocent canine in the world. I rammed the book down the front of my jeans and shot down the ladder.

Sief raised a hand, signaling for me to take it easy. We tiptoed our way to the door that Grisbi had come in, slipping out just as the pocket doors slid open, then felt our way down a servant's hallway in the dark.

The cell phone buzzed in my pocket. I pulled it out, tapping Sief on the shoulder to stop him.

The text from Nina read, "Boyfriends here, 4 of them."

"K. Thx," I texted back.

"Text when u r out."

I leaned to Sief's ear, "Nina says the police are outside."

Cool as milk, he smiled and gave me his cat burglar wink. We came to a spiral stairway, leading up, meant for servants. Thinking we'd take them, I bumped into Sief. He just stood there, deliberating.

"What?"

The door bell chime out front. Grisbi started barking.

"We need to go, Sief, like now."

Instead of dashing up the stairs, Sief fished in the knapsack till he found a Ziploc bag. He pointed at the book. I pulled it out of the front of my jeans. He shoved it into the Ziploc, sealed it, and shoved it into the back of my jeans. "Safer in back," he whispered. "Now. Down stairs. But no hurry."

I hadn't even noticed that the servant stairs went down, but sure enough they did, into a basement kitchen with a door leading out. Sief stalked over, peeped out a window, and opened the door. It wasn't even locked.

I groaned.

He shrugged, put a finger to his lips, stuck his head out, inching up the outside steps to check the way. We could hear people shouting toward the front of the château, and Grisbi barking at them. Sief waved for me. We walked. It took everything inside me to keep from sprinting away. Seconds later, though, we were back at the château wall, hoisting each other up, swinging legs over, dropping down like butterflies.

We eased along hedges then burst out a back gate onto the

sidewalk and strolled off casually. At the end of the street, Sief glanced over his shoulder, let the knapsack glide off his back, and kicked it into the mouth of a street drain. Tools gone.

"Did you really have to do that?"

"Of course. Now come the hard part. The get away."

At the next corner, mimicking Sief, I glanced over my shoulder, whipped off my hat and sweatshirt and kicked them into the street drain. Sief tough-guy frowned his approval.

My cell phone vibrated. I dug it out as we walked. Nina texted, "You out of there? Dog going crazy. Lady threatening to call boyfriends on the boyfriends."

I texted back, "What?"

"Boyfreinds say some one call them about break-in. Now boyfriends threatening to bust door down if lady doesn't open up."

"Where are you?" I texted.

"Werru?" She texted back.

"Walking away."

"K. Me too then. Meet you Metro Ternes."

"BFN," I texted.

"She okay?" asked Sief.

I nodded. We zigzagged our way toward Les Sablons Metro station, the occasional flurry dancing around us. As we crossed the next street, Sief pulled his gloves from his pocket and did the same drop and kick move, sending them into a street drain. He held out his hand. "Gives me the flashlight."

I patted my back pocket, thought a moment, grimaced. "I left it. On the shelf."

He stared at me like he was going to be sick for a moment, then shrugged. Terrified suddenly, I flashed on the French police doing a huge crime scene thing, getting a sample of my DNA, raiding Aunt Mill's, and taking me away to some French kid prison.

We walked on in silence until we turned the corner onto Avenue Charles de Gaulle and crossed over to the Metro entrances. Two policemen were waiting at the bottom of the steps.

Sief and I shared a glance, but we were already too close to make a plan or turn around. The policemen scrutinized us. One spoke into his walkie-talkie. My heart started banging like foo-foo crazy.

*"Excusez-moi,"* I said, *"vous savez où est le Hôtel Inter-Continental?"*

The policemen looked at each other. Sief saw what I was doing and jumped in with his best American accent, "Do they know how to get to the hotel?"

"That's what I just asked them."

"I'm cold. I want to go back to the hotel."

"Okay, doofus, let me talk to them."

The one policeman spoke into his walkie-talkie again while the other nodded his head toward the Metro entrance and said, "Take zee train in direction Gare de Lyon and, *sortez,* unh, exit at *Tuileries.*"

"Thank you. *Merci. Merci beaucoup.*"

He nodded and we rushed down the stairs.

A minute later, standing on the platform, aching for a train to arrive, I couldn't help saying to Sief, "The weird thing is Nina said the police said someone called them."

Sief shrugged. "No matter now."

I nodded. He was probably right. Or so I thought until I looked up and saw Snake-in-Skull coming out of the correspondence passage on the platform across from us.

## 32. Le Marceau

Sief saw Snake-in-Skull at the same moment I did and placed a hand on my wrist. The gangster's eyes latched onto us an instant later. He made a quick cell phone call, to Gruzdeva no doubt, then walked back toward the correspondence passage, blocking our only way out, aside from an emergency exit that would set off an alarm, bringing the police.

A faint rush of air pushing out of the tunnel announced the approach of our train. Snake-in-Skull felt it too. He stopped. If he went into the correspondence passage there'd be maybe ten seconds when he couldn't see us as he ran up the stairs and down onto our side. You could see him thinking about it, thinking about the chances of us jumping onto the tracks and disappearing. He knew the train was a few seconds out, knew we couldn't get on it without him also getting on, so he ducked into the passage.

"He's can't do anything here," I said. "Too many witnesses."

"He just going to follow us till the other vory catch up."

Sief tugged my elbow and we walked away from the correspondence passage, almost to the end of the platform. The train swished in. Sief nodded toward it and said, *"Ba-bien, c'est un em-pay cinquante-neuf."*

"What?"

"Model fifty-nine. That's good."

Before I could ask why that was good, Snake appeared out

of the correspondence passage and stood on the platform at the head of the train. We stood at the tail. A few people got on. A few got off. Snake watched us. He'd seen this movie before. If we hopped on, he'd hop on. If we hopped off, so would he.

So we didn't move. Nor did he.

Sief leaned close, "You got to makes it looking natural because the driver he is watching too."

"Make what look natural?"

He didn't answer. The doors-closing signal buzzed. Sief flicked his eyes toward the back of the train, taking tiny, shuffling, sideways steps. I mimicked him till we lined up just *behind* the last door of the last car. From this distance, Snake couldn't tell.

Just as the doors closed, Sief tugged me past the end of the train and—holding hands—we stepped off the platform. I landed on my feet, teetering over the third rail.

"Onto the train," Sief hissed, jerking me forward, pressing my fingers onto the horizontal grill at the bottom of the train cabin. He grabbed the grill himself, then thrust both feet onto a bumper-sort-of-thing that swept three inches over the track. I did the same, just as the train took off.

"Hold on tight!" he yelled.

Duh.

Because the bumper-thing was set back under the train, it was like riding in an easy chair, leaning way back, only with no chair under you. Railroad ties whisked by below. The station flew past. Snake-in-Skull flew by, too. He was sprinting for the rear of the platform, convinced we'd run for it down the tunnel.

He spotted us out of the corner of his eye, though. Sief leaned close to my ear and shouted, "He seen us." We swished into the dark tunnel, streaks of light flashing past at intervals, wind whistling in my ears. My legs vibrated like spaghetti on the bumper-thing, and my fingers turned white from gripping the grill. Sief actually took one hand off and waved like a cowboy, screaming, "Yeeeeee-haaaaaaa!"

Oh, brother.

Like two days later—time was moving very slow just then—the train hissed into the Porte Maillot station. Sief hopped off. I followed. I thought we were going to climb onto the platform, but he pulled me the other way, back into the tunnel. "They get us on camera if we go that way. *Les flics* will be looking for us cause we riding the wheels."

"Won't another train come and run us down?"

"We got some minutes before that."

"How do we get out of here?"

"Down."

"What do you mean *down?*"

Sief looked right and left into the darkness of the Metro tunnel, saying over his shoulder, "How comes that vory *mec* knows to be at the right metro stop at the right time?"

"I don't know. My guess is they knew who else had the book. They must have talked to the ladies at Librairie Pitollot. That makes the most sense."

Sief walked to the wall of the tunnel and started yanking at the iron grate. "So you gives this book to Madame Millicent when you getting home?"

"Yeah, that's the plan."

Sief growled with effort as he slung the grate aside. We stared into the blackness of a hole just a little wider than my shoulders.

"No way I'm going into a sewer pipe."

"You gots not so many choices, Grace Kelly."

"Don't call me Grace Kelly."

Sief hopped into the pipe feet first and slid into the black.

A moment later I heard his voice echoing up. "Come on. Before the next train coming."

"No way, Sief."

"It's a number nine. I catch you and put you on the sideworks."

"On what? What's a number nine?"

"I mean sidewalk. Number nine is a big *égout*, or like you says, sewer pipe. It got *une manche*—like a path for water—and also a sidewalk to walk on. This one goes along Avenue Charles de Gaulle.

"It smells awful, Sief."

"So does *le coffre*, er, the trunk of a vory's car. You rather go into that?"

He had a point. I could hear the rumble of an approaching train. We'd be in deep trouble if a train driver spotted me. I pulled the Ziplock from my jeans, opened it, shoved in my cell phone, and resealed it.

"Get ready."

I stuck my feet in, sat on the lip of the pipe, closed my eyes, and wormed down until I started to slide. Sief guided my feet as they came out. I did a calypso bend out of the pipe and lost my balance, but Sief pulled me upright.

"Welcome to the rats' kingdom," he said, voice echoing off the walls.

"Don't make this worse than it is."

I couldn't see a thing, couldn't even see the wall of the tunnel, or the watery ick I might have fallen into, though the stench hit like a punch in the nose.

"I can't see, Sief."

"You seeing better in a minute." Sief reached out and placed my fingers onto the back of his sweater. "Just take baby's step." We inched along at first, parallel to the Metro tracks. Sief was right. After awhile I could make out the glint of sewage-stew that was bubbling past us, and the sheen of slime on the walkway, and the bright oval where a pipe let in light, and a row of receding ovals from similar pipes along the way. There was a rumble and then air shot down the pipes as a Metro train roared by up above.

We passed tunnels that intersected from left and right, spewing nauseating mist. Metal signs, like street signs, marked the junctions. Sief put his eyes up to one. I pulled my cell phone from the Ziplock and hit a button so it lit up. Sief read, "rue de Sablonville." He turned left. I grabbed his sweater again. Water sputtered and woofed. Rats squeaked. In the blackness, every sound pierced like a fork in the ear. My eyes kept making stuff up. Same with my nose. It smelled so bad it overloaded my brain.

We passed a pillar of light streaked down.

"It's a manhole, Sief. Let's climb out."

"Too close."

"Close to what?"

"Where we comes in. The more further we goes, the more manholes we maybe could comes out of. The vory can't watch all of them. We needs to gets to le Marceau."

"What's the Marceau?"

"You feel we walking like down a hill, right?"

I hadn't before. But there was definitely a slant to the tunnel. "Yeah."

"Every sewer goes toward Asnières or Marceau. They like big rivers. In old days every sewer goes to the Siene but they stopped that long time ago. Once we get to le Marceau there be like maybe three thousand holes we could come out of. Vory never finds us."

We trudged for hours, maybe more, though along with my

other senses, my sense of time seemed warped. We made a turn then, further on, another. The stewage seem to be moving faster here. A hundred yards into this tunnel we ran into a pack of rats. I could barely see them. Sief ran at them, shouting, and stamped his feet. They squealed in unison. I heard them splashing into the water to swim by us. I made out dozens of heads bobbing past, inches from my shoes. Sief laughed. I held in a scream.

"Sief, do you like this place?"

"What do you means?"

"I mean I'm freaking out. I keep thinking I hear voices and my nose wants to explode and I feel like I'm suffocating. But you seem fine. Like we're walking in the woods."

"We are walking in the woods."

Oh, brother.

We came to a round basin where four pipes fed in, each of them gushing water. All kinds of garbage collected here: tree branches and diapers and cigarette boxes and a bloated cat and soggy socks and plastic bags. I picked up a glass wine bottle and poured out the muck.

"What you doing?"

"My sword," I said, "unless you have a better one."

He kept walking. Something seemed to be bothering him suddenly.

We came to another manhole where water poured down like a waterfall.

"Must be raining up top," I said. There was just enough light to make out his face. He looked worried, like really worried, which made me worried.

"Let's go up here," I said.

"It not that easy." He pointed up. It was impossible to tell how far it was to the surface, but it was way up there, and there was no ladder or metal rungs in the walls. "Not all manholes is the same.  Sometimes *SIAAP* bring ladders to get down and up."

"*SIAAP* are the sewer workers?"

He nodded.

I pulled out my cell phone to check for signal strength. Zero bars.

We trudged on, faster.  The stewage ran faster too, foaming, rising, lapping onto the walkway, soaking my toes.  I noticed dried strands of toilet paper hanging on the wires overhead. They'd been there all along actually, but now I understood why.

"Sief, it's possible for these tunnels to fill up entirely, isn't it?  Like over our heads?"

He said nothing.  Not a good sign.

I'd been holding it together pretty well till then but now I felt jangly and unglued, like I wanted to sob, to shriek, to curl in a ball and hide under a blanket, but mostly I just wanted to be out of here more than anything I'd ever wanted.

We came to a wider tunnel.  Up ahead, in the black, the water thundered.

"We follow this one," said Sief.

"Is that the Marceau?"

"Maybe."

My hair stood on end.  "What do you mean, maybe?  I thought you knew your way.  Are we lost?"

"It is a big city down here.  I don't knows every rue."

I shouted, "It's not a city at all, Sief.  It's like hell.  It's for the dead and desperate."

"What do you think you are, Grace Kelly?"

"Don't call me that!  Don't ever, *ever* call me that again!"

I cut in front of him, marching toward the roaring water.  A dozen steps down I heard a constant high-pitched screeching.

"Bats," I said.

Sief stalked up behind me. "No. Rats. Lots of them. But they will move out of the way."

That was the moment—fortified with rainwater and rising fast—the sewage lapped over the laces of my sneakers. I nearly tossed. As I sloshed forward, some source of light from above illuminated the T-junction where our tunnel joined a huge tunnel where water whooshed by like rapids. Even from twenty yards up our tunnel, I could see, on the other side of the rapids, what looked like a boat landing, complete with concrete dock and iron cleats. Just beyond was a shaft, with rungs leading up and out. It was hard to tell from our vantage exactly how wide the rapid was. Ten feet maybe. It had to be le Marceau. But even above the hiss and boom of water you could hear the terrible screeching.

Sief was right—the sound came from rats. They crawled up the walls and struggled through the current, climbing on top of each other, making a writhing mound of panicked rat-life on the walkway between us and the channel, all fighting to keep from washing into the rapids.

I froze. Sief stepped in front of me and charged forward, stomping his feet and screaming, but this time the rats wouldn't budge. He retreated, brushing rats off. His back was turned when two awful eyes and a pointy armored snout rose out of the water, jaw opening, teeth glinting, scooping up the rats.

Sief saw the horror in my eyes and pivoted in time to see the crocodile crunch a mouthful of rats and sink back under. The remaining rats shrieked in unison. Sief tottered into my arms.

"We got to go another way," said Sief, shoving me backward.

I felt water rushing around my ankles now. "There's no time, Sief. Water's rising too fast. We need to get out now.

*Now.*" I stepped in front of him.

He grabbed my arm, terrified. "Don't be crazy."

I ripped my arm away. "Follow behind me. Right behind me. Don't even think of stopping. We only get one jump. It's got to be a big-big jump—through the rats, past the croc, over the rapids."

"What are you talking about?" He stared at me like I was trying to murder him. I knew if I stopped to explain, I'd chicken out. Some of the rats, which a moment before refused to budge, were leaping in and swimming for the rapids, trying to get past the croc while he chewed his snack. I told myself, *don't think about it, Daisy, just do.*

I charged down, stomping and splashing, my focus glued to the spot where the croc's eyes first appeared. Up came the eyes, the snout, the jaw, opening wide to snatch me.

I pitched the wine bottle down the crocodile's throat, whipping back my arm as his jaw snapped down.

You could see shock in his eyes. Body twisting, belly showing, tail slashing, he shot past us up the channel. We rushed by, rats scrambling everywhere. I came to the edge of the big channel. My toes dug in and I leaped across the roiling water, just getting a hand on an iron cleat on the other side, the filthy rapids foaming over me, trying to drag me away, as two rats, along for the ride, dashed over my head and onto the landing. A moment later, Sief smacked against the lip of the landing, missing his cleat. He latched onto me, his own cargo of rats dancing over his head and scramming.

We hoisted each other up. Four inches of water covered the landing—clear-running from the rain. We splashed through it, grabbed the iron rungs, and climbed till our arms shook, up and up and up. Water dribbled down now. The rain up above had stopped.

When we got to the top Sief put his shoulder against the steel cover and shoved. It wouldn't budge. He caught his breath then went at it again, snorting and roaring, but still the cover wouldn't move.

"Move over and I'll give you a hand."

He shimmied sideways on the top rung as I eased up beside him. It took a moment in the tight space to get both our shoulders against the cold steel. Then we pushed. And pushed. And grunted. And pushed.

Nothing. Not even a squeak.

I looked down, just barely making out the water below. It had already risen three feet into the hole we'd climbed up. We were still hanging a good forty feet above the water, but there was no going back down to find another way out.

I looked at Sief. "How often do the sewers overflow into the streets?"

He shrugged and puffed out lips.

"So it could happen? The water could reach us here?"

He shrugged again. "Maybe. But it probably goes back down."

"How long will that take? I mean for it to go down to normal so we can find another way out?"

"Two days maybe."

## 33. Man and the Sun

I was just getting my head around the idea of hanging there for two days when my cell phone rang. It scared the silly out me. I almost dropped the phone while fishing it from the Ziplock. It was Nina.

"Nina, where are you?"

"At Metro Ternes, worried sick and freezing my buns off. I left twenty messages, you snot. What's wrong with you? We were going to meet up. I'm gonna be in so much trouble it's not even funny. If you're home in bed, I swear I'm coming over to strangle you."

"I wish I were in bed."

"You're breaking up, Daisy. Where are you?"

I turned to Sief. "Where we are?"

"Avenue Hoche near Avenue Beaucour."

"Nina, we're under Avenue Hoche near Avenue Beaucour."

"What do you mean *under*?

"In the sewer. Under a manhole cover. We can't lift it. Come help us, Nina. Come as fast as you can."

"Wait. Did you say in the—"

"Yes. I'll explain later. Just get here."

"Oh, geez. Okay. On my way. I'll call when I'm close."

She disconnected.

"She coming?"

I nodded. There was nothing to do but wait, hanging like monkeys. A car zoomed past up above, splashing water through the holes of the cover. We were so miserable it made us laugh.

Now that my cell found a signal, it dinged to let me know I had nine voice messages and twenty-two texts. It seemed crazy to be checking messages while hanging forty feet above a river of sewage, but there I was. All of the texts were from Nina as were most of the calls, except for three from Aunt Mill.

No doubt she'd gotten back from her meeting and found me gone. She'd be ready to put me on the next plane home by now. All I wanted to do was get back and place the book in her hands and tell her the whole story in one giant, balloon-gasp confession, and then go to bed. And shower. I needed a shower so badly.

"I has to admit, your friend, she make a good *mec extérieur.*"

"Hey. Sief. I'm sorry I freaked out at you down there. I was really scared."

"We have a close call. It is natural."

"How do you know so much about *l'égout* anyway?"

He shrugged.

"Come to think of it, you knew a lot about rats when we were talking in front of that store on rue des Halles, and about the upside down world, too."

He seemed pleased that I remembered, but didn't say anything else.

"Well?"

He shrugged again. "I come down here first time with Zyed. Long time ago. Before he was big cheddar. But when my mom dies and my dad goes away I coming down here again. I even sleeps down here. Yes, the smell is no good, but nobody bothering you. So many places to hide. So dark. Only you and the rats. I thinking I gets closer to my Mom. I thinking, maybe the rats knows about her. They knows about the dead. I thinking maybe they talks to her. I thinking maybe they say to her how much I miss her."

I nodded.

"It's crazy, I know. But that is how I was. See, you still got your mom."

"Yeah."

"So maybe you don't know what it is like. I don't saying it is good. My dad is right. Man is made to be in the sun. I promise him I never go back here. But if it is to help Madame Millicent, then okay. She gave me a place to stay until my dad comes back for me. So I owe her. You understand?"

I nodded. "Thank you, Sief. I'm sorry I've acted like such a big rat. Ever since the first day really. Or, I mean, maybe rat isn't the correct word."

"I know what you means."

"Your dad is right though. Man *is* made to be in the sun."

"I know."

"Plus I don't think you should become a cat burglar. I mean you're obviously a good one already, scary good, but I'd hate to see you turn into Cousin Zyed. I have no right to say that really. It's your life. But it would make me sad. And I know it would make Aunt Mill sad, and probably your mom, too."

He nodded.

We didn't say anything after that until my phone rang. It was Nina. "I'm here. Where are you guys? There's about six sewer covers around this intersection."

Sief yanked off his shoe, shoved it through the grill, and wagged it back and forth.

"Look for a shoe waving at you," I said.

"Huh? Oh, there, there you are."

She disconnected. We heard a horn and some brakes squealing and then Nina's voice blasting down. "Can you guys hear me down there?"

"We're right here, Nina."

"Oh. Sorry. Now I see you. It's kind of dark down there. Hold on." She started tugging from the top, but only for a second. "Wow. That's not coming off."

"We know. Let's try it together."

"Hold on."

We could see her shadow flit away.

"What she doing?" hissed Sief.

"Probably going for help."

"Yeah, but if she gets *les flics* we got troubles. Call her. Call her on your phone."

I fumbled with my cell, dialed.

"Yeah?"

"Nina, you're not getting the police are you?"

"Duh."

"Well, who are you getting?"

"You want me to describe them or do you want to just trust me?"

She disconnected. We waited. About two minutes later— pop—off came the cover. Nina had gathered five boys, all cute, all instantly crushing on her, who came and pried the thing off while she held up traffic on Avenue Hoche with a raised hand and her amazing smile. Sief and I scrambled out. The boys shoved the cover back into place then off we ran, like it was some teen prank, the boys high-fiving, Nina thanking them. Her little gang dispersed as fast as it had formed, the boys no doubt wanting to be away from our awful smell.

I wanted to be away from it too. But it clung tight to us. Dawn wasn't far off. We must have been down there even longer than I thought. A few shopkeepers, rolling up their steel doors, stared wide-eyed as we walked by, stunned by our stench.

Nina, walking ahead of us, literally holding her nose,

shouted, "Come on, follow me, hurry."

"Where you going?" asked Sief.

"Just shut up and follow," she called back.

We did. I'm not sure what Sief was thinking, but I was so exhausted and light-headed that I would have followed Nina anywhere. We traipsed down Avenue Beaucour, cut through a passageway to rue Daru, and shuffled up a footpath into a courtyard. Before I quite grasped what was happening, Nina pressed an apartment intercom button and a crackly voice came back.

*"Oui?"*

*"C'est moi, Tante Benice."*

A buzzer buzzed. Nina pushed open the door and up we marched, our putrid shoes squishing on elegant carpet. As soon as she opened her apartment door and saw us, Tante Benice groaned, *"Nina? Quel horreur!"*

Nina and her aunt had a terse, tense exchange and then Tante Benice waved us in with a titanic frown. For the next hour, Tante Benice lectured us, bossed us around, ordered us into the shower, ordered us to soap and re-soap, confiscated our clothes so she could wash them, putting them through two cycles. She wrapped us in warm towels and oversized bathrobes, Nina included, despite Nina's protests that it wasn't she who smelled. I was never so happy to be scolded in my life.

While Tante Benice was attending to Sief, who took her lecturing with astounding patience, I asked Nina what she'd told her aunt. "I said some nasty boys dumped over a *toilette public* on us and that I barely escaped."

After pushing me into an easy chair with a down comforter, between trips to the washing machine, Tante Benice made it clear, mostly through the tone of her lecture, that she did not approve of Nina and I traipsing around Paris all night with a boy.

I nodded and said, *"oui, madame"* about a dozen times until she tottered off to harangue Nina again.

The comforter seemed like the softest, warmest thing I'd ever encountered and I so wanted to curl into it and let my eyes fall closed, but instead I fished my cell phone from the Ziplock and checked the messages. Besides Nina's and Aunt Mill's there was a new one from Pauline Dumeril. Excited and speaking fast, Pauline said she was sorry to be calling so early but that Dr. Baertich had phoned with some remarkable news about the page I'd left them and could I call her back as soon as possible?

The three messages from Aunt Mill all said the same thing: would I please call her and check in? She didn't seem angry. Her voice was dry and matter of fact. My head was so fuzzy and my eyelids so-so heavy, I knew everything would go better if I just took a little catnap so my brain would be working when I called back. Or maybe it would be better to get home and confront her in person. No reason to go through the same story twice. Every reason to say it all once and be done.

I'm not sure how long I slept. Couldn't have been that long. Nina came and sat on the arm of the chair and handed me a cup of *café au lait*. "You need to get going. Tante Benice needs to go to work. And trust me, you don't want to be here when my mom comes to pick me up."

I nodded. Tante Benice appeared and handed me my clothes, clean, warm and folded.

*"Merci, Madame,"* I said. She walked off scowling. Sief joined us, dressed and ready to go. I turned back to Nina. "What are you going to tell your mom?"

She shrugged. "That I was out goofing around with friends. That I'm sorry I can't always live up to her impossible expectations. That my *fauve*-girl needed me. I certainly can't tell her it was really fun being part of a heist crew, even though I froze my buns off."

"You the best *mec extérieur* I ever works with," said Sief. "We do it again when you done being grounded."

Nina glowed with pride. Seriously. I had to keep my eyes from rolling.

"Go gets dressed," said Sief.

"Don't be bossy," I said back.

A few minutes later, at the door to the apartment, Sief and I gave Nina double-cheek kisses. We knew we were all in big trouble, but that she was likely to get it the worst. I reached out to Tante Benice, despite her pretend parental scowl, and gave her a hug, saying, *"Merci mille fois pour tout, Madame, et je vous prie de me pardonner."* She didn't say anything back, but her scowl went away and she gave me a three cheeker.

On the walk to the Metro, I asked Sief, "You going to be okay?"

He puffed lips. "Sure. I think my dad going to put me in chains."

"After I give Aunt Mill the book and explain everything I'll ask her to call your dad. Maybe that would help."

He shrugged. "Did you call Madame Millicent?"

"Not yet. I was thinking I'll just explain everything when I get home and can hand her the book."

"Up to you. But she probably full of worry right now."

He was right. I was being chicken. I fished out my phone and dialed. She didn't answer the landline so I dialed her cell. It rang twice, then I heard the click of someone answering, but Aunt Mill didn't say hello.

Instead, I heard Russian voices talking in the background.

# 34. Stun Gun Momma

A million chaotic thoughts rushed through my head when I heard the Russian voices, but the only thing I could think to say was, "Aunt Mill?"

"Daisy?" she said back.

"Are you okay?"

"I'm fine," she said, her voice restrained and odd. "What about you? Are you hurt in any way?"

"Me? No. I'm good, totally, and really-really sorry and I can explain the whole thing and I'm on my way home right now so I'll see you in about a minute, I promise, okay, so don't worry about me at all and I'm really sorry-sorry-sorry, okay?"

"Are you alone?"

"Sief's with me. But none of this is his fault. We're heading for the Metro right now so it won't be long and then I promise I can explain the whole—"

"Have you got the book?"

That stopped me. I should have gotten it from the beginning, of course, but for some reason, denial mostly, I hadn't pieced it together. Now that I had, I could hardly walk, let alone stammer, "What?"

"The book. By Jean-Marie Cournac. *Aperçu des secrets diplomatiques.*"

"Um." This was so bad. This meant so many bad things that even a nitwit like me could figure out how bad it was.

"Just say yes or no, Daisy."

"Yes."

"Okay then, listen to me. Listen very carefully. Do not, I repeat, do not tell Sief any of what I am about to tell you. Tell him, if he asks, that everything is okay and that you are going to meet me, oh, say, at the Polidor, alone, for breakfast. He is not invited. Do you understand?"

"Yes. But—"

"Just listen, Daisy. When you've said goodbye to Sief, take the Metro to the Notre-Dame-des-Champs stop. Walk down to rue Vavin. Rue Bréa will split off from Vavin at the next corner. Find number one, rue Bréa, next to the pizzeria, and come up to the *troisième étage*. Knock on the door to the right. Bring the book with you."

"But—"

"I'll explain everything when you get here. Just come alone and bring the book. And don't call or contact anyone else."

"Okay."

"That's very important, that last part. Contact no one."

"I understand."

She repeated the instructions to rue Bréa again and then disconnected.

I must have looked pale. It felt like I had no blood. Sief stared at me. "You okay?"

"I'm good. I have to meet Aunt Mill at a restaurant, but everything is fine."

"Are you in big troubles?"

"Yeah. Big. But I think she's relieved mostly."

He nodded. We rode the Metro together to Concorde, where I had to transfer. As the train hissed into the station I said, "Thanks again, Sief, for everything. I can't say that enough."

"Been fun. It may be awhiles till I seeing you," he said.

"Grounded for life."

"Maybe two lifes." He smiled. The doors slid open.

Leaning in, I gave him a double-cheeker then stepped off the train and headed for the correspondence tunnel, not daring to look back lest I burst open and tell him everything.

I took the Twelve Line south, fighting off panic, trying to think this out. The Russian voices in the background: not good. The address, near Le Dôme, where the vory hung out: also not good. Plus, Aunt Mill's voice sounded much too calm. And she knew about the book. So Gruzdeva had her. That was clear.

The thought of Neckless and Snake-in-Skull forcing her into their car, like they'd tried to do with me, made me furious, but I pushed my fury aside. The fact that they nabbed her meant they were reacting to my having the book, because they could have picked her up anytime and hadn't, until now.

That meant I'd be meeting Samuelson. Because Yursky Gruzdeva—who the gangster appreciation website described as "known more for brutality than brains"—was not up to fabricating an entire eighteenth-century book, and dozens of fake messages in an obscure code, as part of a plan to boost the value of some smuggled diamonds. That's what Samuelson added to the mix. And though I had no proof, I was convinced that Henry Franklin Samuelson was the double agent in Felix's story, who Aunt Mill had ferreted out.

Aunt Mill had put Samuelson in Fleury-Mérogis.

Therefore, he had a grudge. And in fact, what better heist, or con, or whatever this was, could there possibly be than to build on the de la Motte diamond legend? When the thing was finally found out, Samuelson would become a criminal rockstar. The gangster appreciation website would sing his praises. And Aunt Mill would be the donkey.

I heard a buzz and looked up, realizing I'd almost thought

my way past my stop. I darted off the train as the doors snapped behind me. Actually, I'd gotten off at Rennes, the stop before Notre-Dame-des-Champs, in case one of the thugs was waiting for me. They didn't know to the minute when I'd be arriving, so I had some extra time. I circled in on the address, looking over the rues and buildings, scouting. I didn't know exactly what I was looking for, and maybe—since my heart beat like a gerbil's the entire time—I was just stalling.

When I realized I was repeating the same thoughts and circling the address for the third time, I stopped. Scared as I was, I knew I couldn't leave Aunt Mill in there. I took a breath and crossed the street.

The stairs to the *troisième étage*, the fourth floor, were shabby and never ending. My lungs begged for more air by halfway up, but that was fear. No one stood outside the door or on the landing. They seemed confident that I would come and come alone. I stalked right up and knocked, afraid to stop, even to catch my breath.

Neck-less let me in and bolted the door behind me. Down an entrance hall stood a pretty, blond woman in tight jeans, a pink sweater, and fluffy white slippers, holding a baby in one arm and a stun gun in the other. She said something in Russian and waved me into a living room with furniture that looked like it came from IKEA—contemporary and bright. Unlike all the other fireplaces I'd seen in Paris apartments, this one actually had a coal fire burning in it, giving off cozy warmth. The whole crew was there: Gruzdeva, Neck-less, Snake-in-Skull, the guy who followed me at the Palais Royale, and of course, Samuelson.

But my eyes latched onto Aunt Mill. She sat handcuffed to a tubular chrome chair, a blue plastic dog collar on her neck, the kind you use to keep your dog from barking by shocking it. Snake-in-Skull held a blue remote control.

I wanted to punch Snake-in-Skull in the nose so hard his eyeballs would pop out.

But I took my cue from Aunt Mill, who seemed composed in a way I'd never seen before. She looked pale and exhausted, but she was forcing herself to be calm.

"Daisy, my name is Henry Samuelson."

"I know who you are," I snapped as arrogantly as I could.

"And how do you know that?"

"Oh, please, you think you're some international man of mystery? Every kid with an internet connection knows."

I could see a vein pulse on his forehead though his face remained placid. He glanced at Aunt Mill. She gave him the ghost of a smile.

"Let me have the book," he said.

"Let her go first," I tossed back.

"I won't wrestle you for it."

I saw Aunt Mill's eyes go wide then an instant later felt the knobs of the stun gun against my neck. Next thing I knew I was on the floor, legs having gone who knows where, my whole body a funny-bone, head full of fog. I twisted round. The blond with the stun gun stood over me. Her baby was laughing. Must have been hilarious to watch.

"Give him the book, Daisy," I heard Aunt Mill say from the end of a long tunnel. I struggled to my hands and knees. That's when I noticed the other guy. It's not like I hadn't before. There was just a lot to take in and I'd kind of glanced past him. He had on a suit and very expensive looking shoes and stared down at me, appalled. He had a square, clean-shaven face and sat in a mauve cube chair near the end of the coffee table, on which sat a beautiful, black laquered box. I straightened myself up and fished the Ziplock from my jeans and fumbled it onto the table, my hands not quite working yet.

"Sit," said Samuelson.

I sat.

Samuelson took the book out of the bag and flipped through it. "Look at that. In good condition, too. And exceedingly rare." He clapped the book closed, walked to the fireplace, set it on the coals. Flames sprouted and licked at the cover. I caught Aunt Mill's eye, saw her turn down her lip for a nano as if to say, don't give them the pleasure. I kept my face stony.

"There, that's done," said Samuelson. "Now let's talk a bit."

"Why don't you let me explain things to her," said Aunt Mill. "It might go easier if I do."

Samuelson considered a second. The flames rose and the book crackled, cover curling up from the heat, smoke fluttering. Samuelson nodded to Aunt Mill.

She looked directly at me and spoke in an emotionless voice. "It appears you've uncovered a well-orchestrated plan having to do with my research and the Queen's Diamonds. These gentlemen have invested a great deal of time, money, and energy into their plan and do not wish to have it compromised. They will—how shall I say it—use any means necessary to ensure that their plan succeeds. Do you understand so far?"

I nodded. No news there.

The book raged orange-red now, flames expanding to the walls of the fireplace, smoke rushing up the flue, filling the ancient throat of the chimney, spilling out under the lintel, curling into the room. The baby started to cough. Stun Gun Momma didn't like it. She squawked in Russian at Snake-in-Skull, who, it seemed, was her hubby or baby-daddy or whatever. Gruzdeva started hacking too. Bad lungs from dank Siberian jails cells, no doubt. He rose and moved to the big double windows and threw them open, barking something at Samuelson while Snake-in-Skull tried to push the book to the back of the fireplace with a poker.

Aunt Mill glanced at Samuelson as if to say, *is this ridiculous comedy about over?* He gestured for her to continue. She looked back to me. "I have convinced them that the expression 'corpses don't talk' is not entirely true in this instance, since there are people who know about my activities and your association with me. Therefore our deaths, or even our disappearance, would be noted and have significance. Thus our hosts are willing, now that they possess all the other copies of the book, to grant us our freedom in return for our complete silence on the subject of their activities."

"Like Lupatreaux," I said.

Aunt Mill looked puzzled.

"Yes," said Samuelson, "Like Monsieur Lupatreaux."

"That's it?" I asked. "No problem then. I mean, I don't really care. What's it to me? Sell your diamonds. Make history. It doesn't concern me at all as long as my aunt goes free."

"That's a sensible attitude," said Samuelson.

"Just one thing, though."

I could tell from their looks that Gruzdeva and Samuelson were growing impatient with me but I had to play them a little more. Because even through the stun-gunned fog in my brain, I sensed that as soon as they'd completed their sale Aunt Mill and I would be much more useful to them dead, no matter what they said. And I knew with laser clarity the only thing that would guarantee our safety was if we had the diamonds—or rather, if I had them.

"Could I see the diamonds? I've read so much about them and I promise not to tell a soul, but it would just be so cool to see them, even for like a single second. Pretty please. I promise I won't tell anyone. I mean I've already promised that already, right, but I'll double promise just for a single quick look."

Gruzdeva fought through another coughing attack. Hard to tell whether he was laughing or disagreeing or just coughing. He turned toward the open window. Aunt Mill got an alarmed look in her eyes—she knew I was up to something. Samuelson glanced at the man in the nice shoes, who I knew had to be Christophe Babinet, the international art dealer holding the diamonds to give them legitimacy. He shrugged. Samuelson nodded. Babinet opened the box.

They rested on blue velvet that had a space molded for each diamond. The missing diamonds had been replaced by black Lucite shapes, so the whole necklace was represented.

"Oh, wow," I gasped.

I wasn't kidding. They took your breath away. No matter that they probably came from Gruzdeva's smuggler friends in Russia and were still buried under Siberian mud at the time Marie Antoinette's head was severed from her delicate neck—these stones, so arranged, created all the drama of the notorious originals.

I had to get closer.

"They are so amazing."

I had to keep my heart from beating so hard they'd hear it.

"So beautiful."

I smiled wide. I smiled with my eyes. With my toes even. I tried to glow. And I swear the gangsters smiled back—proud of their plan or their product or just hypnotized, like any mortal would be, by the otherworldly sparkle—until I snatched the diamonds from the box, jumped over the table, and dove out the fourth floor window.

## 35. Reid Hall

Gruzdeva grabbed for me, but I shot past him over the guardrail. My fingers clasped it for a nano and my body flipped over, slapping into the grillwork of the railing. Snake-in-Skull caught hold of my finger on the way down, but that wasn't enough to stop me, just enough to make my finger pop.

Unlike last time, the balconies here were recessed into the building so there was little to land on. I tried grasping a stone lip that divided the floors as it blurred by, but that just wrenched my wrist. On the second floor, a sunshade angled out from the building. I went right through it, ripping the fabric, yanking its metal frame from the wall. That slowed me down, though, and probably saved my life.

Down I shot, hitting the pizzeria awning with a timpani boom that would have been funny if it didn't hurt so bad, bouncing off the awning and onto the roof of a workman's van parked out front. People at the Café Vavin across the street gave a communal shriek when they saw me. The folks sitting below the pizzeria awning dove for cover in ten directions.

Falling the second time, as you might guess, was no more pleasant than the first. I curled into a ball of pain, the necklace jammed into my armpit, and slid off the roof of the van. I'd hit my head somewhere in there, probably a few times, so everything was blurry. The voices gathering around me echoed. Part of me wanted to pass out, but part of me knew the Russians were dashing down the stairs as fast as they could. I rolled face up.

Stun Gun Momma was standing right over me. I freaked. How did she get down so fast? I blinked. Now she was looking down from the balcony, screaming at me. Clearly my brain wasn't working right.

I sat up. People bent over me, asking a million questions. The French translation part of my brain had completely switched off. I tried to rise, but my knees wouldn't hold. Some guy helped me up.

"They're coming," I gasped. "I have to go." I ripped away from the guy. My ankle hurt like fire but I ran anyway.

I passed two shops, my brain taking a snapshot of each for some reason—Savon de Marseille, Princess Tam-Tam—then someone popped out of the door to an apartment and I lurched in before the door closed. I hobbled down a hall behind the stairs, past trash barrels, then out a sliver of a door that gave into a tiny high-walled walkway. Somehow, reflexively, even in my near-reptile state, I knew I had to stay off the long rues because it would be too easy for the vory to spot me.

I could hear sirens. Police. Or an ambulance maybe. Spots began to swirl. I started to black out. A surge of fear snapped me back. I climbed over a wall and into someone's postage stamp garden. I plunked down next to a birdbath with a burbling Buddha statue.

"Buddha," I said, wiping blood from my nose. "I got the diamonds, Buddha." I let them slide from under my arm into my lap. "Now that I have these, they won't dare touch my aunt."

"If you get away," Buddha said, with his happy smile. Was he really talking to me? Oh, Daisy, pull it together.

I yanked myself up. I stuffed the necklace down the front of my jeans. Trying to open the sliding doors that led into a ground floor apartment, I woke two hairy micro-dogs who snapped and barked and leaped at the glass doors. Retreating, I climbed over the wall into the neighboring garden, spotted a window ajar, shoved it open and climbed through. I heard a toilet flushing and rushed down the hall to the front door, letting myself out, into the building's lobby, stopping at the main door onto rue Jules Chaplain. I peeped out, looking both ways. No vory.

I limped across the rue, teeth clenched from the pain in my ankle, and lurched down a passage between two buildings. It ended in a tiny entrance way. Locked. Next to it stood a trellis overgrown with ivy strong enough that I could crawl up to a low roof. From that roof I climbed to a higher roof, then scooted along the top till I faced rue de la Grande Chaumière. I scrambled down the bare branches of a tree over a stone courtyard.

On the final leap down, I jolted my ankle and collapsed onto my face. It felt like an ice pick pierced my foot. Tears flooded my eyes. Every part of me throbbed. I was pretty sure I'd broken my ankle, my wrist, a few fingers, and a few ribs. I curled up, giving in to dispare. Then I flashed on that thing around Aunt Mill's neck and snapped upright.

A woman came out a back door to have a smoke. I limped past her, into what turned out to be an office for medical specialists. The receptionist glanced up, mistook me for a patient, told me to have a seat.

I crossed the street to the iron gate of another walled-off garden. Locked of course, with spear points along the top. I got a grip on the top of the wall beside the gate and used the spear points to wedge myself up, squirmed over, ribs screaming, then hung down on the opposite side, bracing for the drop. I must have passed out when I hit. I woke sprawled in a pile of leaves. I couldn't remember where I was or how I got there until I felt the diamonds pressing into my waist and hissed, "Aunt Mill."

I pulled myself up, clinging to the bark of a tree trunk and hopped from one trunk to another, then across a path to a courtyard planted like a mini-version of Hôtel Rohan. Could I have gotten to the Hôtel Rohan somehow? Everything telescoped forward like I was stuck in a zoom lens. Just beyond the ringing in my ears, I could hear my sister blabbing. But why would Clymene be here? Then I heard two Clymenes blabbing. They were talking about some guy who thought he was so special but was really a loser. I laughed, stopping at once because of the pain in my ribs. But still—Clymene—*here, right here.* I wanted to hug her. I really truly did. I shouted, "Clymene!"

Two college girls sitting at a table turned to me. "Who?"

"I—I'm sorry. I think I'm a little mixed up. Are you Americans?"

"Yes. Who are you?" I could see them more clearly now. They wore heavy sweaters and big scarves and black jeans. One of them had a ring in her nose. The other had pink hair.

"My name is Daisy Tannenbaum. Where am I exactly?"

They looked at me funny, but one of them said, "You're at Reid Hall."

I hopped over to them and eased into an empty chair. "What's that?"

"A study abroad campus. Are you all right?"

"Well, I had sort of a fall and my cell phone is nearly out of juice, but I think I still have some euros. Would one of you mind calling me a taxi?"

# 36. Téléphone Public

The two college girls, Chandler and Frankie, called a taxi, fetched me a glass of water, and helped me into the taxi when it came. They thought it weird that I peeped out the door to make sure no gangsters were lurking about, but invited me to drop by again anytime.

Even before I told the driver where I wanted to go, I flattened myself into the back seat so no one could see me. He kept glancing back at me in his mirror. I didn't look like an escaped convict, but clearly I was acting like one. It didn't help that all the way over to the Louvre, I kept leaning up to check the meter, fearing I'd run out of money. Several times, at stoplights, since it looked like the taxi was empty, people rushed up and insisted on getting in and the driver would have to yell at them.

I had him drop me at a place called Café Le Corona, across from the Perrault's Colonnade side of the Louvre. Limping past a thicket of tourists, I parked myself at a back table. On the ride over, I'd worked out what I needed to do. I hurt all over, even worse than the first time—thumb, wrist, shoulders, ribs, neck, skull, ears, eyeballs, ankle, plus overall nausea and thumping that came from everywhere. But I felt something else too. Like I wanted to rip someone's head off.

I pulled out my cell phone. It was dead. A waitress in black and white approached. *"Quelque chose pour mademoiselle?"*

*"Avez-vous un téléphone public?"*

She pointed her chin toward a stairway behind me.

I was in luck. A lot of cafés in Paris don't keep public phones anymore because everyone has cells, but this place had an old meter phone where you pay at the bar after you call. I struggled down the stairs and dialed Aunt Mill's number. After three rings, she picked up.

"Aunt Mill, it's me. You okay?"

"I'm fine. Where are—no, don't tell me. Just tell me if you're hurt."

"Why would I be hurt?"

The phone crackled as someone pulled it away from her. "Listen, you little idiot," said Samuelson. "My Russian colleagues were willing to let you both walk out of here, but instead you foolishly took something that was theirs. Now they insist on killing you both."

"Then why haven't they? Seriously. They could have chopped my aunt to pieces and fed her to that demented baby by now. Oh, but wait, that would cost them millions wouldn't it? Because even though these aren't Jeanne de la Motte's diamonds, they're still diamonds and I still have them. And if your pals so much as touch a hair on my aunt's head they'll never see their precious bling again."

"You've got bravado, kid, I'll give you that. But let me just say, as a fellow American, that what you need to do is march right back here with those diamonds and beg these men to let your aunt go. You have no idea of the viciousness of these people."

"I have some idea. They're *really* scary. Which is why you're in an awkward place. I mean, if something happens to us, why would Gruzdeva keep you around? You're just another person who can blab."

He didn't say anything. I could hear him breathing. "So you want to trade, is that it?"

"In a little bit," I said. "I need to get to a post office with some pictures of these beauties and a list of names and just enough of a little written history so that if afterwards something were to happen to Aunt Mill and I, say we disappeared, then the French government would receive a fat envelope that would make them extremely unamused."

"Come on. You think the delayed letter gambit actually works?"

"You better hope I do. I mean, put yourself in my shoes. I'm tired, I'm scared, I'm all alone in a foreign country, I have this bag full of diamonds and I'm sitting in a *CopySelf* across from a police station thinking, 'The heck with it, just turn the diamonds in and let the police deal with this.'"

"That would be a grave mistake."

"I don't care. The only thing I care about is my aunt."

He was quiet. He might have hit mute and talked to his comrades, I couldn't be sure. Finally, he came back with, "Daisy, I'm going to give you an address."

"No, I'm going to give you one."

"You want to see your aunt alive?"

"You want to see your diamonds alive?" I looked at the clock above the phone. "I'll meet you in ninety-three minutes exactly, top of the hour, at the Place des Vosges. Just you and my aunt. Walk to the center of the garden, to the statue of Louis the Thirteenth. Bring her cell phone with you. I'll want to talk to you and her before I turn over the diamonds. I don't care if the others are waiting in cars around the square, but if they set foot in the park the deal is off."

"I'm not sure they'll agree to it, Daisy."

"That's your problem. Your neck is on the line with ours, so say whatever you have to. All I want is my aunt."

I hung up. It was the hardest thing, hanging up, because I

had no idea if Samuelson thought my bluster was just, well, bluster. And who knew what his vory partners would think.

# 37. A visit with DCSP, DGPN, DCPAF, UCLAT and GIPN

Hobbling the quarter mile from the café to the Porte des Lions entrance of the *Centre de recherche et de restauration* was torture. I hopped on one leg, holding onto stone balustrades and the iron fence enclosing the Cour Carrée. The whole way I just knew vory gangsters would nab me. Twice I had to stop and hold on so I wouldn't toss cookies.

Pauline's eyes bugged out when I plopped the necklace on her desk. That's not even an exaggeration. She kept insisting I tell her how I got my bloody nose, collection of bruises, and the gash on my hand while I kept asking her what Dr. Baertich said about the page from the book.

So I plopped down the necklace and said, "Is the page a fake?"

"Yes. But w-where—?"

"Dr. Baertich said that? Positively?"

"Yes. Daisy, where did you—what are these?"

"Diamonds obviously. How did he determine it was fake?"

"Spectro-imagery—with a computerized camera—he found the ghost of the original text that had been chemically removed. Where on earth did you get these?"

"From Russian gangsters trying to pass them off as the Queen's Diamonds."

After Pauline could talk again, she made about a hundred phone calls. Dr. Baertich came to her office, as did an expert on gems and jewelry. As the questions about how and where I got the diamonds came pouring in, so did their lawyer and their head of security and Pauline's boss and her boss's boss.

Meantime, thank heavens, someone brought water and aspirin. Madame Haron taxied over from the Archives Nationales, arriving just after a doctor. He said my wrist was definitely broken, and my ankle was either badly sprained or broken. My ribs, he shrugged, were going to hurt like *l'enfer* whether broken or sprained. He wanted to take me to a hospital for x-rays, but I said no way.

He would have forced me to go had an array of police not arrived, alone and in clumps, and with them more questions. There were officers from *DCSP* and *DCPAF* and *UCLAT* and *RAID* and even *GIPN*. It seemed like every time I got halfway through an explanation, another police branch arrived. I was getting fed up.

But slowly, or perhaps rather rapidly considering all the bureaus and egos involved, various threads of the story wove together for them. One branch confirmed reports about a girl in Montparnasse who had fallen out of a window. The girl, apparently, had walked away from the fall and disappeared. Another branch knew of a missing person report phoned in by one Felix Henry Chareau-Aghion de Pindenhaus about a woman, one Madame Millicent Gladston, who, according to Monsieur de Pindehaus, was a possible victim of foul play.

Yet another branch knew of a burglary attempt at the Château d'Aubergine in Neuilly, in which, as far as they could tell, nothing was actually taken. After I told them that a rare eighteenth-century book had been taken and then burned by vory gangsters in the very Montparnasse apartment the girl fell from, or rather, jumped out of, a policewoman recalled that a Russian émigré with a baby, at the rue Bréa location, had been cited for burning coal in her fireplace, which was outlawed within city limits as part of an emissions control ordinance.

By this time I'd reached my limit and blurted that my aunt was a hostage and I'd already contacted her captors to trade the diamonds for her release, and that every second I wasted counted against her life. While Madame Haron translated this—over the chaos of all the other voices—I opened Pauline's desk drawers, found a scissors, and cut the diamond necklace in half.

Everyone gasped.

Everyone except a man with a huge nose and crinkled face, dressed in a dark suit, who looked like he'd last had an emotion in 1960. He said in a voice just above a whisper, *"Bravo, mademoiselle."*

I'm not certain what department he was from, he never said, but all the other branches were either deeply respectful or utterly terrified of him. After a moment of silence, Dark Suit asked me if I happened to know the names of my aunt's alleged captors.

"Yursky Gruzdeva and Henry Franklin Samuelson."

He nodded and thanked all the other police for their help and asked them to leave the room and file copies of their reports with him, then flicked a finger at an olive-skinned man in paint-splattered, mechanic's coveralls and a gray hoodie, indicating that he should stay.

He also asked Madame Haron and Pauline to stay, as witnesses and to translate if necessary, then asked me, "How did you contact them?"

"I used a café phone. They have my aunt's cell. If I can get my cell recharged, they're sure to recognize the number when I call."

"Where is the exchange to take place?"

"At the Place des Vosges. There are a million places to

hide and the central area is open and there are always lots of people around."

Dark Suit glanced at Monsieur Picon, which was, as far as I could tell, the paint-splattered operative's name. Picon nodded.

"And you cut the necklace to return it in two parts?"

"That's right. They get half when I see that she's okay and half when she's safe."

Picon said something in police jargon that I couldn't understand. Dark Suit's lip curled downward. Later, when I asked Pauline what Picon said, she informed me that it was impolite to translate, but meant that I had impressive fortitude as expressed in a metaphor about male anatomy.

## 38. Place des Vosges

Once they decided the thing was on, Dark Suit and Monsieur Picon made about a hundred cell phone calls a piece, one after another, shooting questions at me the whole time, while somebody drove us to Hôtel de Sully, which, I had no idea, contains government offices that back up onto the Place des Vosges. The moment we arrived, some geeky guy took my phone, replaced the battery and SIM card, and handed it back to me.

Place des Vosges was steps from Aunt Mill's apartment. She took me here practically my first day, going on about how Henri IV built the place in 1612 and how it was called Place Royale at the time.

About an hour and a quarter after I hung up the phone at Café Le Corona, Snake-in-Skull and Neckless made the first pass in their Mercedes. They drove in on rue des Franc Bourgeois, past Ma Bourgogne, then turned south at Café Hugo and circled around twice. They drove slowly and looked. They looked for me, they looked for policemen, they looked for traps. But the arched arcade surrounding the square cast deep shadows, each arch so thick you could hide an elephant behind it. Dozens of people filled the central park and dozens more strolled past shop windows or sat at café tables—a paradise of witnesses.

On the second pass, Snake-in-Skull got out of the car. He walked the covered arcade all the way around. By the time he got to my side of the square, it was easy enough to duck behind a rack of clothes inside a designer boutique. After finishing his snooping, Snake-in-Skull settled at a table outside Café Hugo, at the northeast corner of the square, and phoned in his report, keeping an eye on things while Neckless drove off in the Mercedes.

With the leaves gone, you could see between the tree trunks, all the way across the park. Another ring of leafless trees surrounded the bronze statue of Louis XIII at the center. Aunt Mill said the statue had been knocked down and replaced several times during this and that revolution, until no one quite remembered what was so horrible about Louis XIII and just left him alone.

At about five minutes before the hour, Samuelson appeared, on foot, through the rue de Birague archway. He too strolled the covered walkways, not acknowledging Snake-in-Skull as he passed Café Hugo, cutting across and checking out the park. Just before the hour, he pulled out a cell phone and sent a text. The Mercedes returned, pulling up on the west side of the garden. I could see Gruzdeva, Neckless and Aunt Mill in the car. I dialed my phone.

"Daisy, don't do this," Aunt Mill hissed the instant we connected. "Call the police and let them handle this. Do not, I repeat, do not get involved—"

The phone crackled as they ripped it out of her hand. I could not see from my vantage exactly what was happening in the car, but I saw Samuelson make his way over. Gruzdeva must have called him over to talk on the phone.

"Is this Daisy?"

"Samuelson?"

"Don't use my name."

"I'm sorry, I have a bad connection. Hello? Is this Samuelson?"

"Yes. But don't use my name."

"Samuelson, will you put my Aunt Mill back on the phone?"

"I'm afraid that's not advisable presently. Where are you?"

I ignored his question. "In that case walk her to the center of the garden, near the statue. I'll call you back when you're there." I hung up.

He rang me back. "You'll need to come to us."

"Not happening," I said, my heart beating so hard I was sure he could hear it.

"That's our deal, Daisy. Take it or leave it."

I hung up again.

He called back and swore at me, but it wasn't anything my sister hadn't said a dozen times.

"Are you finished?"

Oh, that got him. He went on swearing, describing what would happen to Aunt Mill if I did not come immediately to the car. He went on and on, mixing his cursing with: "Did I want to see her alive? Did I think I could get away with their diamonds? Was I so stupid I thought I could escape them?"

"Potty mouth," I said. For some reason that made him dummy up. "Do you have any idea where the local police outpost is?" I asked. "Because I do and I can get there in ten seconds. So stop with the phony gangster hysterics. You're a spy, not a thug. We came to make a trade. Unless you're telling me you've already hurt my aunt, in which case the deal is off. So walk her to the center of the garden by the statue of Louis XIII. I'll phone you back when I see you. Otherwise just drive away and save your breath. You'll need it to talk your way out of whatever Gruzdeva has in store for you."

I hung up. Tears burned my eyes. I knew my taunting might completely backfire. The next seconds dragged like hours.

You can't imagine how relieved I was when Samuelson and Aunt Mill made their way to the center of the square. She limped more than usual, hunched and leaning on an umbrella, but she had that terrible collar off her neck. As soon as they neared the statue I dialed back.

"Satisfied?" said Samuelson.

"See the garbage receptical to your right? Inside the green, see-through bag you'll find a crumpled box of *Alsa macaron au chocolat* under the other trash. It's brown and pink with grease stains on it. Look inside."

I could see them walk over. Samuelson dug through the trash. Funny almost. Toddlers chased past them, voices screeching in real life and a moment later over my phone.

"This is only half of it," said Samuelson, his hand inside the box.

"My aunt is only half free. So, now tell her to walk south toward rue de Birague and when she's at the gate I'll tell you where your other half is."

Silence. He was calculating.

"Of course you could search yourself, since it is very likely I've hidden the diamonds in the park somewhere, but there are over seventy garbage recepticals alone to search. Probably I wouldn't hide them there twice though. That would be dumb. Then again, maybe I would just because you'd think it was dumb."

He didn't respond, but I saw Aunt Mill limp off toward the rue de Birague exit.

"Go ahead," he said.

"Just another moment. She doesn't move very fast."

"Nothing's going to happen. Trust me."

I almost laughed. Instead I said, "Have you ever heard the song, 'Diamonds are a Girl's Best Friend,' from the film *Moulin*

*Rouge?"*

"It's originally from *Gentlemen Prefer Blondes,"* he said.

"Really?" I said. I could see Aunt Mill nearing the south garden gate. "I'll check it out on YouTube. Meantime, walk southeast toward Victor Hugo's house and at the fountain, circle around till you see a stone in the base that looks a bit darker than the rest. If you look closely you'll see a white chalk mark on it. You can easily pry this stone out. Beneath it you'll find a plastic bag. Call me back if you have any trouble."

"We'll be in touch," he said, trying to sound ominous.

"You never know."

Monsieur Picon, standing beside me, barked a command into his radio.

I'd be lying if I told you I saw all of what happened next as his team went into play: a mom pushing a baby carriage near the south gate rushed over and, grasping Aunt Mill's shoulder, instructed her to hit the dirt for safety; a homeless man, napping near the fountain, jumped up and tackled Samuelson from behind. Two tourists at Café Hugo smashed Snake-in-Skull's face into his *crème brulée* and handcuffed him to his chair. Picon, with two fellow painters in coveralls, rushed across the street with police badges raised. Neckless saw them and hit the gas, roaring away, only to find the *rue* blocked at the north end. Somehow, in the foot chase that followed, Gruzdeva got hit by a car while trying to flee.

I only heard all this later, since, as soon as Picon gave his order, I darted out from the column I was behind and rushed over to Aunt Mill. It was at least fifty yards and my ankle was screaming and I looked like a clown bumping along. But who cared? I hugged Aunt Mill for all I was ever worth and she hugged me back. We kept asking each other if we were all right, neither of us answering, just asking over and over—"Are you all right?  Are *you* all right?  Are *you* all right?"—until we both started laughing.

We were all right.

# 39. Inquest-o-rama

The next day and the day after that and the whole next two weeks really, were one huge question-fest. I didn't know so many questions existed. By the end of two weeks, every worker bee in the French government must have filed a report. They talked to me, to Sief, to Nina, to Aunt Mill, to Felix, to Lupatreaux, to Pauline and Madame Haron, to Tante Benice (which they regretted), to Dr. Baertich, and to a bunch of people I didn't know existed.

Mostly I talked with Inspectrice Sophie Baragnon and her assistant Pierre Demy. They were always super-serious, always dressed in tailored suits, always very polite, and *never* willing to answer any of *my* questions. They made it clear that I was to answer questions, not ask them. I started to wonder whether they intended to put *me* in jail.

Sief, Nina, and I had, after all, broken into Château d'Aubergine and stolen a valuable book that ended up destroyed. My claim that I'd planned to return it didn't seem to impress them. The fact that Madame Geromina Henrietta d'Aubergine didn't even know she owned such a book, didn't impress them either. A burglary, in their book, was a burglary.

There were also certain times—for instance when I told them about being attacked by a crocodile in the sewer—that they grew annoyed with me in their polite way. They would ask repeatedly if I was certain I saw a crocodile, did I really want them to enter it into evidence, which, since I had mentioned it under oath, they were obliged to do. Did I realize what an oath was?

But after the first week, I knew things were going to be okay. They asked me not to discuss anything with anybody—but come on. Since they only had time to question me a few hours each day, I talked over everything with Aunt Mill, who was being questioned thoroughly herself. Each evening, Aunt Mill and I would hobble over on our canes and crutches and have dinner at Café Saint Gervais. Then we'd help each other up the endless steps to her apartment, where she'd spend an hour on the phone with Felix.

Felix had contacts with people in government who knew other people in government and he relayed rumors, and rumors of rumors, from inside 36, quai des Orfèvres, where the *Brigade Criminelle* for Paris had its offices. The *Brigade Criminelle* was elated to have an opportunity to prosecute Gruzdeva and Samuelson. Apparently the idea that these two were conspiring sent shivers up the spines of French police officials.

Both Gruzdeva and Samuelson latched onto lawyers and dummied up. But Snake-in-Skull and Stun Gun Momma (who they caught getting off a train in Marseilles with her baby a day after the Place des Vosges arrests) sang like opera stars once the police pressed them. Plus the recording of my cell phone conversations with Samuelson at Place des Vosges, made by the geeky guy from Officer Picon's squad, pretty much condemned the bunch of them. Kidnapping, smuggling, intimidation, forgery, fraud, conspiracy—the collection was impressive.

Christophe Babinet, the art dealer, got a lawyer too, but in the end cooperated, claiming he was an innocent dupe. Buzz from Felix was that the *Brigade Criminelle* didn't believe Babinet, but were willing to trade for information that the vory minions didn't know.

Felix also related a rumor to Aunt Mill about another whole level of *L'affaire*. Apparently the billionaire Stanley Berkman (aka Mr. Jones), whose interest in buying the Queen's Diamonds had started the whole thing, was acting as a "firewall" for the French government. Aunt Mill had to explain that one to me. It appears when rumors arose (at the highest levels of the antiquities market) that someone had recovered a portion of the Queen's Diamonds, certain French ministers thought it would be wonderful if *La France* could possess them. How nice if the glass necklace Madame Haron displayed at the Hôtel de Breteuil, could be replaced, at least in part, by the real thing.

But the risk of buying something of dubious provenance, and the political risk of spending taxpayers' money to do so, was as great today as it had been during Marie Antoinette's time. The French ministers needed a go-between. Instead of Jeanne de la Motte they used Stanley Berkman. So, all this time, Aunt Mill had been working for the French government without knowing it.

Samuelson and Gruzdeva's achievement, though it failed, did not fail to impress everyone who knew about it. Pauline told me Dr. Baertich was in absolute awe. Gruzdeva, for his part, managed to collect all those smuggled diamonds and have the replica necklace made. Samuelson, meanwhile, had pulled off, or almost pulled off, one of the greatest document fabrications in history: an entirely forged book that acted as the key to a set of fraudulent secret messages. He planted both so that their discovery would seem natural—and all to provide plausible provenance for Gruzdeva's diamonds. "No doubt," Aunt Mill told me, "they will be held in high esteem by the inmates of whatever prison they end up in."

Meanwhile, after learning details of the Château d'Aubergine heist, Officer Picon took an interest in Sief, and persuaded him to give up on becoming a cat burglar in favor of becoming a *zombie*, French police slang for an undercover cop. Apparently the skill-set is similar. This new vocation did not, however, keep Sief from being grounded indefinitely by his father. He was forbidden to speak to me, was not allowed to use the telephone, was confined to his bedroom, was allowed out only to go to school and police interviews and no place else. He took all this surprisingly well. I would see him, of course, looking out his courtyard window. Sometimes, if his father was home, Sief would sneak a smile and thumbs up, but if his father was not home he would send down a basket on a string, which I would fill with notes and candy bars and chips.

If things were not exactly ideal *chez* Sief, they were horrible *chez* Nina. She too was forbidden to speak to me, to even possess her cell phone, to linger anywhere after school, to sit down, to pose, to use the internet, to listen to music, the works. When I called to plead on Nina's behalf, her mom said that I should be put behind bars, and hung up on me. We'd have been totally cut off if I didn't receive occasional texts from her via Bruno and Gille's cell phones when she was at school.

The main problem was, Nina resisted. She refused to apologize to her mom, refused to acknowledge that she'd done anything wrong, vowed that if given her freedom she would do the same thing over again, when and if she chose. I texted her, through Bruno, that she should just cave, but she would have none of it. "This is a fight over *la liberté*," she would text back. "This intolerable tyranny has gone on too long."

Oh, brother.

I tried to get Aunt Mill to call Nina's mom, but she claimed that every parent had a style of discipline and, as long as Nina was safe, it was not ours to interfere.

You may be wondering what *I* said to Aunt Mill afterward,

when it became obvious that I'd been lying and doing all this stuff I shouldn't have. Unlike Nina, I apologized my eyeballs out from the get-go, right there at the Place des Vosges, and tried to tell Aunt Mill the whole story, from falling off the roof on, in one giant, balloon-gasp confession. But thirty seconds into my confession, Aunt Mill put a hand up and said she was too exhausted to listen and could we please talk about it the next day. I had to hold my balloon-gasp overnight.

Next morning, over *café au lait* and *tartines*, I started again. Aunt Mill wasn't exactly happy about what I told her, but her questions seemed more about establishing a time line. She was aggravated that she didn't catch on sooner. I ended by saying, "Aunt Mill, please don't send me home, please, please."

She sighed and ran a hand through my hair. "You know, Daisy, you are an extraordinary person. That is why your parents, particularly your mother, wanted you out of that school. Too smart for your own good, growing in great bounds in some areas, lagging in others, with a huge spirit. I so hope I live long enough to see the adult Daisy. I also earnestly hope *you* live long enough to see her. And that's my main concern. You understand?"

I nodded. "But Aunt Mill, I *can* be good. I really can. I just got off to a bad start because I was worried that—"

"—Let's talk about lies."

I looked down at my plate.

"As a rule, they take great efforts to maintain, especially complex ones, and it is rarely worth the trouble, since they never last. I say this as someone with professional experience in creating them. This is quite aside from any moral obligation one has to the truth. It's about trust, Daisy. Trust is the most precious commodity on earth. More valuable than diamonds."

My eyes stayed pinned to my plate.

"You understand?"

I nodded without looking.

And that's all she ever said.

Because she no longer had the code to obsess over in her off hours, we began walking in the evening (limping at first) to look at all the Christmas decorations going up. On the weekends we took trips out of the city, to see all the châteaux. We visited Chantilly, Malmaison, Sceaux, Compiègne, Fontainebleau, and of course Versailles. I can't even begin to describe how wonderful it was to see all these places, each one more ridiculously wonderful than the next. It gave me a pretty clear idea why Jeanne de la Motte wanted to steal those diamonds.

On the Monday after we visited Vaux-le-Vicomte, Aunt Mill and I were notified that we'd been summoned, along with Sief, to the Palais de l'Élysée, which is like the French White House. We were to receive the Ordre National du Mérite from President Hollande himself.

I thought about it and told Aunt Mill that Nina should get a medal too, because she was just as instrumental during the Château d'Aubergine heist as Sief or me. Aunt Mill said it didn't work like that with medals. I said they could keep their stupid medal in that case. To my surprise, after a flurry of phone calls, Nina was in.

Once again, the horrible, gray, going-to-church dress came out of the armoire and once again Aunt Mill fussed over my tights and shoes and hair and every other detail of my shabby being. This time, she had all morning to fret over me instead of just twenty minutes. *Quel horreur*—seriously. She even dug out some pearls and forced me on pain of death to wear them.

Thankfully the taxi finally arrived. We met Sief and his dad in the courtyard and rode over together. Sief looked even more uncomfortable in a suit and tie than I did in my dress. Somewhere along the rue de Rivoli, as we passed the endless glow of Christmas lights, he leaned over and said, "you look beautiful, Grace Kelly."

Part of me wanted to sock him. But instead I said, "Thanks, Sief. You look very nice too."

Nina and her parents met us at the entrance to the Palais de l'Élysée. She of course looked fabulous in a blue dress, white patent leathers, and red Hermès scarf. Her parents looked proud. Like really proud. Not only did *they* look proud but Tante Benice looked proud too. The fight for *la liberté* had been won.

We all got to walk past the guards with their gold helmets, shiny swords, and dour faces. Felix was there as were Madame Haron and Pauline and Officer Picon and a bunch of well-dressed people I didn't recognize.

The whole medal thing was puzzling to me, though. Granted, I'll never truly understand the grownup world but, to hear Felix tell it, the French government thought we'd prevented them from getting into a major embarrassment and didn't really want to throw us in jail for swiping the book at the same time they honored Aunt Mill.

At the appointed hour, President Hollande swept in and shook all our hands, draped us with the medals, and embraced us with triple-cheekers. It was surprisingly fun. No one had ever given me a medal before. Plus the Palais de l'Élysée was cool, with a million gold chairs and marble fireplaces and paintings of dead kings and stuff. Jeanne de la Motte would have fit right in.

I noticed, though, among all the details of that spectacular day, two little things. Nina was standing right next to her mom. And Sief's mom was absent. Maybe that's why I went home afterward, fired up my computer, and wrote an email.

*Dear Mom,*

*I received a medal today from the President of France. I so want you to be proud of me and I'm very sorry I've caused you all the trouble I have.*

*Hopefully, this will help make up for it. The only thing that could have made today better was if you had been here to see it.*

*Love,*

*Daisy*

The next morning I received her reply:

*My darling Daisy,*

*I wish I could have been there too. I am very proud of you. But you know, I am always proud of you, and always will be. I miss you more than you can possibly know.*

*Love,*

*Mom*

Later that night we got the news that Baby-X was born and Mom came through the delivery in once piece. I went into my room and cried. I guess I never admitted how worried I'd been for her. Plus, I had a brother.

A brother!

The very next day I got another email from my mom:

*Dear Daisy,*

*It ends up that air travel is completely safe and incredibly easy with newborns. So, unless you mind awfully, we thought we'd come to Paris for Christmas. What do you say?*

*Love,*

*Mom*

That evening, when I heard Aunt Mill's footsteps in the courtyard below, I rushed to my window and shouted down, "Aunt Mill, they're coming for Christmas. All of them—Mom, Dad, Cly—even the baby."

She smiled up through the raindrops and said, "Splendid. Grab an umbrella and let's go celebrate at Le Saint Gervais. Madame Rose said she was cooking *daube de sanglier à la Provençale.*" And bring your medal. She'll be so tickled to see it."

"What's *daube de sanglier?*"

"Well, come find out."
So I did.

The End

# Daisy's French Glossary

*Bonjour Madame Millicent* — Good morning, Mrs. Millicent.

*Chocolat chaud* — hot chocolate.

*Saumon rillettes* — a type of salmon spread or paté. Yum.

*Gratin dauphinois* — thin sliced potatoes cooked in cream, fit for a prince.

*Roti d'agneau aux herbes* — roast lamb with herbs.

*Figues chaudes à la mousse d'amandes* — warm figs with almond cream custard.

*Paris par Arrondissement* — a pocket map book of Paris by neighborhood.

*Tartines* — yesterday's bread, toasted and spread with butter and jam.

*Café au lait* — coffee with lots of warm milk.

*Truc* — stuff, thing.

*Le Centre Pompi* — the (President) Pompidou Museum of Modern Art

*Gausson Bottier, fondé 1831* — Gausson Boot Maker, founded in 1831.

*Très cool* — Very cool.

*Vers 1925* — Towards, or around, *1925*.

*Bon-bien* — Well-good, or good-good.

*L'égout* — the Paris sewer.

*Poulet en pot-au-feu* — chicken in a pot of fire, a kind of country chicken stew.

*Émigrés* — immigrants or refugees.

*Filles du Calvaire* — subway stop near the site of the Sisters of Calvary monastery.

*rue Quincampoix* — who knows what it means, but it's like really old.

*Le Baiser Salé* — the Salty Kiss night club, famous for jazz in Paris.

*Fauve, fauve-girl* — wild beast, beasty-girl.

*femme sauvage* — wild woman or savage woman.

*Porte des Lions* — Door of the Lions, at the Louvre.

*Louvre* — The huge, amazing art museum where the Mona Lisa lives.

*Quai François Mitterrand* — riverside walkway named after President Mitterrand.

*La Coupole* — famous café where Zelda and Scott Fitzgerald hung out.

*Seine* — The river at the heart of Paris.

*Centre de recherche et de restauration des musées de France* (C2RMF) — Center for Research and Restoration for the Museums of France.

*Croque monsieur* —open-faced grilled cheese and ham sandwich with white sauce.

*"Mon Dieu, Daisy, mon Dieu!"* — My God, Daisy, my God!

*L'Affaire* — The affair, but in this case the events surrounding the theft of Queen Marie-Antoinette's diamonds.

*Fini* — the end.

*Pompiers* – French firemen.

*S'il vous plait* — please, or if you please.

*"Je suis desolé."* — I'm so sorry.

*"Non, c'est vrais, un requin, vraiment?"* — No, it's true, a shark, truly?

*"Mais, oui, c'est vrais. Elle n'est pas mauviettes comme vous."* — But, yes, it is true. She's not like you little weaklings.

*"Tu exagères, 'moiselle."* — You exaggerate, missy.

*"Dans mon bureau, s'il te plait."* — Put it in my office, if you please.

*Serge Lupatreaux, Livres Anciens* — Serge Lupatreaux, Seller of Antique Books

*"allez"* and *"au revoir"* and *"très occupé"* — let's go, good bye, I'm really busy.

*Tuileries* — formal garden in front of the Louvre with lots of naked lady statues.

*Chevalier de la Légion d'honneur* — a knight of the French Legion of Honor. So like a very big deal.

*"Je suis ravie, certainement, monsieur,"* — I'm very please to meet you sir, certainly.

*la Résistance* — underground fighters who resisted the Nazi occupation.

*Châteaubriande* — a type of steak, invented by the chef of some snobby French count named Châteaubriande.

*Coquilles aux Asperges* — asparagus in cream sauce.

*Le Dejeuner sur l'herbe* — literally, Afternoon upon the grass. A picnic scene.

*Pêches à la diable* — peaches poached in a sweet fruit brandy.

Goutte D'Or — like an African town plopped in the middle of Paris.

*l'abattoir* — the slaughterhouse.

*Grand Bain La A--ttu*— the grand public baths of something (letters missing).

*Mec* — guy.

*Aperçu des secrets diplomatiques dans l'histoire de France. Comprenant un point de vue philosophique sur la nature des actions menées avec discrétions et savoir-faire. A l'usage des futurs ministres royaux. Tome deux. Par Jean-Marie Cournac, Duc des Ongles.* — Okay, Let's see if I can do this: Concerning the secret diplomatic history of France. Especially concerned with a scientific analysis and instructions for these [spying] operations. For use by future royal ministers.

*Jambon* — ham.

*Crème fraîche* — kind of like sour cream, only a bit sweeter. Yum!

*"Voulez-vous quelque chose, mademoiselle?"* — Do you want something, miss?

*"Autre chose pour mademoiselle?"* — Something else for the young lady?

*"C'est le crouton, Le Fig. Vous ne devriez pas perdre votre temps à la lecture."* — It is a goat turd, the Figaro newspaper. You shouldn't waste your time reading it.

*"Merci, 'moiselle, a bientôt,"* — Thanks, missy, see you soon.

*Tu-es seule?" "A part mon amie,* Daisy." — Are you alone? Except for my friend, Daisy.

*"Et alors?"* — And so?

*foie gras* — a spread made of goose livers and cognac and really gross looking but so good that you want to die.

*rémoulade* — a sauce of mayonnaise, garlic, lemon, pepper, and other stuff too.

*cornichons* — little pinky-sized pickles that are really yum-yummah.

*"Première édition, Denis Diderot Encyclopédie, publié à Paris, 1765."* — The first encyclopedia ever published. Denis Diderot tried to make a book with everything worth knowing inside.

*"Je cherches un vieux livre."* — I'm looking for an old book.

*Archives Nationales* — The National Archives of France.

*Mais, j'adore le Hôtel de Rohan.* — But, I adore the Hotel Rohan.

*Déclaration des droits de l'homme* — The Declaration of the Rights of Man. It's kind of like our Declaration of Independence, but for French citizens.

*Monsieur le duc* — Mr. the duke, the duke.

*Jardin* — garden.

*Boulangerie* — bakery.

*"Deux baguettes, s'il vous plait,"* — Two loafs of french bread, please.

*"Deux bag'merc'mo'selle'l'suiv."* — Short for, Two loafs, thanks miss, next. French people can speak really quickly when they are in a hurry!

*Fromager* — a cheese merchant.

*Bonne soirée* — good evening.

*Chambolle-Musigny* — a schmancy kind of wine from the Burgundy region.

*une contrefaçon* — a counterfeit or forgery.

*"Tombée ou prise?"* — Fell out or ripped out.

*"Documents ou peintures?"* — Documents or paintings?

*Epicerie* — a prepared food shop, like a deli, that makes you want to buy everything in it.

*"Pourquoi est la tête dans les nuages, Daisy?"* — Why is your head in the clouds, Daisy?

*"Je veux voir Madame Haron, s'il vous plait."* — I'd like to see Mrs. Haron, please.

*"Merci de m'aider, Monsieur, merci beaucoup."* — Thanks for helping me, sir, thanks very much.

*"Mon plaisir, ma petite,"* — My pleasure, little one.

*Cassoulet* — to-die-for casserole of white beans, duck, sausages, and herbs.

*Tabac* — a store where they sell cigarettes, gum, and other small items.

*Gâteau* — cake. As in, let them eat gâteau. (Which Marie Antoinette never said, btw.)

*"Je cherche Madame d'Aubergine, s'il vous plait."* — I'm looking for Mrs. Eggplant, if you please.

*"Vous-êtes Madame d'Aubergine?"* — Are you Mrs. Eggplant?

*"Elle n'est pas ici."* — She's not here.

*"Quand est-ce que elle va revenir?* — When will she return?

*"En Avril."* — In April.

*"Elle revient en Avril?"* — She's coming back in April?

*"Oui, c'est ça.* — Yes, that's right.

*"Où est-elle?* — Where is she?

*"Oh, difficile a dire. Miami, peut-etre, ou Les Seychelles. Elle a des maisons partout."* — Oh, difficult to say. Miami, maybe, or the Seychell Islands. She's got houses all over.

"*Bonjour. Je suis Daisy. Je voudrais parler avec Sief, s'il vous plait."* — Hi, I'm Daisy. I'd like to speak with Sief, please.

*Préfecture de police* — the Paris police department.

*Les Grande manoirs de Paris* — The great houses of Paris.

*Alpaniste* — a mountain climber, but also criminal and police slang for a burglar who comes in from the rooftops of buildings.

*Thirard, marque vingt-e-un* — A French lock company, type twenty-one.

*"Merveilleux."* — marvelous.

*Mec extérieur* — outside guy, the part of the heist crew that watches for the police.

*"Excusez-moi, vous savez ou est le Hôtel Inter-Continental?"* — Excuse me, do you know where the Hotel Inter-Continental is?

*"Grisbi? Vien ici mon chouchou."* — Grisbi? Come here my little cabbage.

*Les flics* — bad guy slang for the police.

*"C'est moi, Tante Benice."* — It's me, Aunt Benice.

*Quel horreur!* — What a horror!

*"Merci mille fois pour tout, Madame, et je vous prie de me pardonner."* — Thanks a thousand times for everything, Madame, and I beg you to forgive me.

*Troisième étage* — third floor, which is really the fourth floor in France. Don't ask.

*"Quelque chose pour mademoiselle?"* — Something for you miss?

*"Avez-vous un téléphone public?"* — Do you have a public telephone?

*Cour Carrée* — the oldest section of the Louvre, one of Aunt Mill's favorite places.

*l'enfer* — the fiery place, opposite of heaven.

*DCSP, DCPAF, UCLAT, RAID* and *GIPN* — French police and security agencies. (Don't ask me what all the letters mean. I doubt the police even do.)

*36, quai des Orfèves, Brigade Criminelle* — the French police unit that investigates major and organized crimes. They are so famous in France that they are referred to by their address at 36 quai des Orfèves, in the heart of Paris.

*Ordre National du Mérite* — a very big, impressive, shiny medal given to people in France who do great things. I'm still pinching myself, trust me.

*Daube de sanglier à la Provençale* — a stew made with big chunks of wild boar (like a big hairy mean nasty pig) and all kinds of vegetables.

## Acknowledgements

Many-many thanks to Catherine Frank and Peter Meyer, and also to Daisy de Plume, Agata Broncel at Bukovero, Nathalie Paris of Natta-lingo, Michael Miller, Lynda Rescia, Kerry Madden, Patrick & Yanou Beggs, Maria & Denis Laloux, Nathalie Massip & Kirk Lightsey, and to all of Daisy's steadfast Facebook and Twitter friends, and of course, eternally, to Lily, Cora and Laura.

Got a moment?  Why not leave a tiny-tiny review of this book on Amazon.  You can't even imagine how that helps an indie author like me.

And, if you missed reading Daisy's first book, **Daisy and the Pirates**, you'll find it waiting for you at Amazon.

Then if you haven't had quite enough of Miss Daisy Tannenbaum, you can visit her website, MY STUPID JOURNAL, at:

http://www.daisytannenbaum.com/

While there, you can join her mailing list.

You can also like her on Facebook and leave snidely comments or whatever.  Or you can follow her on Twitter at:

@DaisyTannenbaum

Plus, if you are so inclined, you can write to her at:

daisytannenbaum@roadrunner.com

## About the Author

J.T. Allen is a long-time screenwriter who sold his first script while living in Paris. He then moved to Los Angeles and wrote several early drafts of *The Lion King*. His television movie credits include TNT's *Geronimo* and *The Good Old Boys*, FX's *Redemption* and CBS's *Death in Paradise*.

The first Daisy Tannenbaum misadventure, *Daisy and the Pirates*, started as a pitch for a Disney Channel movie. Allen loved the character, who was inspired by his two daughters, and wrote a novel instead.

*Daisy in Exile*, the second in the series, started as Daisy's blog, *My Stupid Journal*. In the meantime, this very instant, Daisy has a crack troop of monkeys working day and night to create a third book while she is off getting into mischief, which she (or Mr. Allen) will no doubt tell the monkeys all about.

Printed in Great Britain
by Amazon